For all the lost girls, and the ones who got away

The author acknowledges the Whadjuk Noongar people, the Traditional Owners of the lands, waters and skies where this story is set, and pays her respects to Elders past, present and emerging. She supports the Uluru Statement from the Heart and recognises that sovereignty has never been ceded and this always was, and always will be, Aboriginal land.

Author's Note

During my growing up years, Perth was home to two serial murder cases. Living through those times was formative – it changed our behaviour, the places we went out at night, how we got home after dark. We changed too in response to the shark attacks that happened off our coast every few years. But *The Shark* is a work of fiction and any similarity between the story and real events, or with any person, living or dead, is coincidental. The setting of Cottesloe is real, and locals will recognise much of it, but I've fictionalised some aspects to serve the story. The Broome Street Frangipani House does not exist.

He wakes on his back. Pain and darkness wash through him from the base of his skull, wash away from him and return like waves of black water, like something he should be able to remember. There's a rushing sound and the salt smell of the ocean. Beneath the salt, familiar smells and something more – an otherness.

The rest of him – not his head, still heavy with pain, but his limbs and torso – vibrates with something he can't place until his body is jerked and tipped then rolls back to rest with a new burst of pain and he knows what it is.

Engine hum. The swish of tyres. A vehicle.

There's more pain – his wrists and shoulders. He cannot move his arms. If he could, he'd touch his fingers to the back of his head and the place where he's certain there is injury and blood. Skin and tissue damage he won't think of because they drill fear into him, churning now with nausea. It's not only the movement of the car, and being positioned the way he is, laid out supine across the back seat.

The familiar smells are his. The way he likes his car to smell, and his clothes, his skin and hair. He is meticulous with these things.

It takes this time to understand he is in his own car. He is being driven.

The realisation drills the fear deeper. No one else drives his car. There will be blood on the seat. He needs the car these weekend evenings, for his regular, crucial night drives. But is it a weekend evening? He cannot remember.

His vision is dark and blurred, of the backs of the front seats. There's a new sound now, a frantic whispering hiss. And the smell – the otherness – he recognises it at last as female.

And now he remembers.

He was at home. Outside the house. In the driveway.

Dark. He'd kept the lights off because of the girl. The girl in the golf club car park. The one who'd followed him there.

His heartrate spikes as he remembers. Someone hit him. Someone behind him in the dark outside his house. The girl has an accomplice. There are two of them.

Driving him. Whispering. Scheming in that female way.

What have they done to him?

PART ONE

SUNDAY

1

Raych

Polaris

This is how you taunt a serial killer. How you call him out. You return to his patch, over and over. You don't give it a rest. You are tireless. You wear a flag the colour of blood on your arse, over your heart, and in the depths of your soul, even though you don't believe in a soul any more, not really.

You parade yourself. You are shameless.

You wave, repeatedly, so no one can see you are drowning.

Look, I'm scared of monsters. Monsters with blunt objects and sharp intellects. Monsters with too many teeth. Monsters that come at you so hard and fast you're toast before the first fear hits you. Mate, I'm a gutless wonder. A wimp. A coward. You would not think this now, but I'm the girl who holds tight to the safety rail, who swims inside the shark net, who walks with her keys tight in her fist in broad daylight down her own street.

That is to say, I *was* all of those things. Before the worst thing that could happen, happened.

So yeah, there are mitigating circumstances. Here be monsters. All kinds of them. Anyone who thinks otherwise needs their head opened up by one of those saws they use in the mortuary and examined by a pathologist.

Lucky for me I met Carmen Chase when I did.

Or maybe not.

Sunday was the start of it with Carmen, not counting our three days on the psych ward the year before. It was the day before Dad was due to leave for his work shift, and I was awake way early. A night's sleep had come to be a nostalgic thing, a childhood thing. I'd been listening to episodes five through seven of *Inside the Hunt: Serial Murder* but I was too tired to take in the finer points of criminal profiling and dogged police effort.

I lay in bed and tried for a wank but I wasn't in the mood for that either. Fuck, I was practically a pervert. No one in the state I was in should have been able to contemplate an orgasm.

My mind was firing off the usual random, brutal thoughts as I hauled myself out of bed and down the hill to the beach at Cottesloe for my swim, those thoughts that chew me up on a regular basis. But that morning they were more persistent. Like, I knew Dad had forgotten the anniversary six days from today, and I knew the out-of-the-frying-pan house move was just over a month away. I knew there was nothing I could do about anything, but I still hoped I'd get back from the beach and he'd apologise and admit to being an insensitive prick and say we weren't moving after all.

I mean, I knew it wasn't likely. But that little kernel of hope, the one bit I had left after the last year? Well, it hadn't been stomped on yet.

The heat and the white noise of cicadas followed me down the hill in a rolling wave, but hung back when I stepped onto the grass terraces above the beach. That early-morning almost-cool under the Norfolk Pines, the smell of salt and reticulated lawn, the smudged glimmer of ocean through the trees. It was the end of a week of absent and erratic sea breezes, unseasonal cloud and humidity that ramped up the February temperatures and kept them there. I knew I'd remember the cool later like it was a dream.

The crow in the pine tree I was standing underneath started telling me how suboptimal life was, but I cut it short. 'Guess what, mate? I already know.' It tilted its head and didn't talk back.

The beach was filling steadily: runners and walkers, hardcore early swimmers like me, families with little kids setting up camp between the flags. No one my age from what I could see. It was busy, considering we were all waiting for him to make his next move.

Neil Fraser Lock. Person of interest. *Suspect*, if you listen to the media, which let's face it we'd all been doing for months.

Yep, a serial killer name, like someone had mapped out his fate from birth. Parents, Robert and Catherine. If you're into true crime like I am, or you know your serial killer history, you'll have a bunch of names like his taking up space in your brain. But why should they? What makes them so special they get to do that?

The light on the water was flat. Low cloud that'd burn off later. A sharky light, the surfers call it, because you can't see what's there in the water. I heard the rattle of the shark-spotter helicopter before I saw it, tracking south down the coast towards me. The skin across my shoulders and the backs of my legs flickered and tightened and I thought of the Diana Nyad movie. That incredible swim and all the stuff she had to do to keep safe. Full body jellyfish protection, shark cages and electronic repellents. She'd been Piper's hero – Piper was the better swimmer of the two of us – but now she was mine.

I don't swim inside the shark net nowadays. Those times are long gone.

I hit the water before I could talk myself out of it. Swam my usual fifteen hundred metres freestyle from Cott to North Cott and back with the seagrass scraping my belly and tugging at my fingers because I hadn't gone in deep enough. I was almost at the end of my swim when I saw it – the shark flanking me to my right. I jack-knifed away from it, choked on a faceful of ocean. Then realised it was four big fish in formation and not a shark at all.

FFS, Raych. I caught my breath and waded out of the water. Felt like a jerk until I saw the helicopter, static and hovering, and the shark alarm went off. It was only the second time I'd ever heard it. There was something out there after all.

I stood at the top of the terraces in my red bikini, the water and salt running off me like blood as the beach emptied out. The panicked scramble of bodies as parents hauled kids out of the surf by skinny arms. The red and yellow decked-out lifeguards yelling, 'Vacate the water. Vacate the water, NOW.' And each and every head turned to look at what was behind them in the waves.

Fake-as-fuck shark or not, I still can't watch *Jaws*. But if there's a shark in the water, looking at it sure as hell won't stop it from coming for you.

The previous time I'd heard the alarm at Cott, the shark was a hammerhead, only 1.3 metres long and already heading west into open water when the spotter identified it. This, to my mind, was not enough to warrant a full-scale evacuation of the busiest beach in the Perth metro area, but people were jumpy. This time, I found out later, it was a four-metre tiger shark a hundred metres offshore. It pays to respect a shark, no matter how it appears.

It's all about the sharks, this summer; both in and out of the water.

The stillness of the morning lingered under the pines but I could feel the street at my back, the cafes and punters and passing cars, the smell of hot bitumen and sunblock, the throb of bass from open-topped cars with wanky personalised plates. I swung to face it with my heart still going hard from the beach evacuation, my guts swooping and wheeling like a hot chip frenzy of gulls.

I knew what his car looked like. Everyone did.

It was a reminder, that shark alarm. All of us on the beach were thinking the same thing.

When would they charge him? Would he take another one before they did?

Had the task force fucked up?

Half the suburb was clamouring for a team from Sydney to be parachuted in to fix it, while the other half were up in arms at the thought.

Some days down at the Cottesloe strip I was certain he was

there. In a car, kerb-cruising. Behind glass, victim-selecting. My skin would crawl with his gaze, like flies on dead meat.

And now he had a face, and a name. It was two weeks since Neil Fraser Lock had outed himself to the media. Two weeks since journos had upgraded him from person of interest to *suspect*, and the cops had done nothing to dispute it.

One day he'd be there. One day he'd take the bait, and I'd be ready.

The crow was still there as I left. Disapproving. I swear it was always the same one.

The heat swelled and crackled as I moved out of the shade and schlepped back up the hill from the beach. I'd pulled my combats and top over my already-dry bikini. I took Pearse Street, past the golf club, the way I did every time. I liked to pass the old house, the one we rented when we first arrived in Perth from Sydney, the house that had welcomed us. I didn't get the itch to smash bits of it up like I did most other places.

We lived there from when I was seven to the end of primary school. That was before Dad was seduced by the mining companies, before he amassed his shedloads from the fly-in-fly-out lifestyle and built the cubic monstrosity a few blocks away, where we live now.

The old house was crumbling limestone, rusted lacework verandas and an elaborately sagging tin roof. Now bought up by the same developers that owned the block of units next door, and the blocks either side, all marked for demolition and the new high-rises.

Every second block was a construction site these days. Cott was getting a facelift – or not, depending on how you felt about that. Even the tearooms on the beach and the Marine Parade hotels.

As I passed the empty units, the low sunlight flashed gold on the windows of the corner apartment – I'd smashed a fair few ground floor windows at the back of the block on a bad day, but I'd left the ones at the front – and for a second there was a girl behind the glass. She stopped me in my tracks: I fully believed it was Piper. Piper, back from where she'd gone to that night, and watching me. Too shy to come out and say hey, where've you been for the last year and what the holy hell do you reckon you're doing?

But Piper was never shy, and when I blinked and looked again and my heart settled back down, there was nothing behind the window but an empty room.

Ghost-Piper, hiding out in the shadows. My heart playing mean tricks.

No smashing windows today, though. I'd moved on. That's what I told myself. I kept walking, past the hoardings and construction noise, the dust and hard hats of the block on the far side of the units, up the hill to the corner.

It was hard not to stop there and feel the pull of it, only a few blocks south.

The Frangipani House, I called it – Neil Fraser Lock's parents' place. The Broome Street house we'd been seeing on the news and the internet for weeks. He'd moved back in with them while the cops searched his Bicton apartment. I remembered that particular messed-up news story – the two of them on the doorstep welcoming him home while the media camped out on their lawn. As far as I knew he was still there.

The frangipani trees surrounding that house were the biggest

I'd ever seen, grown almost to the height of the roof. Shit yeah, I'd been down there. In the dark, mostly. Too many times to count. It was so close to home, to where the girls went missing from, and why hadn't the cops searched it too? It was an oversight, it seemed to me. They'd found nothing at his unit but a big fat zero.

I turned north towards home. I was thinking about the coming night, yet another Sunday, about the pattern of girls disappearing, and what I was going to do.

I can't think about him too hard or I lose my nerve. His MO. What condition the bodies have been in when they've been found each time by an unlucky beachgoer. Only once was it a dog walker, so it's not always the way they show it in the movies.

The Polaris task force has never released details, not one whisper of a leak to the media, but there's always someone with a smartphone on the scene these days. The first time, they thought the girl, Christine Taylor-Watkins, was a genuine shark fatality. That is, until other evidence came to light.

It got clear pretty fast that we had our very own serial killer in the Perth metro area, for the first time since the 1990s, the 1980s, and before that, the 1960s. Once again the killer was targeting the Western Suburbs. You can't get a lot further west than where those girls have been taken from, and where they've washed back up.

The victims have all been swimmers. Accomplished swimmers, too. Swimmers with talent and prospects.

I'm not one of those girls. I swim because Piper did. I swim to be close to her.

I swim to make him want me.

Polaris. Named for the explosive Polaris breach of an

attacking shark. Depending on how faint-hearted you are, you can Google it.

Here's the thing about last summer.

You inexplicably come out to your straight best mate on the last day of school, and she says it's not an issue, it won't change anything between you. She says, *It's all G, Raych*, which is her thing she says about practically everything. And you stand there with people yelling their summer plans and banging their locker doors either side of you, knowing she's looking at you with those eyes, but you're too scared to look back at her because you don't know what you're going to see in them. Because she sounds so casual about this thing that's volcanoed up out of you (and why now? You can't for the life of you remember why it seemed such a great idea to say it to her) but you so want it to be an issue, you want it to be a humungous fucking issue. You want it to shoot stars and rock planets and change everything between you.

Can't she see that? Hasn't she felt it, for like, the entirety of your friendship since Year Three when you moved to her school?

And then five end-of-high-school summer parties later, at the beginning of February, she kisses you next to the tequila bottle in Ronnie Lam's kitchen, on a street three blocks north of yours and four blocks west of hers and one block back from the beach. She walks her fingers along your collarbone and around the back of your neck like she's been doing it for years, like she's not your straight best mate at all. She takes your hand and leads you away from the crowd and down the long backyard to Ronnie's parents' pool house. One thing leads to another and another, and you ask her if she's sure and she says she is. And afterwards, in that breathless unbelieving space where everything has changed between you after all, she smiles this smile she could well have been smiling that day by the lockers if only you'd had the guts to look at her. Because she was always a heap braver than you. And that smile has all of the future in it, not only the rest of the summer but all the summers. All of the two of you and nothing else, and more parties, different ones with different people at them.

And then she looks at the time and she swears and starts pulling straight her clothes. She kisses you again and hands you her old iPod, the gold vintage one she's had since she was a kid and takes everywhere. She asks you to keep a hold of it and says she'll be right back, that she has to do this one thing. *Don't go away, Raych.* Look, you want to go with her, shit yeah, you do. You don't want to let her out of your sight because it's like you've only just found her. But she says it again. *It's all G.* And you do what she says and you wait, because you've always been one for doing as you're told (yes, you're the opposite to her in that way too). You wait, and you're buzzing, with your face hurting from its helpless smile and the party a happy blur all around you like lights in the rain. And you want to know what the 'one thing' is she has to do, but you never find out.

Because she never comes back.

She's the second girl to be taken, except no one understands the significance of the first one yet. She's his type and she's in his stomping ground when she goes missing – the killer they now call *The Shark* – and everyone assumes, once they've put it all together, that it's him who took her.

But no one has found her body yet.

So whatever Dad might have thought, I wasn't moving house. I was going to be taken. I was going to make *him* take me and it would be the last thing I ever did.

He was going to tell me to my face what he'd done with her.

Forget the profiling, the door to door, the appeals to the public for thousands of scraps of useless fucking information.

This is how you hunt a serial killer.

2

Carmen

No one notices Carmen

Carmen's frown flickers above her eyes, like she's stood under a fluoro light on the blink. But there's no power in the empty apartments, only the morning sun making a yellow stain on the floor. The golf course man is still there across the street but the girl she knows from the mental hospital is gone. One minute ago they were both right there at the same time, outside the window. Not together; on opposite sides of the street. But still, she doesn't like the coincidence.

She doesn't move from her spot in the corner of the room, at the edge of the block of shadow she stepped into when she saw the girl. Rachel. Names are only for convenience, but Carmen remembers it.

The girl didn't see Carmen, she's sure. The man can't see her, either.

Good. She can use that. It's her unfair advantage, which she needs because the rest of the time, everything is stacked against her.

Carmen has been coming here every day for a week. It took some time, after they first showed him on the news, for her to decide what to do about him and then to find this empty building across from the golf course. She wanted to watch his parents' house, but that was no good on account of the police already being parked out front. This is the best spot, but the golf course is big, and he doesn't work every day. Today is the first day she's seen him.

Neil Fraser Lock. The one the police have been watching. The one they say killed those girls.

It's a shock, seeing him in real life. More of a shock even than seeing him on TV. But still, it's no good with her behind glass and him across the street at the edge of the golf course. She's only ninety per cent sure, which isn't enough.

Neil Fraser Lock is the assistant greenkeeper at the golf course, which in Carmen's opinion, because golf courses are for old people and wreck the environment, is a pointless job. But at least she'll always know where to find him. Neil. She's not going to bother with his whole name each time she thinks about him, and she's been thinking about him a lot.

It was his voice, when they first interviewed him on the news, that made something explode in Carmen's brain, a whole section of it lighting up in recognition. Her face got hot, which never happens, and she had to go to the bathroom and dunk it in a sink full of cold water. Mrs Glasser even noticed and asked her if she was sick.

But Carmen wasn't sick. His voice is distinctive – low and grating with a stop-start hesitation between some words which might or might not be fake – that's how what she'd heard came back to her. 'Not her.' One of only a handful of things she remembers about *that night*.

She never saw his face that night. All she has to go on is his voice and his smell. If she is honest – which Carmen isn't as a rule, even with herself – she doesn't know for sure it was him. Right now he's in shadow under the roof of the buggy he has to drive, but she can see his profile and the sag of his shoulders against the horizon behind. The dark-coloured polo shirt of his uniform with something embroidered on the pocket, which she reckons she remembers from *that night* too. His nose has a bump halfway down it but apart from that, he's ordinary looking. His cropped hair and beard are neat, his eyes invisible behind wire-framed sunglasses. You wouldn't notice him in a crowd or pick him out of a line-up.

He's unmemorable. That's the whole point of him. They're the same that way.

No one notices Carmen.

She knows why they think it's him. It's too obvious, but maybe that's the point. Maybe it's a double-bluff and he's smarter than everyone thinks. Carmen understands how people's minds work – the way they follow each other, like dominoes, falling.

When he moves, his head is tipped forwards to match the slump of his shoulders, his eyes always scouring the ground. But there's an alertness there under the drag of his feet, like he's acting. Maybe they're the same that way too.

Carmen doesn't remember most of what happened *that night*. Only that Alexis was there and what almost happened but didn't. What Alexis accused Carmen of, and what happened after, which was bad.

It took months in the mental hospital for Carmen to tell them what they wanted to hear and admit Alexis was right and she was wrong. That she'd been mistaken because her brain doesn't always remember things, not in a joined-up way like a story. That there was no man in Alexis's room that night, only the two of them.

She had to time it exactly right. She couldn't tell them too soon or they wouldn't have believed her. It was the only reason they let her out, but it was never true, and three months was too long.

She doesn't know how it fits – the killer in Alexis's room. She needs to get closer to him, to hear his voice in real life, to smell his distinctive smell.

She needs to know for certain if Neil Fraser Lock was there that night too.

Carmen looks across at the horizon, the faint contours of Wadjemup, Rottnest Island, and the container ships. She has a good view of it all from this ground floor corner apartment – the ocean, the golf course, the line of tall Norfolk Island Pines, the blue sky.

Carmen likes the quiet emptiness of the rooms. Not two sticks of furniture to scrape together, is what Mrs Glasser would say; one of her wrong expressions that rubs Carmen up the wrong way. Not that Alexis's mother would set foot in a place like this.

There's nothing in here except dust from the construction site on the next block, sand ground into the old carpet, drifts of gum leaves and curls of bark that have escaped inside from the street. Carmen doesn't like the smell of the cockroach baits – it's never the cockroaches that are the problem – but you can't have everything.

She thought no one else came here – even the garages out the back are empty because she's checked – but the first time, last Sunday, someone had been and smashed half the ground floor windows at the back. She doesn't like mess as a rule but the shards of windows, reflecting hard cloudless sky, looked like something different.

Carmen heard a noise and stepped inside, crunching window sky under her boots. The person doing the glass smashing had gone but they'd left a rolled-up sleeping bag and a single mattress and a Coles bag full of clothes in an upstairs room in Unit Seven. The noise was the girl cat in Unit Two, hunting. They've seen each other around, Carmen and the cat. Looked each other up and down a few times.

The girl cat eats the cockroaches. The first time Carmen saw her with one, the cat froze, cockroach-legs sticking out from her mouth like broken twigs, then went right on chewing without breaking eye contact. Carmen likes her for that. She likes that she's a hunter, a good and silent one. Too skinny, but. Carmen has brought a stolen chicken breast for her today, but she's not here.

There are other hunters in the empty apartments. If she holds her breath, Carmen can sense as well as hear them – the vibration they have that's different to other things. A huntsman spider that lies in wait under a broken windowsill in Unit Four. A nest of paper wasps in the bougainvillea against the end wall of the garages. Countless skinks and birds and once, a baby dugite.

Neil has gone now, trundled across to the other side of the fairway, and Carmen steps forwards into the light, up close to the window. The container ships give the appearance of not moving but she knows that's not accurate. They change. Some of them disappear. New ones arrive. One day she counted twelve, and the next day all except one were gone. That one never moves. The stranded one that was on the news after it got damaged in a cyclone and limped down the coast to here. People who say ships limp have got rocks in their heads. Of course they don't. There are other boats too. Today, the early Rottnest ferry, two smaller motor boats and one with a white sail, all on their way to the island.

Carmen doesn't know anyone with a boat. She'd like to leave on one, head west and keep on going. She'd like to be some-where with the horizon all around in an unbroken line. She thinks out there, her mind would be able to breathe. She could find her dad out there too. That's all she knows about him, that he arrived in Fremantle on a boat. Her mother tried to trap him, but he wouldn't be trapped. Carmen won't be trapped either. Not ever again.

She can't swim, not properly, but she could pretend. When you're like Carmen, you get good at pretending.

She pretends all sorts. She pretends she doesn't mind things. Like living with Alexis and the Glassers, the family who adopted her when she was one. Like school; having to repeat Year Twelve because of what happened last year. She pretends things so people won't know what she's really like.

She pictures the deep canyon out there, off the edge of the continental shelf, further than she can see. The water in layers of darkening blue and the sharks deep down inside it. She imagines

Alexis falling into the whirl of slick, muscled bodies and razor teeth, and feels the thrill of it down in her bones. Her fingers tighten around the tin in her pocket.

She shakes her head, blinks, and the vision dissolves.

She knows she's trying to distract herself. It was too much, seeing Neil and the girl Rachel like that. It's confusing, when things happen that way, coincidences that might not be coincidences.

She scans the horizon, the blue line, the ships and the boats, her frown still flickering. Her blood is pushing through her bones in a way she sometimes likes but not today. She can't go now. She can't leave home or get away on a boat to get shot of Alexis or try to track down her dad.

She has to find a way to speak to Neil. To question him.

Because him being there *that night* must have changed what happened. What if Carmen didn't fail like she thought? What if he stopped her from doing it, what she was trying to do?

That girl Rachel better not stick her oar in. Rachel has something going on. Carmen's seen her, out on Marine Parade of a weekend night when everyone knows that's where the girls go missing from.

As if there wasn't a killer on the streets. As if she's got nothing better to do with her time.

She'll be out there again tonight.

Carmen waits until 11 p.m. before she leaves the house, a good hour after Mrs Glasser has turned off every light and gone to bed. She goes the long way around from her room at the back of the house, out through the back door into the yard, past the old bit of wall where the gecko hunts of a night. She can see the

lit-up single pane of the shed window near the back fence because Mr G never goes to bed before midnight, and sometimes
he leaves the light on when he's not even in there. She tiptoes
around the side through the bit of garden where the ravens like
to sit on the fence – and once she watched a butcherbird impale
a frog and eat it – and out the front gate onto the drive, which
is where Alexis catches her.

Carmen, tall and big-boned, has kilos and a good half-head
on Alexis, but Alexis has her ways around these differences.
She'll convince anyone who'll listen – and people listen to
Alexis – that she's the more intelligent, accomplished and all-
around superior person out of the two of them.

'Where do you think you're going, *Car-men*?' She stresses the
first half of Carmen's name in the same projecting way she'd say
the word *retard*, which is what she means. Alexis always talks
like she's auditioning for something, but with Carmen, since
her time in the mental place last year, she takes it a step further
and slows it down until there's a full stop between every word.

Alexis's red hair is loose and damp, not in the usual tight high
ponytail that makes Carmen worry her eyeballs could pop out.
Her skin is pink and shiny under the glow of the streetlight and
she smells soapy and clean. Carmen knows she's put the cream
on her face she does before bed, that she's been listening out for
Carmen from her room at the front of the house. Maybe she's
even got out of bed for this.

It gives Carmen a shudder of satisfaction to know this.

'Out,' she says. 'For a drive.'

Alexis has one hand on her hip, leaning against the carport
bricks. Her eyelid twitches. Carmen only has the car because
Mr G bought it for her. 'Are you sure that's safe?'

Carmen knows a redback spider lives under the lip of gut-
tering above Alexis's head. Course it's not safe, but that's not
the right answer. With Alexis, no answer is the right answer,
because Alexis knows she has all the cards and this can go any
way she wants it to. Her top lip is fat and twitching like a grub,
not quite curling, while the rest of her face is uncannily smooth.
She's had things injected at the beauty place where she works
again.

For some reason, and her reasons are always random, she
steps back to let Carmen go. 'I won't tell if you won't, Car-men.
But remember,' she says, 'I can get you put back in that place
like *THAT.*' She snaps her fingers to make the point, to make
Carmen jump.

Carmen always jumps.

Down on Marine Parade, Carmen parks in one of the overflowing car parks. The night smells of deep fat fryers and car fumes
and makes her nose itch. She waits in her usual spot at one end
of the kids' playground, with the beach and ocean at her back.

The playground is empty, all shadows and sharp angles under
the night sky. The pines block the light from the street, and in
Carmen's long-sleeved T-shirt and jeans and boots, it's easy to
disappear.

She's watching Rachel, inside the front bar of the Beach
Hotel. What Rachel's doing has something to do with the
murder case. Carmen's connected to it somehow too, she knows
she is – has had this sense for months that she knows something
about it. Because it's not only *that night* she can't remember.
There are other times too, when *big things* happen and her brain
can't hack it and goes offline, like whatever's happening isn't

22

real, or Carmen's not real herself. It's only for a few moments each time, but events can be hazy for hours afterwards. She played it down when she was in the mental hospital, course she did. The adolescent unit, because she was seventeen then. They're used to kids with brains like Carmen's in there.

Rachel's not observant because she walked right past Neil today without even knowing it was him. Maybe she doesn't watch TV. Still, Carmen needs to find out what she knows. She's got this feeling something's going to happen, and she needs to keep out ahead of it. It might not be so bad if she does.

She sits on the bottom of the slide, can see stars between the pine branches, and sense the lorikeets up there. They're like noisy little kids at sunset but quiet now it's dark. And no, she's not hot, even though there's no sea breeze tonight and it's twenty-eight degrees. Carmen's never hot.

She watches the rich kids across the street, with their flash clothes and shiny hair and bare arms and legs, at the art deco Beach Hotel and the Ocean View Club around the corner. The pub is chucking out, the crowd deciding whether to go hard or go home, when she sees Mrs Craigie through the windows of the front bar. She has her back to Carmen, but Carmen's eyes lock onto her short black hair and those green dangly earrings she wore one day last week.

Mrs Craigie is the new PE teacher at school, only six years older than Carmen and one year older than Alexis; twenty-four, which is too young to be married, in Carmen's opinion. Mrs Craigie can be a bitch to people, especially if you're not good at sport. Either that, or the other teachers have already told her what Carmen is like.

Giant SUVs are rolling up now like it's the morning school

run, people disappearing into them in groups of two and three, and Carmen loses sight of Mrs Craigie in the exodus from the bar.

No one walks home any more.

Rachel ricochets from group to group amongst the crowd on the club balcony. There's a queue already down on the street to get in and a whoosh of music each time the main door opens.

Rachel's not in her usual daytime outfit – khaki combat pants and tiny singlet tops and white Converse sneakers – but the same short skirt and heels all the girls wear. She's small but she stands out, because of her dark gold hair and skin and the red of her dress. Her hair is in a sticking-up quiff, like a boy from the 1950s, or the 1980s. She must have to work at it, to get it to go like that. It's the opposite to Carmen's hair, which Alexis, when she's being mean, tells her is like a baby's hair.

Rachel waves her hands around like crazy when she talks, Carmen can see her do it even from here. Like she's writing her name with a firework, or she thinks her words aren't loud and clear enough when anyone who's met her would know they are. Carmen remembers that, from last year.

The killer takes girls on nights like this, in the early hours of the morning. From down here on Marine Parade or one of the side streets that run off it, from outside one of the hotels or the Ocean View Club. Everyone knows that. It's a concrete fact. Rachel will know it too.

Some days Carmen feels the throb of it like eyes on her back. Someone out there. Someone watching from the shadows, the same way she's watching Rachel. But whenever she looks there's no one there.

No one can understand how the person gets away with it,

in a place like this where everyone knows everyone else. The kids who go out on Marine Parade all know each other from the private schools they go to or the surf club or tennis club, or because of their parents' rich friends, or from working a summer job in one of the cafes or hotels.

People haven't stopped going to those places, that's what interests Carmen. They've done the opposite. It's only the tourists from interstate who are scared. The locals want to support the businesses, is what it says on the news, but Carmen knows it's more than that.

They think they're better than the killer, is what she reckons. As if they know whoever's doing it isn't from around here. They think they can stop the killer from coming back to their patch. It's not denial, exactly. It's confidence, from the money they have, the schools they go to, the jobs their parents have.

They think they're safe. But Carmen knows they're not.

Carmen doesn't come from one of the suburbs the rich kids come from, or go to one of the private schools they go to, but Mrs Craigie did before she ended up as a teacher at Carmen's school. That's a thing she likes you to know about. She told them all that on her first day.

When they say the names of the dead girls on the news, they do it in this dramatic way that makes you realise they don't really care. It's funny, to listen to them talk that way about people you know. It's what happens when you live in a place like this. Even if you don't go to the right school, the degrees of separation are small. It stands to reason you're going to know one of those girls, or know someone who does, or even know all of them.

That's what Carmen tells herself.

The feeling from before, that something is going to happen,

is still there. Rachel walks to the end of the balcony and grips the rail, staring down at the street then out towards Carmen and the ocean. Carmen's legs get heavy when Rachel looks her way, as if her blood is full of iron filings instead of cells and she wouldn't be able to move even if she wanted to. But Rachel turns away and hasn't seen her.

Rachel was raging when she arrived on the ward in the mental place, fully messed up. Calling everyone the c-word at top volume, even her dad when he came in on the third day. She had it all going on on the outside, while Carmen kept everything in.

Rachel only stayed in those few days, which was not in proportion to how crazy she was when she came in, but maybe that was the point. Carmen didn't tell them anything when she was in there except for what they wanted to hear.

Just past midnight, the club door opens and spits Rachel out onto the steps, in the middle of a tight knot of girls. Two of them head for a waiting car while Rachel stands and sways. A third girl, taller than Rachel with a long plait of hair, tries to get Rachel to go with them but she won't, until at last the girl gives up and the car with the three of them pulls away.

Rachel went to one of the schools and dresses like one of the rich kid crowd when she comes out here, but that's all it is. They know her and some of them think they're her friends, but she sets herself apart. Carmen hasn't worked it out yet, what's different about Rachel or why she comes here at night. Not yet.

Still, she feels something whenever she sees it – another person who doesn't fit in – even if it's Rachel's own fault. The feeling only lasts a second and then it's gone.

Rachel walks around the corner into the first side street, unsteady on her feet as if she's drunk too much but Carmen doesn't reckon she has. She keeps moving, up the street and away from the beach, the sound of her heels echoing. There's no one else out here now except Carmen, who rises to follow her. Rachel's a shadowy blur receding up the dark footpath – you'd only see her if you knew she was there.

Until she crosses under a streetlight and the red of her outfit blazes for a moment, like a sign.

Carmen steps out of the dark from between two parked cars. 'What are you doing?'

Rachel swears and spins to face her. 'Jesus fuck, that took years off my life. Do I want to be thirty already? Don't do that.' She's stopped halfway up the hill under a streetlight, next to a two-storey house that takes up most of the block. Carmen can smell their garbage.

Rachel's vaping, her other hand pressed against her sternum, genuine shock or putting it on, Carmen can't tell. She's dressed up for something or someone in the red dress. Not one of the rich kids at the club, Carmen doesn't reckon. She's taken out her piercings – the one in her nose and bottom lip, the extra ones in her ears – but the tattoos are there, snaking up her left arm like someone's scribbled all over it with a black pen. Words, phrases, line drawings, all in different sizes and styles. Carmen can only read the words in big letters: *woman on the edge*, and a girl's name, *Piper*, repeated over and over. The scars are there too, faint lines in the light.

Rachel's eyes dart up the empty street, across the dark windows of the house, back down to Marine Parade. She lives in a house like the one they're in front of but Carmen's not supposed to know that.

'Get lost,' Rachel says. 'I'm busy. Plus it's rude to stare.' She picks a flake of something off her bottom lip and blows out a slow stream of smoke. But her eyes won't stay still, roaming the street. She's got the same edginess she had in the hospital, as if nothing's changed about her in a year. Electrical, like a storm is coming.

'What are you doing out here?' Carmen says again. She swings around to show her – the lights from the hotel at the bottom of the hill, the dark pines, the deserted street. Houses shut off behind walls and gates. 'S'not safe, is it?'

Rachel snorts and sways, still pretending drunk, one hip cocked and one foot in front of the other like someone in one of the magazines Alexis reads. Carmen doesn't know fashion but Alexis'd kill for those shoes. Rachel's make-up shines where the light catches it, winged eyeliner and a shimmery tan. 'What are you, my mum? I don't have one of those.'

'I know that,' Carmen says. 'Course I do.' It was the one fact about them in the hospital that was the same. Carmen tells everyone her mum is dead because it's not as bad as the truth – that she didn't want Carmen and gave her up when she was a baby.

There's a blast of music and laughter from the club and Rachel flinches. A car passes on Marine Parade. Rachel's eyes follow it until it's gone, and she shivers in the hot humid air.

'Were you following me? You can't follow people. Especially not people you've been on a psychiatric ward with. They might get the wrong idea.' She arches one eyebrow like the back of a cat, like a challenge, but it's no big deal to Carmen. Course they remember each other, because of what happened on the ward. And it was three whole days.

Rachel sucks in another lungful and breathes it out. Carmen catches the sweet smell of the smoke. 'You shouldn't be out here, Rachel,' she says.

Rachel stares at her. 'It's Raych. I don't like Rachel. I can't remember yours and I'm not going to apologise for that, either. And why the actual fuck would you care if I'm out here or not?'

'Because. It's late. S'not safe.'

Another car passes at the bottom of the street. Rachel watches it until it's gone. She swallows. 'Listen, I'm in the middle of something. So fuck off, okay?'

What's she in the middle of? But Carmen thinks she knows. She remembers Rachel's desperation in the hospital, how big it felt – bigger than the room they shared, bigger than the whole place. And that place was full of desperation.

She steps towards Rachel. 'I can give you a lift. In my car.'

Rachel frowns, rubs her bare arms. 'I don't want a lift from you. I'm waiting for someone. You got a problem with that?' She tries to shoo Carmen away with her hands. 'Piss off. I've got a lift. It's on its way.'

Carmen stands her ground and checks the street – parked cars, no lights inside them, nothing moving. Rachel makes an impatient sound. 'It's an Uber,' she says.

'Is not. You only live a few blocks.'

Rachel's glossed lips pop open. 'Jesus. So you're a stalker now?'

Things are blooming in Carmen's senses, too big. The smells of things, the sounds. She can hear her blood in her ears, that sound and pressure inside her head she doesn't like. She breathes and tries to calm herself. Why should it matter to her, what Rachel's doing? But it does.

A third car passes on Marine Parade, slows for the corner and stops as if to turn up towards them. A white station wagon. It waits there. There's no other traffic.

Carmen's seen the station wagon before. On the news. Everyone has.

The white car idles for what feels like minutes but can only be thirty seconds. The driver's face is turned up towards them, bleached pale under the streetlight, staring. His dark hair and beard merge with the shadows inside the car. Before he changes his mind and accelerates away.

Carmen feels the shock of it like icy water, seeing him again. Neil. She turns to Rachel, who watches him speed into the dark. Rachel's shivering again, transfixed. So she does watch TV.

They've both seen him, but neither of them will say it.

'I know what you're doing,' Carmen says.

'Huh? No, you don't.' Rachel tries to glare but it doesn't come off.

'It's not gunna work. You can't do it.'

Rachel fidgets with the vape thing, looks away. 'You don't know what I'm doing. You have no idea.'

'You shouldn't be out here,' Carmen says again. She moves towards her, sees the goosebumps under Rachel's tan, how scared she is.

Rachel steps back out of the light. She trips and recovers. 'Back off, you're freaking me out. I've got a mate in the police, you know that? I'll tell her about this, about you.'

Rachel's bluffing – she won't tell. Carmen bluffs her back. 'Wouldn't bother me.'

'No?'

'Nup.'

'Bullshit.' Rachel walks backwards down the hill and Carmen

follows. It would bother her, if Rachel spoke to the police about her. If Neil has too. If he's told them anything about *that night*. It was bad enough what Alexis told them. Carmen doesn't want to go back inside that place.

She's not going back inside anywhere.

Another car slows on Marine Parade, coming up from the south. It indicates and turns. A flash SUV with dark tinted windows. A rich kid car this time, but Rachel hasn't called anyone. Its headlights are on high beam and for a second Carmen is dazzled and can't see. She wants to reach out and pull Rachel off the street.

'What do you know about him? Neil?' Carmen blurts, too late.

Rachel's distracted now, looks over her shoulder at the car. 'Fuck. No.'

The SUV pulls up close, a metallic grey Prado. The passenger window slides down.

The man in the driver's seat has red eyes. Dark shadows on the planes of his jaw. Gritted teeth. 'Raych. What in buggery are you playing at?'

Rachel has her arms wrapped around herself. 'Dad. I was only—'

'Get in the car.'

'But—'

'Get. In. The car.'

Rachel glares at Carmen. 'You don't know anything.'

Carmen opens her mouth to tell her she does know; she's figured out what Rachel's doing. It's clicked into place and filled her with a panic she doesn't understand. But Rachel climbs into the car and then the man is talking to Carmen, asking her if she needs a lift and where she wants to go.

Rachel's dad. Carmen remembers him.

But she backs away and shakes her head. She's not getting in the car with him. The window slides upwards, the Prado pulls out from the kerb and it leaves.

Carmen remembers that first week in the hospital better than the other weeks, which were all the same. Most of all, she remembers how much Rachel wanted to be dead.

3

Raych

What's a girl to do?

Carmen and me, we were choosing the shark. My little variation on choosing the bear – in the ocean instead of the woods. Only we didn't know it yet.

I mean, imagine you're alone and unarmed in a forest or the bush. It's dark and there's no one around. Who would you rather meet, a bear or a man? When that was doing the rounds online a couple of years ago, practically everyone I knew chose the bear.

And look, none of what the two of us have done would have happened if we had normal parents, normal families, normal lives, okay? If Piper hadn't been taken. If I was a different person. If I'd never met Carmen.

Too many bloody buggery ifs. I do know. But no one should

be surprised at us taking matters into our own hands. What's a girl to do, apart from that?

Carmen's family situation is shit, from what I've made out. I'm not saying that's an excuse, but it's not nothing either. She was adopted by a family with one other daughter, an uptight bitch who resents her, and the family are weird and religious. Makes me appreciate Dad a bit more, if I'm honest. And that's me reading between the lines, because Carmen doesn't talk about that stuff. Carmen doesn't talk full stop, not if she can help it.

Dad and Max, that's my younger sister, they're not around so much. Dad's either up north on a fly-in-fly-out shift or at the office. Max is at school or swim training or sleeping over at her best mate Kylie's place – whatever she can do to avoid spending time with her messed-up big sister, which is fine by me. Mum's not around at all. She drowned when I was six and Max was one, in the Pacific Ocean off the northern NSW coast, though if you ask me there was more to it than a straightforward drowning. The Valenti women have all died young. That's Dad's side of the family I know, but Mum and me, we were Valenti too.

So Dad's a FIFO single parent and I reckon he was feeling it. This doesn't excuse his actions here, but hey. It's those mitigating circumstances again, radiating outwards like the spokes of a wheel, or jellyfish tentacles, or just plain bad vibes, wrapping around us all.

I mean, what is it about these suburbs between the river and the ocean? Surely we've had our share of serial murder of women and girls? There aren't that many of us who live here, for a start. Not compared to LA, say, or Sydney.

It seemed like something was saying to us, over and over, you have too much, you've had too much for too long. Too much privilege. Too much sunshine and luck. You haven't appreciated it. You haven't been thankful.

We're going to teach you.

We're going to take your children.

It wasn't like other parents in the Perth metro area were locking up their daughters by this time, far from it. Maybe they should have been, but life had to go on. Plus we weren't going to take that victim-blaming BS; we'd never have tolerated it. Everyone going out along that Cottesloe strip was pushing crazy by then. The drinking had an edge to it, a ramped-up urgency, a big *FUCK YOU* to the killer.

It wasn't only me.

Dad went to town yelling as he drove me the few blocks home, away from the pines and the dark tilt of the ocean. *Blah blah blah* reckless and *blah blah* brainless . . . There you go, there's a taste. He was aggro at Carmen too, for not getting in the car, and she wasn't even there. Dad and I can hurl abuse for Australia when it's called for, when we're off-the-charts mad, which he was.

Dad's words bounced right off me, anyway. I'm armour-plated these days, don't you know? No one can hurt me any more than I've been hurt – except for one person, and I was still waiting to meet him.

I didn't know why Dad was combing the streets of Cott or how he'd found me, but he had, so I had to suck it up. He'd caught me at it, on one of my fishing-for-the-serial-killer nights out. Not that he'd guessed what I was doing. I'd got in the car because I didn't want a stand-up fight with him in full view of Carmen – I'd remembered her name but don't forget, this was the first time I'd seen her since our three days on the psych ward together last year. I didn't know the circumstances of her going in there, let alone them letting her out again.

Had Carmen figured out what I was doing, back there on the street? *What do you know about him?* She'd waited until the last second to say it. But how could she have figured it out? She didn't know about Piper. I wasn't on the ward long enough to talk about Piper, and I sure as shit wasn't making a lot of sense at the time.

There was no way Carmen could have guessed, not unless she was as fucked up as I was. Another big if, although possible. I didn't know her well enough at that point to know, and what were the chances of us both being fucked up in the exact same way?

I could still see her there on the street, her hair shining dark in the moonlight, skimming the shoulders of her steel blue long-sleeved tee. The steep angle of her fringe over one eye and the way she was always tucking a slippery fold of it behind one ear. I could see the white car again too, idling under the streetlight on Marine Parade like it was spot-lit in a movie. All the hairs had stood up on my arms the moment I'd seen the indicator go on. They were still that way now, as I sat there letting Dad's words crash over my head.

The car was a white station wagon, no distinguishing features except WA plates, too dark to see the model or make or rego number. They're everywhere, white commercial vehicles like that, and believe me, I notice cars. There was nothing exceptional about this one, apart from Lock behind the wheel.

His pale bearded face had been turned up towards us. Had I imagined the anticipation on it, the searching gaze in his dark eyes? Was he too far away for me to have seen that?

Carmen recognised him too, I know she did. But who wouldn't have? We'd all seen that car on the news.

People noticed, first up, that an unmarked car with two detectives inside was parked opposite Neil Fraser Lock's Bicton apartment, watching him twenty-four seven. The neighbours who'd noticed started taking the detectives coffees, FFS. Then one of them called the media, and they started watching him too. We all did.

We saw how often he drove his car around the Cottesloe backstreets, late of a night and early morning. How quiet, solitary and singular he was, how he didn't have a girlfriend or boyfriend, how he never went out with his mates.

And then he came out one afternoon and spoke to the journos.

My ex-cop contact Zee wouldn't confirm or deny it, but Lock said to the media and I'm guessing the police, that he hadn't killed anyone. That he was driving the streets of Cott to keep us safe. He was worried for us young ladies – that's what he called us, like he was twice his actual age – out on the footpaths, alone and vulnerable. He wanted to look out for us, to make sure we got home safe, so he drove the streets in a grid, circling back again and again to Marine Parade because that's where the girls were going missing from.

Mate, I'm no young lady. There's not a chance the cops believed his BS, either. I mean, sure, he'd grown up in Cottesloe – his parents' house was there on Broome Street – but he didn't live here any more. Whether he was killing us or saving us, he was an outsider. Either way, it had been two weeks now. They'd taken apart his apartment, his car, his known associates (few), his work and his life, looking for evidence, and hadn't found it.

Dad was quiet again, making the turns, the Prado humming smooth on residential backstreets with his Dad-worry filling the furthest corners of the car.

Lock and the surveillance, especially now he'd moved back with his parents, had been *the* topic of conversation in the bar and the Ocean View Club tonight. That and when, not if, the task force would be relieved by an interstate team. If I'm honest, before that night I'd never believed Lock was the one. It was too easy. He was some weird, unfortunate dude the cops had chosen to pick on. It wouldn't be the first time, not by a long shot.

But sitting there in Dad's car, remembering the face of him, turned up towards me and Carmen, I finally believed it.

That Neil Fraser Lock was *The Shark*. That he'd taken Piper and those other girls, and got away with it for all this time. That I'd been *this close* to meeting him and getting what I'd wanted for the last year. And maybe I would have, if not for Carmen.

Now, sure, I wish I'd trusted my instincts about him. But that was then. I didn't know any better. I didn't know what was to come.

'Earth to Raych!'

I turned to Dad and blinked. 'Huh?'

'Did you hear one word of that?'

The left-hand garage door yawned open in front of us, the sweep of Dad's headlights picking out the oil stain on the floor inside that tonight looked like blood, and throwing the shadow of the boat on its trailer up the front of the house. The boat that was too big to fit and crouched on our driveway like the chromed penis extension it was.

He was selling it, hadn't Dad said that? Before the move.

He'd clicked the remote but we were stationary on the drive with the engine idling. There was a moon out, two-thirds full. The moon wasn't something I usually noticed but I kept doing it and didn't understand why. What was Dad waiting for? I wanted to get inside to my room, get my head around things and decide what to do next.

'Did you?' Dad said again.

I kept my eyes on the house. 'You bet, Dad.'

He nodded. 'You bet. Righto.' He rubbed a hand over his face and shook his head. 'Unbelievable.' His nose looked bigger, reddish in the light from the dash. Had he had a drink? Two beers, maybe. A two-beers nose. But there were red blotches climbing his neck above the collar of his shirt – off-the-charts mad blotches. Maybe that's all it was.

'I'm this close, Raych.' He held a finger and thumb up in front of my face. 'Honest to buggery.'

'No, you're not. You're not close enough.' An unaccustomed haemorrhage of honesty on my part. 'You're way off.'

'What's that supposed to mean?'

'Nothing. Forget it.' I looked away, at the wing mirror. 'Objects in the mirror are not as close as they appear.'

'Is everything a joke to you?'

He was veering into that deadened tone I hated and I suddenly wanted to cry. I bit down on my lip and took a slow breath in.

Dad frowned out of the windscreen, staring down the house like he was contemplating the move up north. Contemplating the place we'd leave behind and where we were going next, when all I could think about was Neil Fraser Lock, and Carmen.

True, I hate our Cottesloe house. Cubic, concrete, and architect-designed with metal-shuttered windows in two tones of grey. Dad had the builder match one of those two greys to his MacBook Pro, which tells you more than you might care to know about Dad. Check this out, world. Take a look at our small, dysfunctional but prosperous family in our multi-million-dollar home, all paid for by the unconstitutional pillage of Nyamal Country. If things were different, and that was an off-the-charts if, I'd be ecstatic to be moving. But not out of town. Not like this. And not now.

Dad kept the car in Park and stayed silent. Uncharacteristically silent, which made me nervous as well as impatient. I figured he was waiting for me to say something, to give him some explanation for tonight, which I was never going to do.

Any normal person would've felt relief, that Carmen was there on the street and nothing had happened to me. But I didn't, hell no I didn't. She'd fucked it up for me, is the way I saw it. I didn't know then what it had started, us both recognising Lock in his car and saying nothing. Carmen, consciously or not, stopping him from making that turn up towards me.

But what was she doing there in the first place? Following me up a dark side street after midnight on a Cottesloe Sunday night, pretending to be concerned for my welfare when she wasn't. Believe me, Carmen is not someone who cares about her fellow humans. It's not how she's put together.

I stole a sideways glance and cleared my throat. 'Dad?'

'Talked to your sister this weekend?'

'She hasn't been home.'

'And you'd know that, would you?'

I inwardly rolled my eyes. 'She's been at Kylie's, where she always is. I'm guessing she's back now, asleep in bed.'

He nodded as if to say, 'Where we'd all like to be.' I wasn't in the mood to be guilt-tripped but he turned and looked at me and I could see he wasn't drunk, not even two-beers drunk; he was just tired, like he hadn't slept. I remembered he was on shift from tomorrow, now today, and had an early flight.

'Change of plan,' he said.

It was the tone of it. My fingers sprung into fists like they knew before I did what he was going to say. 'No. Dad—'

'Got the call tonight,' he said. 'Went to find you and tell you but you weren't back. Panicked. Stupid bugger.' He grinned, sheepish, which was a shitload more than I deserved. The grin went out again like a light, and I felt pretty low in that moment I can tell you. I imagined what his face was going to look like when I got what I wanted and disappeared down the rabbit hole after Piper.

Then he told me he was bringing the move forwards. That the house in Port Hedland was ready ahead of time. 'A fresh start. That's what we all need. Six days, Raych. Next Saturday. That's when the movers will be here.'

'But Max's—'

'The race is off. I've told Max she's not swimming. That's the end of it.'

The Rottnest Channel Swim. Max had been training for it for the last twelve months. The first time she'd be old enough to swim it.

The same day as Piper's anniversary, a year to the day since she was taken. And now the move.

The rush started at my shoulder blades and the backs of my knees. I fumbled the door open and half-fell, half-bolted out of the car. I needed to break something. But not in front of Dad.

I wasn't moving house.

*

Later, a shitload later and I honestly couldn't say what time it was, I washed up on Piper's old street in Peppermint Grove, opposite the deli. I'd been at the back of the empty units on Pearse Street again, smashing windows with discarded half bricks and rocks. It was four storeys and I'd done the whole of the ground floor now; if I went back for another shot I'd have to start climbing stairs. I was sweaty and emptied out, but calmer.

The night slash morning was moonlit dark and I swear was still as hot as the daytime, not a breath of Freo sea breeze to cool things the fuck down. I had my notebook with me, scribbling at full tilt everything that had happened since seeing Carmen and Lock on the street.

I'd changed outfits at home and walked from Pearse Street. Up the hill and down, over the footbridge – no trains and barely any highway traffic. Past the primary school and on away from the highway to where the peppermint trees grew thick and gnarly and ancient on watered grass verges and I could smell the river.

Piper's parents ran the Korean deli from way before she and her sister were born. The family lived in the back rooms of the sprawling house, one of those old homes on giant blocks the developers are rampantly sniffing out and bulldozing. Verandas all around it and a spreading tin roof under trees that dropped flowers and leaves and fruit all year and never got pruned, even when her family still lived there.

They built the shop up from nothing into one of those corner places where people queue all weekend. Where the neighbours have stand-up fights with punters over the parking and traffic, until they realise they like the convenience of 24/7 lattes and kimchi and cinnamon scrolls on their doorstep.

Not that it was like that now. It was a ghost-deli, a shadow of its former self.

One of Piper's posters was still in the front window of the shop, bleached pale from the year of sun with one corner curled away from the glass as if I'd slipped back in time. *Have you seen Hana Piper Lee?* The words caught in my throat like I'd said them out loud. Her dad had insisted on both names, but Piper never used her Korean name at school, and I'd worried people would miss it. The posters were in every shop and business between the river and the ocean, for months. We designed them in her dad's study, me and him. I'd taped that one up in the window myself.

The media made this huge deal about Piper's family, the hardworking immigrants done good and their terrible tragedy, as if a girl going missing from a less industrious mob from an outlying suburb would have made it less of a crime.

It made me sick, all that bullshit, and I know her parents hated it. Not that it made any difference. They still never found her.

I sat on the lawn across the street from the house. I always ended up here, outside Piper's house. It was the only building apart from our old place on Pearse Street I didn't want to tear down or smash up.

When we landed in the Pearse Street house from Sydney in the middle of the school year, everything seemed too bright to me. Even the teeth on the other kids at primary school were too bright. Mum was inexplicably dead and it was like there was this hole in the sky wherever I went that was as big as the hole in the ozone layer. That's the best way to describe it even though back then I didn't know what that was. The class teacher had told everyone not to ask me about my mum but all that did was make the hole seem bigger. Until this little person materialised next to me on the first day and asked me straight out what had happened to her.

Piper did it in this no-bullshit way that told me she got it, about the hole above our heads, that her family was in some way broken too. She slipped her fierce hand in mine and started defending me to anyone and everyone who'd listen, and although I didn't need defending, I wasn't going to argue with Piper because right away I could tell she wasn't someone you argued with. It was like she already knew me, like we'd always been friends. And we were, from that day on. Best friends for ever.

Except I loved her. I knew that right away too. Just because you don't have words for it, aged seven, doesn't make it not true.

FOR SALE/UNDER OFFER was still on the front lawn of Piper's house. It had been there a month. It was different in the moonlight, not as horrific as during the day when I usually sat here, but I still wanted to take an axe to it. The requisite tanned face and sparkling teeth of the real estate agent in the corner with her mobile number in giant digits. The lawn was neglected now, brown and unwatered. You'd think no self-respecting sparkletoothed real estate agent would let that happen, wouldn't you? But I guessed no one was interested in the lawn. I wondered when the demolition sharks would move in.

The front yard of the place opposite was plush by comparison, springy green buffalo grass with no prickles where I'd sit with my back against a jacaranda tree – I had done in every season and at pretty well every time of the day and night since Piper had gone missing. The people who lived in the house never came out or complained, never said a word to me, even when they were arriving or leaving in one of their two BMW four-wheel-drives, which is how I knew they'd guessed who I was. In the daytime the sounds of the family filtered out from behind the shaded windows. Tonight the place smelled of pool chlorine as well as the briny river. The dark was alive with the sounds of crickets and frogs but the house behind me was silent.

I leaned back into the hard trunk of the jacaranda and covered one eye so I didn't have to look at the real estate sign. I knew where Piper's family had moved to – as far south as they could get without dropping off the edge of Australia into the Southern Ocean.

It was a betrayal. I mean, okay, they didn't want to run the deli any more. I got that. And they were scared for Tami, her sister. No one knew back then why the killer targeted the girls he did. But to sell up and move away when Piper still might come home? How could they do it?

They were as bad as Dad, wanting to rip home away from me like a Band-Aid with the move to Port Hedland.

Don't get me wrong, I could see why Dad wanted it, to get his girls as far from here as he could. But why the urgency? Why couldn't he give me time? It felt like the world was collapsing in on me. I was still going to fight him.

I pulled Piper's gold iPod out of the pocket of my combats and turned it over in the moonlight. I knew every dent, every scrape and scuff, though I'd never once charged it up. I know, okay? I know that's weird. What can I say – it was the gutless wonder in me. I still carried it everywhere while my phone mostly languished in my room. I'd deleted all my socials; shit yeah, they were too painful to look at. No one called me these days anyway, not apart from Dad and Max, who I was usually trying to avoid, and Hazel, the one friend who refused to give up on me.

When I started going out on the Cottesloe strip again after Piper, I had to keep reminding myself people's reactions were about them and not me. I mean, some of them avoided me like we'd never even been friends, like Piper's tragedy was something they'd catch if they got too close. Some needed me to act as if nothing had changed, while others cried mascara tears at me in the toilets. But some of them were okay. They thought I was finding my way back to them, that I'd do it in my own time.

Hazel, though. Haze knew something was up. Max's mate Kylie's older sister, the girl at the end of a night out who'd always try to make me go home. I wasn't about to explain it to her, either. Some nights out on the strip I swear I'd feel Piper alongside me, one minute rolling her eyes at one of the characters from school, the next asking me WTAF I was playing at. I could taste it, how close I was to her, to the last time anyone saw her and what happened next.

I'd get that close and then lose it, like seeing her retreating through a crowd in a dream. And believe me, I've had my share of those bastard dreams.

The last time I saw her was there, in the pool house at Ronnie Lam's party on John Street. The way I still remember it, Piper's breathless and smiling, her eyes wide and shining and that crooked canine tooth snagging her lip as if she wasn't one hundred per cent sure if it was okay, what we'd just done. As if she was looking to me to reassure her that it was.

The worst thing, which whenever I let myself think it makes me feel like the most self-obsessed person in the world – because it's not the worst thing, not by a long shot – is everyone thinking I was Piper's best mate and not knowing the other half of the story. The biggest half, even though it had happened in the shortest time.

They didn't know I loved her. They only thought she was my friend.

As a friend, Piper was bossy, funny, fierce and opinionated. The rule breaker, the class disruptor, the girl who wanted nothing but to swim for Australia. Who gave the fat middle finger to the stereotype of the quiet, studious Asian girl who kept her head down. Who didn't give two shits what you thought of her, who sang out of tune 90s tracks at top volume with her headphones on.

As a girlfriend? I don't know. We didn't get to find that out.

I'd have given anything – *done* anything, no holds barred – to solve the mystery of Piper. Of *her* as much as what happened after she was taken. I didn't know her enough. We hadn't had our time.

And I wanted to know where she'd been going when she left Ronnie's party that night. What was so important it took her one block to the beachfront and the steps of the Ocean View Club – the last place she was seen before she vanished? Not a place she'd ever been, as far as I knew. She didn't hang with that crowd.

What was so important she didn't ask me to go with her? Was it because of me, because of us getting together for the first time?

Did she wish we hadn't done it?

There was a crow on Piper's threadbare lawn, creaking its wings in the moonlight and stabbing its beak into the sand like it owned the place. I told it to piss off and wreck someone else's lawn, but it flapped up onto the real estate sign and stared me down.

'You following me or what?'

Didn't crows sleep at night? I blinked, and frowned. Shit, that wasn't moonlight – it was daylight already, the morning bleeding into the sky like rain. My spiral notebook had imprinted itself on my hand while I slept. I didn't want to go home yet but I knew I had to. Dad would freak out if he got up and found I wasn't back, and I had to check the news.

Okay, Lock hadn't taken me last night – he'd got spooked, by Carmen or the cops or something different. But I had to know he hadn't taken someone else.

Stopping him was part of my plan, after all.

It took months for the police to flag the possibility of a serial killer on our patch. By the time they did, Piper had already been missing six months. Alarm bells had gone off with her disappearance, sure, but it wasn't until Mo, who vanished months later from the same spot, that the task force was set up.

The first victim, Christine Taylor-Watkins, a 19-year-old state water polo player, disappeared from outside the Beach Hotel after victory drinks with her teammates and uni friends. When her body washed up on Leighton Beach the next morning, it was thought she'd left her friends for a late-night solo swim and had a run-in with a great white or a tiger shark. It was the obvious assumption, even in winter – she was wearing a thermal rash vest and bikini bottoms, a neat pile of her clothes left folded on the sand at Cott. A reckless swim, for sure, like something out of *Jaws*, and the media made a big deal of her name at the time. Her injuries were horrific, it goes without saying. Everyone knows you don't go swimming alone at night, not off our beaches.

When Piper disappeared, the red flag was that she was last seen on the steps of the OVC, right next door to the hotel where Christine had been drinking. On the security footage that got released later, the footpath and steps were mobbed with people saying messy goodbyes to their mates. Piper was there one second – talking to an average-height male figure with dark hair, blurry on the CCTV, that no one has been able to identify – and the next she was gone.

Too similar to Christine to ignore, except Piper's body has never been found.

Mo was six months after Piper, a surfer up the coast at City Beach whose body showed up a week later at Scarborough, prompting speculation she'd been held for some days before she was killed. Four months later Maya, number four, washed ashore at Swanbourne. In an epic fail, the media labelled Maya *The Christmas Victim* when her family were Hindu. She was a twenty-one-year-old dive champion, studying Sports Science and living her best life.

They were swimmers, every one, with tall swimmer bodies – narrow boy-hips and broad defined shoulders – but there was more to it too. A bearing, forward motion, a length in their stride. Did they know they had it? Did others see it? I don't like to think about what it meant, why they were all of a type. But it's why he takes them, I know it is. It's what makes him want to take them down.

I don't have it, are you serious? No way. I fake it. I fake it like everything else.

The police had never released specifics – of the killer's MO, the state of the bodies, the injury detail – and Zee my ex-detective mate would never tell me anything. For my own good, she said, as well as that of the investigation. But someone has to be the one to find the body. Details get leaked, shared, obsessed over, speculated about all over the internet. By Maya, three things were clear. The killer kept these girls for up to a week before killing them. He restrained them, leaving ligature marks on their wrists and ankles. And the one detail Zee did tell me, for obvious reasons: there was no reported evidence of sexual assault.

If you read what's out there – and I did, because how could I stop myself? – the brutality of these killings isn't something we've seen before in Western Australia. The attacks appear to have been frenzied and prolonged, the cause of death likely blood loss but difficult to determine.

That was when I woke up to it – after Maya. That the deaths were getting more frequent. That the task force was getting nowhere. I'd done my time on the ward by then and I was back home with Dad, but I wasn't what you'd call sane. I was un-hinged and looking for answers. Where was Piper? Why hadn't her body been found? Did the killer still have her?

I needed action, and if the cops weren't going to bring it, I'd bring it myself.

I'd get him to take me and I'd find out what he'd done with Piper, even if I died trying. At the very least, I might save the next girl.

So that's what I did, at the end of every weekend night. I was the last girl standing, looking for trouble. I'd trip my way through the back-street dark with my shoes in my hand, looking for company. I'd hover on corners and under streetlights. Watch for his vehicle, listen for his footstep or the click of a car door.

As the weeks ticked by with no new victims, I got to be

superstitious about it. I didn't miss a single weekend night. Each time I was the last girl on the street and the killer didn't take me, I was saving someone else. I didn't know why. I didn't *care* why. It was another night ticked off. Another girl saved.

It's my only consolation, each time I go out there and he doesn't take me. That he hasn't taken another girl. I had to hope last night was the same.

So whatever Dad had decided, I wasn't giving up on my plan. Far from it. I was going to ramp it up. And that meant tracking down Carmen, who I reckoned knew more than she was letting on.

Because now I'd seen Lock and he'd seen me. Now it was even more personal than before. And next Saturday was Piper's anniversary. Enough was enough, and I couldn't do it on my own.

If he wasn't going to take me, then *we*, Carmen and me, would take *him*.

PART TWO

MONDAY

4

Carmen

Most people don't believe Carmen about most things

At school Monday morning there's a special assembly, and the rumours and whispers unfurl around Carmen, flung between the bodies of her classmates as they pack into the gym. *Mrs Craigie. Mrs Craigie. Mrs Craigie.*

Missing from the front bar of the Beach Hotel. Last night.

Carmen keeps her face blank and still so no one can see what's happening inside. This is something she's good at, but it's hard today; the gym is too hot, too sweaty and agitated and full to bursting with everyone's reaction to the news.

The principal delivers the facts only, no emotion, which Carmen likes, but she goes on to remind them Mrs Craigie was a valued and respected member of staff, which isn't true for everyone. She introduces Detective Jared Rosso and his sidekick, who are here to interview staff and students in her office. Carmen knows Detective Rosso, and Detective Rosso, worse luck, knows her. A stickler for rules and procedure except for when it's in his interest not to be, he's the one the Glassers called *that night*, the whole reason she ended up in the mental place. She knows too that this, today, is a waste of time, because if the killer has taken her, Mrs Craigie is already in the past. All of them, including the principal, whether they've noticed it or not, are talking about her in the past tense.

Detective Rosso tells them all to keep calm and not speculate, which is stupid and pointless because it's all anyone can talk about for the rest of the day. Not that the other kids talk to Carmen; they steer clear of her, like everyone does. Even Rosso doesn't ask to speak to her, which is a relief.

But it's weird for Carmen, Mrs Craigie going missing after seeing her through the front windows of the hotel last night when she was busy watching Rachel. It makes something itch down in the marrow of her bones, something to do with the other murdered girls, not only Mrs Craigie. She feels like this for the whole day, and at lunch she can't go into the music room because it's locked and she can't find Mr Ayele, which is bad because she needs to go in there today. Drumming in the music room is one of the things that helps her stay calm.

She drives straight home after school and walks to the beach instead. She nearly turns south towards Leighton but she mustn't do that, not now, so she goes to South Cottesloe. South Cottesloe is the crappy part of Cottesloe where the rocks are, and seaweed, south of the tea rooms and groyne and down past the golf course. The beach there is almost always empty except for a few dog walkers, and today there's no one.

Even from South Cottesloe, Carmen can see as far as Leighton, the flat stretch of it before Port Beach and the sticking-up things on the docks at Fremantle. And now she's not thinking about Mrs Craigie any more, she's thinking about Christine. The first one to die. Six months before *that night*.

Carmen didn't know Christine's name back then, of course she didn't. Carmen was just there, walking on the beach. She used to do that all the time, in the early morning between the night and the day, before everything started happening. Because things wash up. Dead things, sometimes. Interesting things.

Christine was on the sand at Leighton, stretched out flat like she was asleep, smelling of scrubbed-clean ocean. Carmen had never walked that far down before – she always turned the other way, north towards Cottesloe and Swanbourne. She doesn't know why she carried on that way. The waves were small, constant and quiet. It seemed like they'd spat Christine's body up for her and no one else. Because Christine wasn't asleep, Carmen could see that. Her arms and legs weren't right and her skin looked nearly white in that empty light that makes everything like a grainy photo, almost like you could see through it to what was underneath. Of course, there were places you could see what was underneath, on account of Christine's injuries and how she'd ended up there. And as well as the ocean smell, once Carmen got right up to her, the finest trace of blood.

Carmen can hack things most people can't, but if she's being honest, there are days even she doesn't like to think about Christine too much. It was July and Carmen was shivering, even though, as a rule, she doesn't mind the cold any worse than the heat. There was no one else there and she took a long time looking. Maybe that's all it was.

After she was done that day, Carmen walked away and kept on walking, first along the beach and then the footpath. She didn't see anyone, so she thought no one had seen her. But when she thinks back, there's that same sense she gets more and more these days – someone out there, watching her and waiting, the same way she watches everyone else.

Back home, Carmen stands in front of the bathroom mirror, one of those over-the-top ones with light globes around the frame that belong on *The Kardashians* or in an actor's dressing room. Except two of the globes have blown so now it looks like a mouth with two teeth knocked out.

Carmen has good teeth. They're her best thing apart from her brain, which is mostly good, except for those times when the stress gets too much for it. Those times it's like a screen going dim, consciousness going offline. Things happen at a distance and later she doesn't always remember them, like last night after talking to Rachel on the street. Carmen knew it would happen. It's normal for her, when *big things* happen. At least she remembers getting into bed and not waking up somewhere different like some of the other times.

Alexis goes to her Pilates boot camp and Mrs G to the supermarket on Monday afternoons, so Carmen knows she's got an hour, an hour and a quarter if she's lucky, of the house to herself before they get back. Without one or the other of them looking over her shoulder, telling her to do her homework, or in Alexis's case, doing or saying something mean.

By now, Carmen has a good collection of Alexis-inflicted

scars. Her favourite is a jagged one across her right elbow that looks like the coastline where WA meets South Australia, the Great Australian Bight, and was made with a pizza-cutter. She takes one of the sharks' teeth from the tin she keeps in her pocket and traces the line of the scar, the shape of the coastline where the ocean has bitten into the land. She tells kids at school it was a bite from a reef shark. She knows they don't believe her, but she's stuck to that story since it happened in Year Four.

Most people don't believe Carmen about most things.

When Alexis was eleven and Carmen was six, Alexis took Carmen to the old monkey bars at the edge of the school grounds, before anyone else got there, to see which one of them could hang upside down the longest with her eyes closed. Carmen knew she could do it; it wasn't even hard. But as soon as she started, Alexis grabbed Carmen's feet and flipped her off the bars, and she landed on her arm and broke it.

At first Alexis was frantic and tearful. It was an accident. She didn't mean it. She was sorry. But once the adults arrived she changed her story. The school nurse believed Alexis that Carmen had fallen from the monkey bars after swinging too hard and kicking her in the face. Carmen protested, first to the nurse and then the school principal, but by then Alexis had given herself a fat lip with her own school shoe and it was a question of evidence.

The pain in Carmen's left arm was a swamping thing that got bigger and bigger, all through the waiting and talking time at school until, when Mrs G was driving Carmen to the emergency department, Carmen's brain did its thing and the pain disappeared and didn't come back. The next day, with her arm in a cast, Carmen could only remember a few random things about the day before: the colour of the nurse's shorts at school, the sound of Alexis's fake tears, the smells in the emergency department waiting room.

The entire incident was confusing, and a lesson in Alexis's reach. Because Alexis is careful. She only lets people see what they want to. Mrs G believed the school, and Carmen was branded a liar, so she decided she might as well keep it up. She lied about why she hadn't done her homework. She lied about where she'd got chocolate bars and lollies she'd shoplifted, and the cigarettes she sold or gave away but never smoked herself. She lied about why she wasn't at school, and where she went instead. And in those two years – the first year of primary and then high school, the years she overlapped with Alexis – it was best not to be at school at all.

Carmen never told on Alexis again. But it was the first time she realised the benefit of her brain doing what it did, that pain could go offline the same way other things did.

At the mirror now, Carmen examines her nose; how broad it is and the constellation of freckles on it that never changes with the season. There's a reason she looks and feels different to everyone else. It's more than being adopted by the Glassers, and the way her brain works, and not being believed about anything. There's more to the story, but Carmen hasn't been able to find it out, on account of not knowing who her dad is, and of her birth mother not wanting to meet her.

Carmen's mum wouldn't even let the agency tell Carmen her first name when she contacted them. It was an unusual name, they told her. Too easily recognised.

All they would tell her was she was born in Armadale Hospital and the surname on her birth certificate: Chase, from her dad. She knew she didn't come from one of the rich kid suburbs and she's not surprised her mum didn't want to meet her or see her ever again, but at times she can't help thinking about it. She was only one when her mum gave her up for adoption.

How would she have known back then what Carmen was really like?

On the Levenson self-report psychopathy scale, Carmen scores a 2.9 out of 5 for primary psychopathy and a 4.3 for secondary psychopathy. She can't understand why the 2.9 is so low. She's repeated it several times but it's always the same.

When Carmen was a little kid, she thought her dad could be a bull shark, on account of the shape of her nose. She found a picture, in one of Mr G's *National Geographic* magazines, of a bull shark with a pale snout and spots that looked like her freckles. She cut that picture out and kept it.

Of course, she knows now that's not the case, about the shark.

While the house is empty, Carmen turns on the small TV in the kitchen. The afternoon sun through the blinds makes everything into stripes, and heats the room up so the lemon cleaning fluid Mrs G uses on every surface gets up Carmen's nose. She watches the end of a documentary on apex predators and trophic cascades, which is her best subject in all the world and another thing that helps her stay calm. Today it's saltwater crocodiles, which aren't her favourite, but she still watches. She likes sharks best, and David Attenborough, because of his quiet, whispery voice.

She still remembers the marine biologist from AQWA, the WA aquarium, who came to school in Year Eleven and spoke to her class. He showed them a speargun and knew all about the deep canyon and what lived down there. He listened to Carmen and answered her questions, and didn't think they were strange. He was like the next best thing to David Attenborough himself.

Carmen likes the parts of these documentaries that have Alexis hiding behind her starfished fingers as if she's the biggest wimp out, when Carmen knows for a fact she's not and it's all an act. The chase parts when they show you the predators missing out two or three times and going hungry before at last they get one. Carmen always leans further and further forwards on the couch at those parts if she's watching in the TV room. Once she fell off, but that doesn't happen today, in the kitchen.

It's not the killing Carmen likes, it's the stillness before it happens. The control. Carmen would like some of that for herself, but you can't say that to people, not without them getting the wrong idea. The reason big predators are at the top of every food chain isn't only because they're more powerful than everything else.

It's because they're good at waiting.

At the end of the documentary, she watches a jumping spider on the windowsill outside the kitchen while she waits for the news to come on. She likes the way they move, like someone has filmed them and is playing them back at twice the speed. She'll have exactly enough time to watch the first news story and switch it off again before Mrs G and Alexis get home.

Carmen and Alexis aren't allowed to watch the news, not since the murder case. Mrs G thinks she's protecting them, her birth daughter and her adopted one, from what's happening out there in the backyard of their suburb. She polices the television, phones and the internet as if they live in the 1950s, but she can't be everywhere at once. Alexis goes to work in that beauty place and to her exercise classes at the gym and the pool. Carmen goes to school and the library. Mrs G keeps track of them using their phones, but Carmen keeps hers switched off and pretends the battery has run down.

Mrs G calls Alexis a VSP, a *very sensitive person*, as if the rest of Perth doesn't give two shits about girls getting got so their bodies wash up on the beach and afterwards the council has to do a big clean-up. She says she won't have evil in the house, but Carmen's not certain she's talking about the murders when she says it.

Mrs G only cares about what happens inside her own home.

The news starts and Carmen rests her chin in her hands and her elbows on the fake-stone kitchen counter and gets close enough that the static from the old TV screen tickles the end of her nose. First up is always the murders, and today is no different. Every time she watches, she waits for them to bring up the killer. To discuss the MO and signature, to speculate about the killer's psychology and geographical profile – where they're from and why they hunt in the places they do. To interview the experts who've been flown in to crack the case.

But they never do. They go on about lines of enquiry and public appeals for information, numbers of investigating officers and the lack of physical evidence, day after day, without saying anything at all. There are no experts from interstate or overseas, only local detectives. Sometimes they show Neil's parents' house or him driving his car.

Carmen is certain the police have no clue. It annoys her too, that everyone assumes the killer is a man, even if so far the weight of suspicion points to Neil. It's bad enough that men take the credit for things women do all the time without people encouraging it.

Today they show Mrs Craigie's picture again, and the four girls before her, against footage of Cottesloe, shot from above with a drone. The water is aqua in the shallows and navy out deep, and Carmen knows that drone footage was taken with tourists in mind, not the bodies of dead girls.

She shuts off the TV and has a moment of not being able to draw her eyes away from the black screen, the pictures of those girls stuck in her vision like sunspots. She wonders what it's like in your brain, that instant when your life is ripped out from under you.

Carmen often wonders about things like that.

People have been calling the killer *The Shark* since the second body showed up. That was the third victim, according to what they say on the news, which is never the full story. The name and the Polaris task force are on account of the injuries sustained by the victims, which anyone knows about by now if they read what's on the internet.

The police will be mad, Carmen reckons, about the shark name. It makes the killer into a monster, a bit of a legend. For sure, most people will hate that, but some might not.

She doesn't mind the shark name too much. It fits.

Carmen's still staring at the TV screen when she hears the front door open and Alexis talking at maximum volume over the top of her mother. She didn't hear the car pull up and has only enough time to slip into the pantry and pull the door closed, which considering Mrs G has been grocery shopping, isn't the greatest of hiding places.

But Mrs G unloads fruit and vegetables into the fridge and the fruit bowl, puts the kettle on and fills the teapot from the canister on the kitchen counter, so Carmen is safe. She's backed into the furthest corner of the pantry with the two middle shelves pressing into her back, one above and one below her waist.

Alexis, Carmen knows, will already be sat at the breakfast bar, her handbag on the seat next to her and her hands folded in her lap, waiting for her mother to bring her whatever she wants. Carmen can't see them, only the flitting of shadows through the louvred pantry door, the kitchen sounds of tap and kettle, shopping bags and fridge door. And Alexis's sing-song voice, lecturing her mother about her favourite subject:

Carmen.

'Oh, but this is disappointing,' Alexis says. 'She's been watching this, hasn't she? In secret. I thought Carmen was doing better, Mum?' Alexis's sentences all go up at the end like she's asking you a question, when really she's telling you the answer.

'It's still warm?' Alexis adds. 'She'll have been watching the news, I'll bet. The *investigation?*'

Alexis won't say the words *murder, killer, dead* or *victim*, but Carmen knows that's all for show like everything else about her. She can picture it, Alexis bent forwards at the waist to place the back of her hand against the TV screen. The fake shock in her eyes and the static pulling at the tiny, fluffy hairs there. Mrs G clicks her tongue, whether at this revelation about Carmen, or at Alexis being Alexis, Carmen can't tell.

'And I thought she was doing *so* much better,' Alexis goes on, in her daytime TV show voice. 'Since Christmas. Don't you think?'

She doesn't. She's building up to something.

Mrs G says some words Carmen doesn't catch. Carmen takes a step closer to the pantry door. She hears Mrs G pour Alexis her tea – a slice of lemon, no milk – the clink of the teaspoon, the clank of the cup in the saucer.

'You'd never guess how bad she was six months ago, would you? I was thinking she could maybe get her own place soon; she's eighteen now, after all.'

'I don't think so, Alexis,' Mrs G says. 'Carmen needs to finish her schooling. You know my stance on that.'

Carmen knows she's a job to Mrs G, that this obsession with her finishing school is for appearances, like everything else she does. She's heard the things Mrs G says about her daughter behind closed doors. The way she encourages Leo, Alexis's fiancé, to keep a tight rein on Alexis and not to trust her. Alexis would be shocked, Carmen reckons, if she knew what her mother really thought of her.

'But how long's that going to take?' Alexis says. 'What if she has a relapse and has to miss more school? She was *unhinged*, those first few months of last year.' This is one of Alexis's favourite words when discussing Carmen. Her voice gets dangerously high-pitched when she says it.

'She was depressed,' Mrs G says. 'Diagnosed and treated.'

'She had a breakdown. Same difference. What if she has another one?' Alexis picks up her cup and puts it down. 'She was in that place months before she admitted she'd lied. What did that psych say? We need to watch for signs? This obsession with the *investigation*, for example. Not to mention the grisly things she likes to watch on TV when she thinks no one's looking.' Alexis lowers her voice but it's still loud and clear. 'I think she watches them to provoke me.'

Carmen would roll her eyes if there was anyone to see. She runs her hands over the pantry door, and hooks her fingers into the louvres from the inside. The door's not heavy. She could rip the whole thing off its hinges if she tried.

The kitchen tap goes on and then off again. 'I doubt that, Alexis,' Mrs G says.

'Perhaps she doesn't need to move *out*, exactly? Perhaps she needs to go back inside—'

'No, Alexis.'

But there's no stopping her now. 'She makes me feel unwell, Mum,' Alexis says. 'You know she does. I still get the headaches. She makes me feel unsafe in my own home. It's how uncommunicative she is, how furtive. Her lurking and creeping around.' She sighs. Carmen is familiar with this, Alexis in full Princess Di mode. 'You weren't there. I still have flashbacks to that night.'

Carmen waits for it.

'It's like living with a wild animal in the house.'

Mrs G and Alexis finish their tea and Carmen escapes the pantry without them knowing she's been in there. She's only just got into her room when the doorbell rings and Mrs G calls her name from the front door.

'You're wanted. Police,' Mrs G says when Carmen reaches her, an expression on her face that could be actual physical pain.

'Why?' Carmen's brain searches through all the things it could be about.

There are a lot.

'I don't know, Carmen. Don't keep them waiting.' She says they're in the drawing room, her ridiculous name for the front lounge room where no one is allowed. Except the police, it seems. Carmen knows it's Rosso in there from his obnoxious fruity cologne before she's even opened the door, and Mrs G's bum-faced expression is because of the car out front, and the neighbours. Rosso and the Glassers go to the same church but Mrs G won't be able to spin this into a social visit however much she'd like to. She clop-clops back along the hallway to the kitchen as Carmen sets her face and opens the door.

Rosso has dark stubble and eyelashes and checks his hair in available shiny surfaces when he thinks no one's looking. The other one is the same as this morning at school – a young woman with freckles and straight blonde hair whose eyelashes are the opposite of his and so fair they're transparent. He's big and she's tiny, both in dark suit pants and light blue shirts. Rosso says their names even though he knows Carmen knows who he is.

How can she not? Detective Rosso is Carmen's sworn enemy. The person who got her put in the mental place. The reason she was stuck in there for three months. The person who caught and returned her each time she escaped, which was four times in total before they figured out how she was doing it. She doesn't trust anything about him.

He doesn't try to shake her hand, which is good.

'Sit, please.' He nods at a chair opposite the couch, which is pushing it when she lives here. Why have they come? Is it something to do with *that night*, or because they know Carmen never liked Mrs Craigie? She can't be the only one at school who didn't.

'Do I have to talk to you?' she says.

'It would be best.' There's a smile waiting behind his lips but he doesn't let it out. 'You want to help us find your teacher, don't you?'

Wrong question, Carmen thinks. But fine. She's not going to tell him anything. She sits in the chair. She doesn't like this room, which always smells of new carpet, and now Rosso's cologne.

'Your mum not staying?'

'She's not my mum.' He knows this. 'I'm eighteen. She doesn't have to.'

Rosso frowns. 'You may have someone else present, if you want that.'

'Like a lawyer?'

Now he smiles. 'I doubt you need one of those.' He's got a folder open on his lap, printed sheets of paper Carmen can't read. His partner beside him is sat up straight with her notebook out. Carmen needs to be careful. He clears his throat. 'I understand there was a . . .' He glances at the file in his lap. '. . . an incident, between you and Mrs Genevieve Craigie?'

Carmen's feet get hot, and under her arms. How do they know about that? One of the kids at school today. She wraps a hand around the tin of teeth in her pocket – it's the right size for that, for whenever she needs to reassure herself it's still there.

Rosso flips pages in his folder. 'Three, no four, of your classmates have reported this exchange between you and Mrs Craigie outdoors on the school oval. She called you a—'

But Rosso's partner whispers something and he changes tack. 'Yes. Quite.' He looks up at Carmen. Her face is hot now. 'She bullied you. You could have reported it. But that may not be relevant now. Carmen, another witness – one of your teachers – has said—'

'Which one?'

'I'm sorry?' A tightness in his stubbled cheek.

'Which teacher?'

He holds her gaze. She doesn't blink. Almost anyone at school would lie about her given the chance.

'This *staff member*,' he continues, 'reports that you've been following Mrs Craigie in your car. You parked next to her in the Number Two Car Park on Marine Parade last night.'

'No I didn't.'

'You were not aware of that?'

'Is her car still there? It's a big car park.'

His eyes go narrow as he stares at her. 'Yes, it is. You're not a suspect in this inquiry, Carmen. But *if* you were following Mrs Craigie—'

'I wasn't—'

'. . . you may have seen something without understanding its significance. I'd like you to tell me, please, if you recall anything unusual in the car park last night. Someone else showing an interest in Mrs Craigie, for example.'

When Rosso says please it's not the way most people say it – it's like he knows you'll do what he says. But Carmen can't do what he says because she didn't see anyone in the car park.

She grips the tin in her pocket and stares at him until he blinks. He's looking at Carmen the way he might look at a snake or a spider he doesn't know how to deal with, which she remembers from before and likes. She considers a lie, making up someone in the car park. She's good at lying. It's not rocket surgery – you only have to get from the back foot to the front. Make your eyes go big and never look to one side or up at the ceiling, because everyone knows that's what liars do if they watch TV.

But she doesn't lie. 'There was no one.'

He doesn't believe her, she can tell, but what can he do? He asks her a few more questions, about school and Mrs Craigie, about what she was doing there last night, if she went inside the bar or the club, which of course she didn't.

She says she parked and walked on the beach by herself and the woman writes it all in her notebook, which makes Carmen feel weird down inside her bones and wish she'd made up something bigger, something over the top outrageous to see if she'd write that down too.

And then it's over and Carmen's shoulders drop and she opens the front door and lets them out. Rosso leaves her a card with his name and direct number on it, as if they're on the same side when it's obvious they're not and never have been. She slips it into her pocket before Alexis or Mrs G can get a look at it.

But now she's thinking back to last night. Was there a person in the car park she didn't see? Is that what the feeling is, the sense of someone out there in the dark? Was there someone watching Carmen, while she was watching Rachel?

Of course Carmen is looking for a way out – from the Glasser household, from Alexis's campaign of terror, from having to finish high school a year later than everyone else. There's no shame in it. And Alexis is right about one thing. Carmen's eighteen now. She can do what she wants.

The problem is how to do it. Because Carmen is a particular kind of person. She knows she wouldn't cope on the run. Where would she go? How would she deal with life, and worst of all, people?

Carmen's not the kind of person who'll save the day and be a hero. If anything, she's the opposite. Even if she wanted to save the day, even if she *could*, there's the fact of not being believed about anything.

She goes back to her room and opens the tin in her pocket and takes out the tooth she found on Christine's body that time. She knows which one it is. The tooth was just there, snagged in a rip in Christine's rashie. Carmen had a job to pull it out.

She was worried Rosso was going to ask her about it, that someone at school had seen her with it. She didn't want to tell him about finding Christine's body and she can't remember now where the tin came from. One week she didn't have it and the next week she did – the day after *that night*.

Carmen's not going back inside the mental place. They kept her in there for three months because of Rosso, plus that's how long it took for all the risk assessments and forensic assessments and everything else. It took Carmen telling them what they wanted to hear in the exact right way so they believed it. And Alexis could make things worse for her at any time.

The thing about Alexis is, if you push her too hard up against something she doesn't want to hear or know about, she'll do almost anything not to hear or know about it. Maybe Carmen can use that. Plus, there's the new development of Neil. She doesn't have that figured out yet.

Carmen has schemed about killing Alexis for years. More than ten, which considering her age, is a lot. She's imagined countless times where and how she'd do it. Whether there would be blood or not, and whether she could do it without having to physically touch Alexis. Whether she'd want Alexis to know why she was doing it (yes, every time) and whether she'd confess afterwards to having done it and explain why she did. She's wondered too where Alexis's body would end up and whether she'd want anyone to find it.

But *that night*, when she tried, it went wrong.

What Carmen remembers about *that night* is being in Alexis's bedroom with her body filled with so much adrenaline it was like a bottle under a tap that was already full but the tap was still on. There were those words she heard, 'Not her,' in Neil's voice, and the dark blue colour of his polo shirt. And then Carmen was crouched on the floor with Alexis in front of her, flat on her back with her eyes open and terrified. Alexis's lamp was raised above Carmen's head like she was about to bring it smashing back down. The power cord was dangling where she'd pulled it out from the socket, and Carmen had one hand at Alexis's throat, which is weird because she'd do almost anything to avoid touching Alexis.

That's how Mr and Mrs G found them. Apart from that, all Carmen knows is what Alexis said afterwards, the conversations in the kitchen she overheard, first between Alexis and her parents, and then between them and Rosso after they called him. The next day Carmen was on the ward in the adolescent unit and Mrs G was telling her how lucky she was Alexis hadn't taken things further and she hadn't been charged.

Alexis had some injuries to her head and neck, but by the time Carmen got out of hospital three months later, they were gone.

Carmen knows what she was trying to do, so why didn't she do it? Did Neil stop her? And if he did, why did Alexis lie?

She waits for the house to go quiet and then she steals a slab of cooked salmon for the girl cat and slips out of the front door unseen. She'll tell them later she went to the library. She goes to the empty apartments and puts the fish down on a broken piece of terracotta tile. She stands back from the window in the front corner apartment, watching the golf course and waiting for the cat to smell the fish and come.

When the girl cat comes, she steals into the room like smoke, keeping to the shadows like she always does. Carmen likes that they're the same that way. The cat's hungry and the fish disappears in five bites.

Neil doesn't come today, the same as last Monday. He was out late last night, that's why, driving his white car around the streets of Cottesloe. And something happened after that, because how else did Mrs Craigie end up gone from the front bar of the Beach Hotel?

Where is Mrs Craigie now? Is she already dead?

Carmen would prefer it if she could remember the whole of last night after talking to Rachel. There might be something important in it. She remembers going to her other place, the one no one knows about. It was still dark when she got home and went to bed, and the light was on in Mr G's shed. She remembers the bottom of her jeans being wet when she took them off. But by this morning, they were dry.

If Carmen's not going to save the day and she's not going to do a runner, what's she going to do instead?

It's not as if she did nothing when she found Christine's body. Of course she did something. She walked the whole way to the payphone on the highway and called it in. Anonymously – the cops didn't need to know who she was – but she still made the call to triple zero. She didn't know the Crime Stoppers number back then. Her teeth were chattering which wasn't a thing she remembered ever happening before, and the woman on the end of the line kept on asking her if she was okay.

She couldn't tell them her name on account of the shark's tooth she'd taken and a few things she'd done before. Not big deal things, small run-ins with security guards at shopping centres and once the police, all before Detective Rosso came on the scene and stuck his oar in. But Mrs G wouldn't have liked it, Carmen giving the police her name for something like that, a dead body. And Alexis would have found a way to take advantage of it.

This time, Mrs Craigie's body hasn't even washed up yet. So why is she thinking about her so much? It's because of Rosso, and Neil. The police might arrest him, and how will Carmen talk to him then? They might already have done it.

It's no wonder Carmen was depressed after *that night* when she was in the hospital. She shouldn't have tried to kill Alexis. But worse, she shouldn't have failed. She should have done it quicker, and better. She should have finished the job.

5

Raych

Fight Back Club

There were seven missed calls from Haze when I got home Monday morning, the first at 6 a.m. She called again as I checked the news on my laptop and I figured she wasn't going to stop.

'I've seen it,' I said. 'I'm looking at it now.'

Sometime after Carmen and me had seen him on the street, Lock had taken another girl. Genevieve Craigie, a 24-year-old PE teacher from Carmen's school, last seen in the front bar of the Beach Hotel.

'Are you okay?' Haze said.

WTF did people keep asking me that? No, I was not okay.

'Raych? Say something.'

'Like what?'

'We saw her. She . . .' I heard Haze swallow. 'She was right in front of us.'

We hadn't talked to her, interacted with her, had never met Genevieve Craigie, but I recognised her picture as soon as I saw it. A face in the crowd, someone who went to the same places we did. Haze was right, it was too close, but not in the way she thought. I felt sick, hot, like I was burning up. Genevieve was the first to be taken since I'd started my mission. The first time I'd failed. And I knew. I knew he'd have taken me instead if Carmen hadn't been there.

I didn't know what to do. If I should be calling the cops or not, telling them we'd seen him, but how would I explain myself? And how would it help? Genevieve was already gone.

'It's not like we knew her.' Even I could hear how lame that sounded.

'So what?' she said. 'It could have—'

'But it wasn't.'

'The police will want to talk to us, I guess.'

'Why? There were about a hundred other people there, Haze. Look, I have to go—'

'Is this about that thing I said?'

'What? No.'

'Because I said I was sorry. I am sorry.'

'It doesn't matter.'

'It does. It was dumb.'

'It wasn't—'

'Let me say sorry, okay! For fuck's sake.'

'Okay.'

'So, are we good?'

Of course we weren't good. Nothing was good.

'Sure, Haze. We're good.'

My head was a mess trying to decide whether to talk to the cops or not about Lock and his car on the street, but in the end I didn't do it. I played the good daughter and saw Dad off instead. He gave me three hundred bucks on the doorstep while the Swan Taxi waiting to take him to the airport idled in the street.

I slid the cash into a pocket – six brand-new fifties – without looking like I was too interested. I'd let it go about the house move. I knew I'd got off light last night, plus I was back inside my room before Dad even woke up. Let him get out of my face. I had shit to do.

The morning sun was behind Dad on the step and the shadow of the boat on its trailer fell around him like a pool of oil. He was in his work high-vis and boots, his face invisible under the brim of his hat. The taxi behind him had its window open and the local talk radio was all about Genevieve Craigie. People were calling in and trashing the police investigation, half of them saying Lock was the killer and had her stashed somewhere, and why hadn't they made an arrest? The other half said it couldn't be him and were calling for the task force to be replaced by an east coast team.

One old dude phoned in to say the deaths were all shark fatalities and the whole murder case was a hoax – a man-hating conspiracy cooked up by women who no longer knew their place.

Say that to my face, you ignorant old fuck.

Dad hovered with Dad awkwardness on the doorstep – that awkwardness honed to perfection over the last twelve months.

He'd been gone so much this last year – extra shifts, last minute changes – but that went both ways. I leaned in the doorway, arms crossed, willing him to go.

'Righto. Last shift, before—' He trailed off and coughed. Looked at his feet in his work boots. At least he had the decency not to try and look me in the eye. 'It's Marble Bar, or near enough, same as always.'

'I know.'

'Bloke'll be round to pick up the boat Thursday. Keys are in it and I've sold him the trailer. He'll drive it away.'

'Fine.' I had zero interest in what Dad was doing with the bloody boat.

He rubbed a hand over his face. 'Got anything to say about last night?'

I scuffed a heel and looked up at him. Chewed the inside of my lip. 'No, Dad. Won't happen again.'

Liar.

To be fair, he didn't look like he bought it. He bent down to pick up his carry-on bag and the light caught his face. His brow was creased with anxiety and there was a shine of sweat on his nose. He'd cut himself shaving and there was a bruise on his jaw next to it, like he'd whacked his chin on something.

I felt the guilt again, wondering what he'd come back to next weekend.

He straightened and shouldered his backpack. 'I'll be out of mobile range once I get out there, but it's a short one: six days. The movers are booked for Saturday. So all you and Max need to do this week is pack up your stuff, and—'

I bashed a heel against the step over and over while I waited for him to finish. But he didn't. What was he failing to say?

Don't do anything I wouldn't do? Don't go chasing serial killers?
One of those old clichés. *Don't trash the house* was more like it.

'You can go now, Dad. Your taxi's waiting. Don't miss the flight.'

He frowned and stared at his boots some more. Rubbed a thumb over the shaving cut. Opened his mouth and closed it. Maybe he was going to suggest I make one last appointment with that therapist, the anger management one whose lamp I smashed and no one asked me to pay for it. Or he wanted to say, *Me and Max, we only want what's best for you.* Or, *We miss Piper too,* the same thing Haze had said the last time I saw her that she kept apologising for.

Instead he said, 'Spend some time with your sister this week. A fresh start, that's what this move is about. For all of us. And no going out after dark. That's non-negotiable. Consider yourself grounded till I get back.'

Legit. His parting shot. My heel stopped its bashing and I felt the arguments stack up in my throat, my blood ramping for a fight. But screw Dad. He was away for the week. He couldn't ground me.

And he'd forgotten Max was leaving for swim camp today.

'Sure, Dad. Whatever,' I said, and lifted a hand in goodbye.

He tipped the brim of his hat back and squinted at me. 'Not getting sick, are you?'

'I'm right as rain.' A half-truth this time. I shut the front door behind me as the taxi pulled away.

Max wasn't back from camp until Friday. The movers were coming Saturday. Piper's anniversary.

I had one week.

*

I schlepped the long hallways back to my room in bare feet, showered, dressed, made coffee, and by the time I'd done all that Max was leaning on the wall across from my room, beside her open door, waiting. Bright-eyed and pony-tailed and a head taller than me, with her boy-swimmer shoulders and tiny waist. 'I need a lift,' she said, in that tone.

'Good morning to you too, Maxie,' I said. 'Ready then?'

She side-eyed the matching large and small rucksacks next to her, like *duh*, of course she was ready. She was her father's daughter. She was zipped and organised and track-suited ready. She was an alien, not a teenager. I was the only person who ever copped any attitude from her.

'Awesome. We'll take Dad's car.' I turned on my heel and glimpsed the inside of her room through the half-open door. The boxes, the bare mattress, the empty built-in robes. 'You already packed up your stuff?'

She gave that a fat sigh. 'I'm not here, like, all week?'

'But you haven't been home. When did you do it?'

Max was always at Kylie's. A big sporting family, a whole one with no missing parents. A water polo team of siblings including Haze and her older brothers and sister. There was no competition.

'I've been here,' she said. 'You just never notice.' She yanked her bedroom door shut to cut off my view. I knew Max wasn't stoked to be moving. She was no different to me in that respect. But she'd never admit it to Dad. 'And keep out of there while I'm gone!'

Little shit. Except she was bigger than me. And I guessed the aggro was fair.

She hefted both her rucksacks and I drove her to school in

chunky silence. 'Did Dad give you cash for me?' she said as we pulled up behind the line of buses inside the gates.

'Shit, I reckon he forgot.'

She gave that the bullcrap stare.

'You won't even need it. Not on camp.' But I slipped her two fifties as she climbed out of the car.

She swung her bags off the back seat and grumbled thanks through the open passenger window. Took a look over her shoulder then turned back to me and hovered, chewing on a thumbnail.

'What?'

'You're going to pack up your stuff, right? For the move?'

I put the Prado in Drive. Kept my foot on the brake. 'You bet.'

'Okay. Just ... don't do anything ... Be careful, okay?' She frowned.

'You know me, sis.'

'And remember I'm staying at Kylie's Friday night, before the race. You don't need to pick me up.'

'Got it.' I nodded. 'No, hold on.' I put the Prado back in Park. The people carrier behind me edged closer. 'Dad said you wouldn't be swimming. He said—'

'I've worked for it. I'm not letting the team down.' She set her jaw like Dad and looked away. 'Dad's having a conniption, that's all.'

A what? Who used words like that? And Ms Perfect *never* went against Dad. I leaned across the passenger seat. 'No, Max, you know what? Dad is worried, and maybe you could—'

'Fuck off, Raych.' She smiled sweetly for the watching teachers and stalked away. The car behind me leaned on its horn.

I guessed she wanted to swim pretty bad. Maybe she was a real teenager after all.

Back at home I opened up her room and stepped inside. It wasn't like she'd left a hair trapped in the door. The déjà vu took me back to a year ago, three days after Piper went missing, and what I'd done here.

You know those days when you want to rip off a few heads and leave them lying around for other people to trip over? Instead, I smashed the fuck out of my younger sister's room and ended up in hospital. Every swim trophy, every globe in every string of flowery fucking fairy lights, every picture frame with her junior champion face in it. Not forgetting the glass top of that dressing table.

A meltdown with teeth. You imagine stuff like that to be cathartic, but I can tell you from repeat experience it's not. I could still feel it, standing there looking at what was left of her stuff. Max's room had always been neat. Now it was boxes and stripped back furniture. It even smelled clean, like she'd sprayed and wiped, when the cleaners would do that. Freak.

After I'd done the smashing, and I was out pinballing the streets with my lungs raw as burnt rubber, all I'd wanted was to do it again, do it some more. Go bigger and harder.

It was either that or the worst thing. Which is how I found myself on a demolition site for the first time, smashing windows with a rusty metal star picket I'd found, so I wouldn't smash myself up. When the cops arrived I wound up on the acute psych ward because Dad was on shift that week and out of mobile range for two more days. And yep, I blamed Max for that too, which was likely harsh.

I left the door to her room open now, because I knew she'd

be pissed about it, and went back to mine. I wove my way between toppling stacks of true crime books that had so far failed to give me the answers I wanted and flung myself onto the bed. Piper would've hated the books I was reading – the classics like *In Cold Blood* and *The Stranger Beside Me*, the obsessive and beautiful like *I'll Be Gone in the Dark*. Despite us having started up KCSI together in Year Five – Killer Crime Solutions and Investigations – Piper did not like dark things.

Yeah, I don't like to think too hard about that either.

We set up KCSI because we each had our own mystery to solve. I was certain my mum had been killed by a shark, but Dad would only ever tell me she'd 'drowned peacefully' which made no sense at all, even to the six year old I was when she died. Piper wanted to find out why her dad kept having affairs and stop it happening so her mum wouldn't leave and her family wouldn't fall apart. Her family did fall apart, but that was later, because of what happened to her, not because her dad was a serial adulterer. At the time it made us feel better about our own unfathomable things if we could help other kids at school solve theirs. Back then, I wanted to study criminology when I got older and set up as a cool girl PI, even after Dad told me that wasn't what criminologists did for a job. Admittedly Piper and me only got to the bottom of one dead cat mystery (a hit and run) before we were shut down by our class teacher for being 'age-inappropriate'. She didn't want to do it any more anyway, not after we found the cat.

I prodded a book stack now until it leaned and avalanched. *Helter Skelter* slid the furthest. The books weren't helping me, even I could see that. They were only pushing me deeper. The thing about the rabbit hole of true crime is, it doesn't only show us what we're afraid of, but what we're afraid of turning into.

I knew what Max thought. That I was a drama queen. The family trouble-maker. The cause of all Dad's stress. And fair enough, maybe I was. But it was different for her when Mum died – she was only one. And sometimes I wondered, was there more to her attitude with me than that?

Max had been weird in the days after Piper went missing. Avoiding me, not giving me a straight answer about whether she'd been there that night or not. She was way underage, but Kylie's older siblings were always holding court at the OVC. Not Haze – we were all underage back then, and Haze was not a rule-breaker – but the others. Max and Kylie would hang out in the kids' playground across Marine Parade some nights, or flirt with older boys on the steps of the club until the bouncers chased them away.

Max felt guilty, maybe. But was it survivor's guilt, or something more?

Sometimes I thought she must have seen Piper that night, that she had to have seen *something*. But the police never interviewed her.

At the time all I knew was this thing beyond imagining had happened to Piper and no one had answers for me. And back then at least, I wished it had happened to Max, and not to her.

Mate, whatever you're thinking about me, I bet you a thousand dollars I've thought worse.

I got a park out front and was halfway to the door of the surf club when Haze yelled out, 'Raych? Wait up.'

Shit. Too slow. She'd parked in the spot behind mine. 'We'll be late,' I said.

'You're late every time!' I could hear the eye-roll. Fair enough. I'd been a punctual person, back before the chaos.

Fight Back Club was the self-defence club for women, girls and non-binary folk my ex-cop mate Zee had started up six months before in the surf club gym. It was ex-homicide detective Zee's response to the situation we found ourselves in, sponsored by the Beach Hotel and some of the Marine Parade businesses.

She'd intended it to be all about strategy – how to stay safe at home and at work, on public transport, out at a bar or on the street. Zee taught us to be mindful; to assess our environment, available exit routes and other people; to lock our car doors as soon as we got inside. Like, you can have a key fob configured to unlock only the driver door and not all of them. How to avoid trouble before it happened, basically.

Only when she reckoned we had a handle on all that did she teach us some defensive moves: what to do if, despite your best efforts, things escalated. How to make a scene, how to get out of a choke hold, the most vulnerable parts of your attacker's body to target in a fight. We learned what you can legally carry or have to hand that could be used in self-defence (baseball bats not included. We each now carried our car keys everywhere and slept with a 3-cell Maglite next to the bed).

Zee never intended to teach us to fight, but it got clear pretty quick what we wanted was to fight.

Maybe today it'd calm me the fuck down.

Haze caught up to me in the lobby. 'Hey.'

'We're late, remember?' I was not up for speculating about Genevieve Craigie.

But she grabbed my wrist and hung on. 'Two seconds, Raych. Jeez.'

Haze could be Max's twin, the same swimmer shoulders and dark hair. She'd been a good mate. It wasn't her fault she wasn't now. I couldn't hack it, that's all. The situation. The circs. The memories.

'The new Marvel movie. We should go,' she said. 'Tomorrow night. I know it's not till Saturday. I mean ... the day.'

She meant it for Piper. Piper loved those movies – girls kicking butt. But I felt like a bitch today and I was following through on it.

'Too busy,' I said. 'Packing up my life to leave town, or did you forget that?'

Her face fell. 'Seriously? Too busy for a movie for Piper?' She still had hold of my wrist. Her fingers were warm. Her eyes raked across my scars and the tatts and I snatched back my arm.

'Yep, seriously.' I pushed past her and into the gym.

Haze didn't like my tatts, although she was the one who'd suggested we get them in the first place, after Piper disappeared. Piper had this jellyfish tatt on her shoulder and I guess when Haze suggested it she figured we'd do something similar. Haze got a seahorse, a discreet dark curl on her ankle that mirrored her dark hair and eyes. I got Piper's name in thick black cursive, the Marge Piercy quote and other stuff. Next came the line drawings of hearts and trees and houses with flames coming out of them, erasing my skin bit by bit as I kept going back.

Things hadn't exactly been cool between Haze and me after that.

It scared her, I got that. *I* scared her. I'd been a normal teen-ager before – hanging at parties, outdoor movies, the beach.

Loving the person no one knew I loved. Making plans for uni, a life, the future. Now I wasn't. End of.

And I didn't like to be judged for it.

'You in the room, Valenti?' I was zoning out in the gym and Zee was onto me.

'Yep.' I blinked and stood straighter. She didn't buy it.

We were practising palm-heel strikes, but it wasn't calming me down, it was doing the opposite. There was too much craziness in my head – thoughts of Max and Piper at the OVC, Genevieve Craigie, Carmen and the killer on the street last night. *Suspect*, I reminded myself; not yet charged. The gym felt too small, the press of amped-up bodies too close. Haze was across the room and looked as distracted as me, flicking the end of her plait like it was bugging her and trying to catch my eye. I struck out and my opponent, Farah, yelped.

'Valenti!' Zee yelled. 'The dead giveaway is in the word practice. No force.'

No special treatment from Zee, no matter who I was. I respected that about her, at least on good days, but today wasn't one of those.

Farah gave me the evils, one arm up to her face. I squeezed out a sorry and she curled her lip. Zee stepped between us, ever the de-escalator. 'Time out, Valenti. You're done. Go take a shower.'

Fair enough. Getting mad never helped me fight better, only meaner; I'd already given one person a blood nose today. I stood down and tucked my hand in my armpit, the palm still smarting. More worried looks from Haze I pretended not to see.

I'd showed up today to quiz Zee on the investigation. A last chance attempt to ditch my plan after seeing the news. Because surely they'd arrest him now. They'd find her in time and save her and he'd be charged.

Zee cornered me on my way back out of the changerooms. 'All right? How's my pocket-rocket doin'?' she said in her Sydney Homicide via London Met hybrid drawl.

'Fucked off.'

'No shit, girl.'

I yanked my bag up my arm. 'Got a minute?'

She glanced past me, distracted, to where Farah was in a huddle with two girls I knew from school. 'We're doing coffee tomorrow, yeah?' she said.

'Sure we are, but . . .' I almost bailed, but it needed to be now. 'This can't wait.'

She narrowed her eyes, searching mine, and gave me one of her slow 'okays'. 'Be with you in five.'

I turned out of the gym doors, blinking against the shock of light, and took the footpath to the giant sundial above the beach. The sundial works, once you get the hang of it. There's barely ever anyone there, but I guess the beach at Cott is the main event. I sat on the limestone wall, the spot Zee and I always brought our coffees to, gripped the warm stone either side of me and squinted out to sea. No whitecaps today – the weather was still weird. Flat blue ocean below a horizon-stripe of cloud, a backdrop to the container ships that were always there. The hot easterly wind buffeted me with the scents of dead grass and the street behind, snatching the cries of gulls and the ever-complaining crows. The sky above was immense summer blue.

Some summer.

'What's up?' Zee made a face as she sat down. Grabbed hold of the baseball cap she was wearing, gave up and yanked it off. 'This goddamn wind.'

Even with her face screwed up Zee was striking. Lashana Lynch by way of Cush Jumbo. Shame she was married to a man.

I'd said that to her face once too. Husbands are so twentieth century.

Zee must have made one badass detective. She had the best brain I knew – better than that detective inspector husband of hers IMO – and looked like a Bond girl. It goes without saying I mean that in an empowering, non-misogynistic way. So shoot me, I like a Bond movie. Get over it, he's not real.

'Have they found her?' I said. 'Is he in custody?'

It came out quick and desperate. Zee's face shifted, a shadow passing across it that wasn't a cloud. I knew right away I'd blown it.

'You watch the news, Valenti, yeah?'

'It's all been Genevieve Craigie going missing. Nothing on Lock. They've gone quiet on him.'

She lowered her brow at the ocean and growled her reply. 'There you have it.'

It wasn't a leap to guess what she thought about it – I could tell from the set of her jaw. 'But he's still under surveillance, right? Did they see where he went? Where he takes them?' I teetered on the brink of saying it. *He was out there in his car again. I was out there too.*

'You know I can't tell you these things, hon.'

'But it's been weeks they've been watching him. How can they not have seen something? What does it mean?'

'For you? Patience, my friend. Or nothing at all.'

'But when will they make an arrest? Charge him. I need to know. What does Jared say?'

Jared was on the Polaris task force and was as tight-lipped as Zee, but that didn't stop me hoping one of them would slip up one day and accidentally on purpose tell me something.

She put a hand on my forearm, the rings on it glinting in the light. 'You know I can't. You know not to ask. I feel your pain, honest to god, but I can't.'

I glared down at my Converses, bright white in the sun, my feet hot. The tears were stacked in my throat but I wouldn't give into them, not in front of Zee. 'No, you don't. You don't get it. I'm this close.' I held up a finger and thumb in her face and felt like Dad in the car last night.

She closed a fist around my hand and lowered it. Her eyes were dark and worried. 'This close to what? I thought you were doing better.'

'Nothing.' I shook my head and pulled my hand away. 'You're right. I am.'

I didn't know what had made Zee leave the police in Sydney. She was on a pension, but only in her thirties. She'd been homicide, like Jared was, and I figured something had happened to her, some trauma of the job. She'd hinted it was psychological, not physical – it for sure didn't look physical – but she'd never said.

'You need to look forwards now.' She leaned closer, her growl softer. 'You've got your life ahead of you, yeah? The move up north—'

'Not going to happen.' I stared straight ahead. 'Not the same day as Piper's anniversary.'

I felt her shift next to me, her shoulders lift and drop. 'Yeah, that's a little insensitive,' she breathed. 'Okay, listen. This is it, all you're getting. This and then you stop.'

I sat silent, the rough limestone imprinting itself into my palms and the backs of my legs.

'There's not going to be an arrest,' she said. 'The team has been instructed to scale back surveillance.'

I swivelled my head. 'What?'

'There's no physical evidence. And last night . . . Lock has an alibi.'

'No. That's wrong.' I was screaming it inside – *I saw him.* 'There's got to be an explanation—'

'Yeah. Like, he didn't do it.' Her words were flat against the wind.

'No, Zee. Listen. He must have—'

'No, you listen!' Her tone made me flinch – Zee almost never lost her shit. 'A team watched his parents' place all last night. He was out in his car around midnight and then at home, where they alibied him. There was no window of opportunity.' She shook her head. 'I'm sorry. Let it go, Valenti.'

It couldn't be right. The already messed up day spiralled away from me, the horizon tilting. 'But they think it's him? You all think that?'

'We *did*. Yes. But now . . .'

'So he's got an accomplice. Or Genevieve is something different. Or his parents lied.'

'No. It's impossible, hon. It can't be him.'

'Bullshit. It is him. Five women have died, Zee. What will it take?' She wouldn't say it, so I did. 'He'll kill her. He'll kill her and take another one. You wait.'

*

I stayed staring at the water long after Zee went back to the surf club, the midday glare stinging my eyes. The easterly had dropped like a switch had flipped and the sense I had was of things suspended, that February vibe when it's too hot to move, my options narrowing down like someone was choking off my breath.

Zee was right. It was an impossible series of crimes for Lock to have perpetrated. It was impossible full stop. How did he take them from under everyone's gaze in a place where we all knew each other? How did he transport them and leave no traces in his car? Where did he keep them, and where did he kill them?

And how did their bodies wash up so precisely, as if he chose each beach for a reason, when the cops and the Surf Life Saving helicopter had been patrolling from the air and the waves and the street all summer long?

Max found a baby green turtle once on Leighton Beach. It was alive, with a damaged flipper, and when Dad took it to AQWA to see if they could save it, the marine biologist there said they get washed thousands of kilometres down the coast after cyclones. I didn't know anything about the ocean currents out there but even I knew they weren't predictable, that you couldn't rely on them to do what you wanted with a dead body.

So yeah, the whole shitshow was impossible. But I knew. I knew it was him.

I'd ask myself later if I should have come clean to Zee, told her I'd seen Lock out on the street the night before. If it would have made a difference, would have saved anyone or changed the way it all played out.

But the surveillance team had seen him too, and right then, what I needed was to back myself, not wimp out. I was so convinced Lock was the one, I'd have done pretty much any-thing to get to him, to prove I was right.

So I did.

I didn't know where Carmen lived but I didn't reckon it was far. Stalker Carmen knew where I lived, after all. And I knew where her warped interests lay. She's a creature of habit, likes things a certain way, likes to be in control. I remembered that, from the ward. You see things, in a place like that, even over the course of a day.

After a few hours of searching, I found her in the empty units across from the golf course. The ones where I thought I'd seen Piper the day before, where I'd later gone back to take out all the ground floor rear windows.

Carmen wasn't looking out of the glassless rear windows onto the deserted back lane and garages, she was at the front, in the corner apartment that smelled of old dead gum leaves and musty carpet. I knew which way the broken glass had fallen and I tiptoed around it, silent, in my old faithful, scuffed-to-buggery sneakers.

I was desperate but I knew desperate wouldn't work on Carmen. I mean, Carmen's not like me. She's cautious, not impulsive. So I turned myself way down, like a Bunsen burner on the lowest flame before it snuffs itself out. I'm adaptable if nothing else.

She was standing at the front corner window, a black baseball cap pulled low, in her usual uniform of dark jeans and boots, and the blue long-sleeved tee. She was looking out across the street. Looking out at *him*, I registered with a kick to the solar plexus. 'Fuck,' I said. 'Some view.'

She spun around, eyes wide. I'd never seen Carmen caught off-guard before and she recovered quick, plastering her face over with its usual blank slate.

'Didn't mean to creep up,' I said. I did, but I didn't want to piss her off. I needed her on side.

She shrugged like it was no big deal, but I knew it was. A blood vessel flickered in her throat. The carotid artery maybe, I don't know. It was a big one, anyway.

I'd discovered her vantage point, hadn't I? I wondered how long she'd been watching him. Lock. Wondered even for a second why the police hadn't used this place for surveillance. But the golf course was huge. He'd only be out there across from this window a fraction of the time.

I wanted to ask her about it, about him. How long she'd been watching him, what her interest in him was, her story. The questions teetered in my brain like the towers of unread books in my room. But I had to tone it down. Get a hold of myself and play it cool.

Carmen was squinting away from me now, past Lock to the line of shipping on the horizon. The ocean was flat, the long smear of cloud still there. I didn't know what she could see out there and I couldn't think of the first thing to say to her now I'd found her, which isn't like me at all. I was saved by the cat. A slinky dark tabby, skinny as fuck. She rubbed around my legs, scared the living shit out of me and I squeaked like a mouse.

Carmen looked at me like I was a jerk. I could see the challenge behind it, like yeah I'd crept up on her, and yeah I'd pissed her off, and now the cat had turned the tables. I pressed the heel of my hand to my sternum to calm myself the fuck down. 'Cute,' I said. 'Is she yours?'

It looked like she was debating whether that deserved an answer. 'She's no one's,' she said, like, yeah, stupid question.

'Good on her.' I held her gaze, trying to figure out what was going on behind her face. She was different to last night, less agitated, like she knew her ground here. I tilted my chin at the window, at Neil Fraser Lock under a straggle of tea trees between the fence and the golf course fairway. He was jabbing an oversized fork into the lawn under the trees, aerating it. Like it was another day at the office when it so wasn't.

He straightened up, wiping a glitter of sweat off his forehead. I got the impression he was dawdling there, under the patchy shade, like he couldn't hack the sun. He didn't look made for physical work but maybe he was stronger than he appeared. It was so out there, seeing him do an actual job. All I could think about was Genevieve Craigie and where she was now. I wondered for the first time how Carmen felt about it, the PE teacher from her school going missing.

'What's the deal with him?' I said. 'You part of the police effort?'

She didn't answer.

'Why are you watching him, I mean?' I said. 'It's not proper surveillance if you only do it part of the time.'

'I'm not doing *surveillance*.' She said it like there were air quotes around the word, and made that *huff* sound she makes through her nose. Gave me this flat passive-aggro glare and turned back to the window, but only halfway, like she didn't want to turn her back on me. It was this weird reversal of the night before, us watching Lock instead of him watching us. She stood right in the corner with most of her body hidden from the street behind the window frame, and I realised it was her I'd seen through the glass the morning before.

So that made three times in a day and a half. I wanted her to tell me what she was doing here, whether she'd meant to stop him on the street last night. But I knew I had to change tack.

Lock bent to his fork again, rammed it in in a way that made me flinch. 'They're going to stop surveillance,' I said. 'The Polaris team. Or they already have. They don't have anything on him.'

She kept staring out the window but the outline of her body tensed like an animal. I knew I'd got her attention.

'They don't reckon it's him?'

'Fuck knows what they think,' I said. My jaw clenched. 'Do you believe in capital punishment? For people like him?'

That stunned me; it came out of nowhere. I'd stepped up close to the window without realising it, right alongside her. If he'd glanced up he'd have seen me, but I didn't give a shit, not then.

There was this painful pressure up under my ribs – so painful it felt good. I swear if I'd had that star picket on me I'd have been across the street and caved in Lock's skull myself. I could feel the jarring blows in my fingers, hear the wet sounds of them, register the shockwaves travelling up from my hands all the way to my throat.

A sound came out of me, an animal sound, and I took a step back. My heart was bashing out this fucked-up rhythm, churning my blood around like a sickness. Jesus. That wasn't the plan.

Carmen was looking sideways at me like I'd shocked her twice in as many minutes. She'd shifted a step further into the corner. She hadn't answered my question about capital punishment, either. I wanted to tell her I was fine, or I would be when I got the answers I needed. I wanted to tell her my plan, to explain who I was and why I needed her to help me – that all

I wanted was to make him tell me the truth about Piper – but I knew I couldn't.

She wouldn't like it. She'd think I was out for revenge. That I wanted to kill him. I didn't – at least I didn't think so. Not then. But Carmen liked calculation and control; she was the opposite of me. I knew that, even then.

I had to make her think this was about Genevieve, about someone we might be able to save. I mean, I still didn't know what she wanted with him, but here was the suspect right in front of us – even the police were in agreement about that – and time was running out. I needed to set a fire under everything, to turn that Bunsen flame way up without Carmen noticing.

I didn't plan to start lying to her. She's not someone you want to lie to, or try to manipulate. You can't beat her at that game. But I didn't know that, not then.

'What if we did it?' I said. 'Asked him questions, if the cops won't do it.'

She didn't move, but she was listening, I could tell.

'We could find out where he's got her. Genevieve Craigie. She could still be alive. We could save her.'

Carmen swivelled her head to stare at me, but her eyes were blank.

'I mean, she's your teacher, right?' I took a step closer and she shrank back. 'What if she was a mate of yours? Or your sister? Would you do it then?' But the sister thing wouldn't work with Carmen, would it? She was adopted by that weird family. I wasn't sure the friend thing would either. So I said, 'What if it was my sister he'd taken? Would you help me? My sister's a swimmer, did you know that?'

I looked from her to him, out there across the street. How

impotent he looked, lurking in that feeble strip of shade. And sure, I regret it now. I don't know what I was thinking. It didn't occur to me how drastically things had switched between Carmen and me from the night before. How that day I was playing right into her hands.

I said, 'We can do it. Make him talk. If we don't, any one of us could be next.'

TUESDAY

6

Carmen

Another coincidence that can't be one

Carmen's up early. It's a Tuesday, which isn't as bad as a Monday, but still. There's school, with PE today, which even without Mrs Craigie she still hates, and Alexis to manoeuvre around while she's in the house. Alexis has an early shift on a Tuesday, so it's hard to avoid her without Carmen being late for school.

She's in the bathroom, finishing getting dressed. There's a skink on the wall outside, warming itself up in the sun. Carmen would like her life to be as simple as that – survival, one moment to the next. She can't hear anything in the rest of the house yet, good, but there's a smell of coffee from the kitchen. Her tin of sharks' teeth is balanced on the edge of the sink; she keeps it with her all the time now, for reassurance, since Detective Rosso and his questions. She's had the best ones out, the biggest ones, holding them in the palm of her hand.

She cleans her own teeth, thinking back to Rachel finding her in the empty apartment building yesterday, out of the blue. Afterwards, at sunset, Carmen made her way through the streets to her other place, where she can hear the water and there's space for her thoughts. She needs to think them now, with Mrs Craigie being missing. She went like the girl cat, silent and sticking to the shadows so Rachel wouldn't follow her, and she didn't. There's a boat there, an aluminium dinghy no one uses. The place isn't far, but it's in a direction no one expects. It's not near home, or school, or the library, and Carmen doesn't have a boat of her own and she can't swim well, so why would she go there?

Carmen has always wanted swimming lessons, and Alexis has always made sure she didn't get them.

Mrs Craigie's body hasn't washed up yet. There was nothing on the early news about her. Carmen had to switch the radio off before the broadcast had finished, Mrs G swishing past her room in a cloud of morning stress and perfume, but it would have been big news. It would have been first.

The police have stopped watching Neil, like Rachel said. That's the big news. But are they watching someone else instead? Rachel still reckons it's him, Carmen could tell from the way she looked at him after she said it.

Carmen doesn't know what to make of Rachel. Asking for her help like that. It's got nothing to do with saving Mrs Craigie, Carmen could tell that too. But why would Rachel lie? What does she really want? Carmen said no, anyhow, to Rachel's off-at-a-tangent, shot-in-the-dark plan.

She thinks back to the night before last. The two of them

out on the street with Neil watching from the driver's seat of his car. It's weird how fast things can change. Everything can. It already has.

He only looked at them for thirty seconds but Carmen doesn't know if he recognised her or not. If she didn't see him *that night* maybe he didn't see her. Still, she doesn't know if he was looking for her out on Marine Parade or looking for Rachel. If he was concerned for Rachel's safety, the way he tells journalists he is when they interview him on the news. She doesn't know if it's a lie or not, when Neil says that.

It was strange, the two of them seeing Neil and neither of them saying a word about it. Why does Rachel go out there, every weekend night? Is it because she still wants to die like she did when she was in the hospital? Is that what her plan is for? If it is, Carmen can think of better ways to do it.

Carmen should stay away from Rachel like she stays away from everyone. But was it a coincidence, that the two of them ended up in the mental place at the exact same time? Or, to be accurate, three days apart.

Carmen doesn't believe in coincidences.

She'll have to add that to her list of things to find out.

Today is bad, after all, because when Carmen opens the bathroom door, Alexis is right there, her hair in its tight ponytail, her eyes like blue marbles, the pupils small and black. She's leant against the door frame with her arms crossed and her head on one side. Her lips in a gluey line, like a school bully on one of those high school movies or TV shows, which is what she is. 'Take your time, Car-men,' she sings. 'You put yourself together so beautifully, after all.'

Carmen looks down at herself. She's dressed – Carmen's always dressed unless she's behind a locked door – but she can't help looking where Alexis's eyes have gone, to her dark jeans and T-shirt. The line of dried salt near the bottom of her jeans and the stain on the toe of her boot that's still visible, like a sunspot in your eye, even though she's polished them a heap of times since it got on there.

For a second Carmen sticks there in the doorway so Alexis can't get past, the smell of the things Alexis puts on her face and body getting up her nose. She could say it, that Neil was there *that night* in Alexis's room, that she knows Alexis lied, and if he hadn't been there she'd be dead by now. But she's conscious of the kitchen, right next door: Mr G finishing up his coffee and reading the *West Australian* at the table, Mrs G loading the dishwasher – how expert at multitasking she is, how she doesn't like the radio on in the mornings, how she listens out and doesn't miss a thing. And apart from the clink of dishes and the beep of a vehicle reversing out on the street, silence.

Anyhow, what would be the point of reminding Alexis about that night? It would get a reaction out of her but that's all. Carmen hesitates, and she's distracted by a wedge of light falling across the hallway that's not usually there. She sees it because Alexis's bedroom door is open opposite, the morning sun shafting in through her patio doors where the curtain isn't drawn right the way across. But it's even more annoying than that, the curtain bunched together in the middle of the rail like Alexis couldn't decide which way to pull it. The bottom of the curtain that bit too long for the window, slumped on the floor like something curled up dead or asleep.

Alexis keeps her bedroom door closed at all times, and locked when she's not in the house, so the inside of her room isn't something Carmen's seen often at all.

But she did see it – a year ago. *That night.* She looks at the lamp. The one on the bedside table that ended up in Carmen's hand, lifted high above her head. The ugly green glass shade with a crack in it above the heavy metal base. The shade that cracked in half like an egg instead of shattering into pieces. She sees that someone has glued it back.

That's how Carmen remembers it. The sound of the lamp falling was what woke her in the night, even in her room way back at the other end of the house. Because Carmen doesn't sleep well, and if there's something to hear in the quiet she's going to hear it.

The lamp had fallen before Carmen got inside the room. And that's not all. The patio doors were open on one side; she remembers the feel of the night air on her face.

Neil was in there before her.

The blood in Carmen's brain stops and starts again and she shakes her head. Her brain isn't remembering right. It's got things around the wrong way like it so often does. She went in there to kill Alexis. Neil came in and stopped her doing it. That's what happened.

She thinks all this in a second, even as Alexis is already reacting, stepping back across the hallway and pulling the door to her room closed. There's a mixed-up look on her face as she turns back to Carmen, as if she knows what's in Carmen's brain. She can't know, but it gives Carmen a lurch of satisfaction to think she's unnerved Alexis, even for a moment. She won't say anything about *that night*, she decides. Not yet.

It's only as she steps aside for Alexis that She sees her

expression change and reanimate, the hunted morph back into the hunter, as Alexis sees past her into the bathroom.

'Forgotten something, Car-men? Let me help you with that,' she says.

Carmen lurches back into the bathroom and lunges for it at the same time, the object she's left there: the tin of sharks' teeth that's always in her pocket, still balanced on the edge of the sink. But Alexis is too close and bumps up behind her, like a car rear-ending another car. Carmen grabs for it but the tin falls to the bathroom floor, and the tin springs open, and the teeth . . .

Carmen never swears out loud, only inside her head, but if she did, she'd do it now. The inside of her head is full of rushing as she scrambles to pick up the teeth skittering from under her hands, grabbing too hard so one of them slices open her palm, and another one her thumb. Alexis snakes a hand towards the last, spinning on the tiled floor. But Carmen grabs her wrist and twists it, leans in and snatches up the tooth. 'No.'

She gets them all back in the tin and the lid closed before she registers the silence in the room, the blood from the cuts on her hand, the drops and smears of it across Mrs G's white tiles. She needs to stand up, to wash the cuts and find the pack of Band-Aids – Mrs G will be calling out to them any second to watch the time. But Alexis is between her and the sink, both of them crouched on the floor. It's only then Carmen notices Alexis staring down at her wrist. The bloody prints on it from Carmen's fingers.

Carmen stands up, careful to avoid the smears of blood, because she's got to stop backing down from their confrontations. Still, she waits for Alexis to say something – about her being a freak, and obsessed with the forbidden murder case, or worse – because maybe Alexis knows about the tooth she found on Christine's body. Maybe she followed Carmen to Leighton that day and saw her. Maybe she knows other things about Carmen too. She waits for Alexis to open her mouth, to sneer, to run next door and show her mother the blood on her wrist. But she doesn't. And when Alexis stands up, their heads are close, and Carmen sees real fear on her face.

It's only there a second, then her eyes get hard and blank again, all emotion wiped away. Carmen has the tin behind her back now, slippery with blood. She wants to put it in the pocket of her jeans but she can't, not until she's cleaned it.

Mrs G calls from the kitchen, 'Carmen. Alexis. To school, to work. Away with you both. Chop chop.' And Alexis steps backwards out of the bathroom and in through her bedroom door in a rush of air and light and slams it shut.

Carmen runs the cold tap and watches the blood swirl away down the plughole from her hand. Was it the blood that unnerved Alexis, Carmen grabbing her like that, or the teeth? Or did she see *that night* on Carmen's face as she looked across the hallway?

Either way, something has changed in the house. Carmen senses it like an electric charge.

Alexis is afraid of her.

Despite Mrs G's *chop chop* from the kitchen, Carmen doesn't go to school. It's that kind of a day. She has things to find out.

It was real, the fear on Alexis's face. Not fake, like so many things about her. This is how Carmen knows she's right and the lamp memory in her brain is wrong. She went into Alexis's room to kill her that night but Neil stopped her. That's what happened. Alexis must remember it too; that's what's scared her.

Carmen puts Band-Aids on her cuts and the tin of teeth back in her jeans' pocket and sets off in the direction of school, with the usual things in her backpack – her lunch, her metal water bottle with the dent in it, and the other things. She parks in a shady spot far enough from the school gates she can watch everyone go in but not be seen. It's reassuring, to know they're all inside but Carmen's not. Once the bell has gone and everything is quiet again, she turns the car and doubles back.

Mrs G will get a phone call. But Carmen knows she might not be going home tonight or going to school ever again – it depends on what she finds out today, and what happens next. If she needs to, she'll come up with a lie; she's got all day to think of one. And if she never goes to school again it doesn't matter. She'll miss Mr Ayele and drumming in the music room, the one time Carmen feels like herself, but that's the only thing.

She puts Alexis and Neil to one side in her brain and she goes to the library, where they know her and are never surprised to see her. She has a note from her Media and Computing teacher, about research, that she wrote and signed herself. No one ever checks.

Tucked in amongst the smell of books (the one smell Carmen doesn't mind), the stage-whispering pensioners getting help with their online forms, the toddlers and the noisy knitting club (Tuesdays at eleven) she is calm. Libraries are no longer quiet, but today this is what Carmen needs.

Camouflage.

There's a room divider next to the computer where she's sitting, pinned-up quotes that make Carmen think of the words tattooed on Rachel's left arm. *An apple a day keeps anyone away if you throw it hard enough.* That one is perfect for Rachel, except Rachel's apples would be rocks, or cannonballs, or set on fire before she threw them, like bombs.

It takes Carmen most of the day because she doesn't know what she's looking for, not at the start. But she's not in a rush, and she doesn't stop looking until she's sure. She finds what she needs after lunch.

It's a shock – another coincidence that can't be one. Another piece of *that night*. It's part of the reason she feels connected to the things that are happening, and to Rachel.

Piper. That's why Carmen missed it. It's not even the girl's real name. She understands Rachel's death wish now, why she was raging when she arrived at the hospital. But Rachel can't know how they're connected, not apart from those few days on the ward. She'd have said something to Carmen if she did. She'd have told her the truth, instead of pretending she wants to save Mrs Craigie. That was stupid, but it doesn't matter now.

Carmen won't tell Rachel what she knows. She should have stayed away from her, but it's too late for that now. She has to keep her away from Neil. She can't risk her finding out about *that night* or going to the police. She can't risk Rachel connecting the two of them, Carmen and Neil, until she knows more.

Carmen waits outside the front of Rachel's house, between the brick wall at the side and the giant boat on a trailer that takes up most of the drive. The drive is the colour of beach sand, the chrome on the boat brilliant with light and impossible to look at in the sun. She can smell hot garden and hot bricks, but it's cool in the shade where she waits, as if the hull of the boat is the pale underside of a whale.

Apart from the boat, the house doesn't look like anyone lives in it. Both garage doors are rolled down, the metal shutters out front are closed and everything is pressure-washer clean. But there are two cars in the garage – she's seen them through the narrow high-up window around the side – one the grey Prado from the other night, and one a fire-red Mini that must be Rachel's. She knows Rachel's in the house because she can hear someone moving around and there are voices coming out of a rear window – not Rachel's voice, the radio, or a podcast, but Carmen can't tell what they're saying.

Rachel comes out of the front door half an hour before sunset in her usual combat pants and sneakers with a spiral bound notebook sticking out of the front pocket and her hair standing up like she's put some effort into it. She takes off walking fast like she's on a mission, and Carmen follows. She keeps well back and stops on every corner like they do on the spy shows on TV.

Rachel zigzags blocks like she's pretending she's going somewhere else, but after two turns Carmen speeds up because she can guess where she's headed – the golf course. But she's left her run too late, because Rachel's cutting across the footy oval now, in full view of anyone out on the golf course or the adjacent streets. All Carmen can do is follow and try not to be seen.

What does Rachel want with Neil? What's she going to do about him? Carmen thinks again of when Rachel first got onto the ward, the out-of-control vibe of her, the shouting, the things she got a hold of that first day and smashed on the floor. Her mind goes to yesterday at the empty apartments, Rachel pretending she wants to help Mrs Craigie when that was never what it was about.

The sun is sinking into the ocean, the horizon stripes of orange cloud. Rachel disappears across the golf club car park towards the clubhouse. Carmen's too close and hangs back. It's packed in there – lights blazing, tables and chairs, a queue of people at the bar. Neil will have finished his shift. Most likely he's gone home and Rachel's missed him. Or she's here to have dinner, to meet someone else and not him.

Maybe there's nothing to worry about.

The light's fading and Carmen risks a few steps further. She opens her mouth to call Rachel back but Rachel disappears around the side of the building where a sign says *deliveries*. Carmen's annoyed now, telling Rachel off inside her head. It's been a long day with too much in it – the tension is stretched like a strand of hair pulling at her scalp. She hears a car door slam, and an engine start up. She gets closer, and then she sees it.

Neil's car – Carmen recognises it. It's coming from behind the clubhouse, around the corner where Rachel disappeared. He's finished his shift. He's going home.

Good. Carmen keeps her head down and keeps walking. The car passes her, Neil in profile as he drives. She'll see who Rachel's meeting and then she'll go. But when Carmen rounds the corner, the staff car park has one empty car in it and nothing else. Nothing except Rachel's notebook, splayed open on the bitumen like a run-over squashed-flat bird, a magpie or cockatoo.

Carmen picks up the notebook, swings one way and then the other, but Rachel is gone. There's no trace of her and the back door to the clubhouse is closed. Rachel is in Neil's car. Carmen feels the fact of it worm down inside her. It's the only explanation that fits.

She can't keep up on foot, but she tries. She cuts back across the oval, the pulse in her head pushing harder. There are lights on for footy training, everything unnaturally bright, the shouts and running feet and thud of the ball too loud. The baseball bat lies in the brown grass where a girl has dropped it, her dad for a moment distracted by his phone. Carmen picks up the bat as she passes, ignores the dad's shouts when he sees her, already too far away to catch. She's not thinking any further than what happened in the car park and Rachel being in Neil's car. Has he taken her? Is that what he wanted, the other night on Marine Parade? Carmen needs to get there and see.

When she does – because she's far slower than the car – it's full dark, and Neil is stood at the bottom of the driveway, staring into the back of the car. The unmarked blue police sedan that's been across the street from the house isn't there.

Neil doesn't hear Carmen as she moves down between the frangipani trees at the edge of the drive. He doesn't sense her coming, and neither does Rachel, which is Carmen's unfair advantage over them both. By the time she gets down there he's unlocked the car and Rachel has opened the door and they're looking at each other. He's stood there and Rachel's inside the car, and it's silent apart from a dog barking a few houses away and a clicking sound. Rachel has a pen and she's clicking it, over and over. It's annoying. It must be annoying him too. There's the smell of the frangipani flowers, but also his smell – his sweat plus the soap he uses – and that's what confirms it for Carmen. That he was there *that night* in Alexis's room. Because one thing she never gets confused is smells.

And all she can think, now she's watching them, is what she found out this afternoon in the library about Rachel's friend Piper, the name tattooed on her arm. All Carmen's senses are booming too big and too loud and she doesn't know what either of them is going to do next.

She tells herself it's because she's concerned for Rachel's safety, the same way she was when they were out on the street the other night. She knows it's more than that but she doesn't have time to think about it. It's complicated. Rachel's a complication.

It's easiest to take him, and not Rachel. Carmen comes at him from the side as he looks the other way.

It only takes one fast swing of the bat, and he goes down.

7

Raych

The first time I think we've killed him

The baseball bat was pink, metallic and kid-sized. I couldn't figure out how we'd got here, to the bottom of the driveway of the Frangipani House, Lock's parents' place, with him lying like a dead lizard at my feet. I didn't know Carmen had seen me get into his car.

She stared down at him, that intense frown she has. The baseball bat dangled from a hand. There was a smear of blood at the tip I'd have bet real money was not there before she whacked him, and I started to hyperventilate. There was more blood, too, a trickle like mud oozing out from one of his ears.

That's a bad sign. Everyone knows that. That's a really, really bad ...

'Fuck.' The scorch of bile at the back of my throat, the rattle of my pulse. 'We need to do something. Call someone. The ambos or something. Do you reckon he's—'

'Breathing,' she said, letting go of the bat. It hit the drive with a clang. He hadn't moved, on his back between his parked car and the house. I was picturing blood spatter, fingerprints, DNA evidence. Imagining true crime docos and podcast episodes. Carmen twitched her nose like she used to do when it was feeding time on the ward. She bent towards him. 'Alive.'

The car's interior light filmed the concrete driveway, leaking out from the car door I still had hold of. I clunked it shut, extinguishing the light. Leaned against the car and tried to breathe. 'What did you do it for?' I said.

I didn't know Carmen owned a baseball bat. She's not the type. I've said it before – she's not impulsive. If I'm honest, she's how I imagine him to be.

Calculating. And not in any way sporty.

'Thought he was gunna do something. He can move fast when he wants.' Her eyes slid away like she'd said something she shouldn't have. 'You can't talk, anyhow.'

'What?'

'Smashing things.'

I scowled at her, my breath still ragged. 'Yeah, *things*. Not people. Plus, I don't do that now.'

She made that *huff* through her nose that meant she didn't believe me. She was wearing the black cap I'd seen her in the day before, her too-warm-for-February dark jeans and boots, but she radiated cool like always, in contrast with the hot night and Lock's sharp, distinctive sweat.

This is what Carmen is like. She's purposeful, focused. Her attention lands on things and singles them out, cuts them away from the pack. She's like a feral cat, hunting, a torch you grab in the night when the power's out, the Eye of Sauron. There are better comparisons but I couldn't think of one because the situation was too tense.

'Carmen? I said we should—'

'S'not my fault you've got a death wish, Rachel.'

'I do not have a death wish.'

She swivelled her frown my way. 'You do, though.'

'It was plastic cutlery. How many times do I have to say that?'

The house behind her loomed like it was listening in. Were they in there, Lock's parents? Why hadn't they come out after him? She made the *huff* sound again, bent over his face with her head on one side like a bird. The metal bat had stopped its roll just short of the closed garage doors. We could take it with us, get rid of it. Call the ambos anonymously from down on the highway.

I craned my neck back up the driveway. The angle and curve of it, the buttressed frangipani trees and their massing of flowers, meant I couldn't see the street from down here. A car passed, a flicker of lights through the branches, and my heart gave a kick.

'Was the surveillance team up there when you came in?' I asked her. 'The cop car?'

'Nup.'

So they'd stopped watching him, like Zee had told me. It wasn't late, but quiet enough it could have been 2 a.m. There was no sound at all except my breath and Carmen's, a dog barking from down the street. The night came on fast in these north–south running streets, shaded all day by their Norfolk Pines. The moon was a few days off full and the waxy light from the frangipani flowers made the house appear darker, but who was to say there wasn't someone behind those blank windows?

'What do we do with him?' I whispered. 'What if someone comes?'

Lock was still breathing, and Carmen was examining him in a way that made me nervous, like he was a high school science experiment.

She looked up at me, and honest to god, she smiled. It was the first time I'd seen Carmen smile in all the time I'd known her and it dried up the spit in my mouth like a lemon. It had me trawling back through the past few days because I should have seen that smile coming. Shouldn't I? Like, seriously? How come I hadn't?

'We search the house,' she said. 'Check no one's seen us. And we take him.'

'We what?'

'You heard me, Rachel.'

She leant in closer to him, her chin propped in a palm, the smile transforming her face. Then she dropped the smile and got to her feet. 'We take him now, while he's out.'

Her eyes moved over him, up past me and his car to the top of the drive and the street, back again to the dark house behind her. I'd asked her what she meant, Take him where, but she wasn't listening and she didn't answer. She was already calculating, thinking ahead, onto the next part of the plan.

What plan, though? We didn't have one. I went over the last few days, the times I'd seen her. Was all this, Carmen following me and knocking the dude out, because of something I'd said? I'd asked for her help yesterday and she'd said no. Whatever I was thinking at the time, it wasn't this.

I was only now getting the circulation back into my legs after my ride in his car, pressed flat to the floor. I hadn't prepared for this. It was enough, I thought, that I'd leaned on the horn to draw him back out from the house after he went inside. That I'd banged on the back passenger window with the flat of both hands until he unlocked the car, with that look of calculated surprise on his face.

I hadn't got as far as the next step – I guessed I reckoned I'd run like buggery – but clearly Carmen had.

'Did you mean to get in the car?' she said. 'Or did he—?'

'He came back while I was looking for clues. He'd left it with the doors unlocked in the car park.'

'A trap,' she said, gazing down at him.

'No, not a ... Okay. Maybe.' She was holding my notebook and the cover had a big crease where it'd been folded back. I'd dropped my pen on the drive when she hit him and I couldn't see it. 'Where did you get that?' I said. 'Did you look in it?'

She shrugged and handed it back, didn't meet my eye. There was stuff in there about her, but whatever. It had fallen out, maybe, when I scrambled into his car. I looked past her to the double garage, the porch and blank staring windows.

She followed my gaze. 'You should check no one's in there, Rachel. Check no one's seen us.'

'Why do I have to do it?'

Only then did it hit me as strange, that Lock had left the house dark when he came back out to me and unlocked his car. I was trying to remember if he'd turned a light on when he first went inside or if he hadn't. Was there a porch light? Had one of the windows lit up?

If it had, it was now dark.

I was getting this crawling feeling up my back like a million bull ants. Legit. Or centipedes. Centipedes would be worse.

'I can do it,' Carmen said. 'If you don't want to. Someone has to wait with him, but.'

I took in Lock at her feet, flat out on his back with his mouth open like he was already on a slab. Still bleeding from one ear.

Still breathing.

'Listen, we don't have to stay with him,' I said. 'We can get out of here. Do a runner while it's dark so no one sees us. Call the ambos from a public phone.' There was this little whine in my voice I hated but I couldn't stop it. 'What do you think?'

But she was bent over him again and I could see what she thought of all that in the set of her shoulders. 'We're taking him,' she said, like he was a prize she'd won and wouldn't let go of. 'You wanted to ask him questions. You said—'

'Not like this! And has it maybe not occurred to you he's got Genevieve Craigie stashed somewhere? What's going to happen to her?'

'We're taking him,' she said again. 'He's the one.'

'Right. Okay. I'll check the house.' Fuck. She was impossible to argue with. My teeth were gritted in a way that irritatingly reminded me of Dad. I wished he was here and hadn't gone on shift. Why was he always gone when I needed him? Then I remembered how pissed at him I was.

'Do it fast. Check the street after, check the police didn't come back. It's a blue sedan.'

I rolled my eyes but she didn't see and it didn't help. I knew it was a blue sedan but it wasn't going to be there. She was already reaching down to unclip his house keys, the bunch attached to the belt loop of his uniform. I still couldn't see my pen.

'I'm not breaking in there,' I said.

'You don't have to.'

'I don't reckon they're in. His parents.' But I was only telling myself that. They'd alibied him two nights ago, was what Zee had told me. And okay, there were no lights on inside the house, no flickering TV screen, and no one except Lock had come out when I leaned on the car horn. But the lawn was clipped and watered, the driveway under the frangipani trees swept clean of dead flowers. Carmen held out his keys.

And the thing is, I took them.

It was like watching these two versions of me from above like a drone. The first was standing in front of Carmen, hands on hips, arguing the point. *That* Raych had her phone out already, calling triple zero to get the paramedics out. She was giving them the address and telling Carmen to pull her head in, she wasn't on the ward any more, she didn't need to act like the insane person she was doing an awesome job of impersonating.

But that Raych wasn't arguing loud or hard enough. She'd already lost her nerve and put her phone back in her pocket. Because alongside the fucked-up-ness of it all was something else. I mean, hadn't I wanted to search this house? Hadn't I questioned for weeks why the cops hadn't done it?

So *this* Raych – the real one – took hold of the keys Carmen handed her, ignored the ramping of her pulse and turned towards the house.

*

There was no sound from inside as I climbed the steps up to the porch. No security light leapt out at me. I cupped my hands around my face at the windows either side of the front door and all I saw was shadowy hallway.

Empty.

It was still freaking me out that the house had been dark when he came out to the car. Carmen hissed at me to hurry up from down on the drive, and I jumped.

I tried the keys. The first one slid in, which I wasn't expecting. I turned it, and my heart was like how thunder sounds when the lightning is right on top of you. I didn't want the door to open; I didn't want to go inside. Because what if there was something of Piper's in there, something that proved she was dead? But also, I wanted to go in there more than I'd wanted anything at any time. This was the house the cops hadn't searched. And even though it was a year since she'd gone, what if there was a hidden room here, a basement under a floor behind a reinforced door? What if, in a twist of fate, I was the one to find it?

Piper could be in there. She could still be alive. Or Genevieve Craigie. But Piper, out of all of them, might be the special one. The whole time I was thinking this I was also thinking, No, Raych, *come on*, and my hands shook so hard the keys fell out onto the floor as I pushed open the door.

If it was true, we could call the police and the ambulance like I wanted, and all of this would be over and we could go home.

But that's not what happened. I pushed the door and stepped inside, over the keys on the doormat, and first up I thought the house was empty. The air was cool and smelled of furniture polish, and weirdly, Anzac biscuits. A laugh bubbled up because the moment was extremely tense and maybe I'd imagined the biscuits. Until I heard the voice and stopped dead.

It was Lock's voice, coming from further inside the house. 'No. That's not how I like it,' he was saying. 'That's not how it's done.'

I stood there, one hand gripping the edge of the door. I couldn't have moved if someone had told me the place was on fire. He had a girl in there. He had Genevieve in there and I had to do something. And then he said, 'You have to put the milk in first.'

He was talking about tea, FFS. And it wasn't Lock – hell no, it wasn't. Lock was unconscious in the driveway behind me. It wasn't the same voice, it was deeper. It was Lock's father, it had to be, talking to his wife.

You'd think they'd have gone away, the parents. Surely any sensible people would do that after their life was taken apart by the police and the media. After their only child was outed as a suspected killer. But they'd stayed.

It made me wonder if they thought he'd done it. But he'd moved in with them, and there was the alibi Zee had told me about. I'd only seen them that one time on the news – a clean-shaven, wirier version of Lock and a woman with glossy dark hair. Not as old as I expected, like they'd had him when they were young. I hung there in the hallway but didn't hear anything more. How come they hadn't come out of the house when Lock arrived back in his car? Weren't they wondering where he'd got to?

Then Carmen called out, 'He's waking up. You need to come now,' and my muscles unfroze with a jolt. Jesus, she needed to keep her voice down. I backed out and picked up the keys. Pulled shut the door as softly as I could.

I made sure it was locked and I turned my back on the house

and started back down the steps, and I tell you what, it was the hardest thing I've ever done. It didn't matter that the house wasn't empty, everything in me was screaming at me not to leave. I was gripping the keys so hard they cut into my hand, and all the things I might have found in there were lost to me.

So I picked out the key to the front door and I prised it off the ring and slid it into my pocket past my notebook. I saved it for later, for a time I could go back when no one was home. And when I got back to the car, Lock was still flat out on the driveway, and Carmen had bound his ankles and wrists together with cable ties.

Who carries cable ties with them? I noticed Carmen's backpack on the drive for the first time, yawning open. What else did she have in there?

'Is that the reason you got me to check the house?' I said. 'So you could do that?'

She was inside his car with her back to me, reaching across the back seat to open the opposite door. She shrugged one shoulder as she reversed out, her face a neutral mask as she held out a hand for the keys.

'Did you touch anything inside?' she said.

'They're in there, Carmen. His parents,' I hissed.

'Did you touch anything?'

'Don't you care? What if they come looking for him?' I glanced up at the house and shook my head. 'The outside of the front door. And these. Nothing else.' I hesitated then dropped the keys into her hand. Thought for a second she'd notice I'd taken the door key, but she didn't blink.

The living areas were towards the back, I guessed, the bedrooms at the front. Maybe his parents hadn't heard him come back, but they had to be wondering where he'd got to. I looked again at what I could see of Lock in the dark. He was on his side with his wrists bound behind him, the pink metal baseball bat nestled against his leg. 'We need to get out of here,' I said. 'Now. We'll have to leave him.'

The cable ties were thick and black, the kind you'd find in a warehouse or holding bits of fence together. Or cable, Raych. You'd literally have to hacksaw through them to get them off. He wasn't waking up anytime soon, not from what I could see.

I thought back to the victims, the ligature marks on their bodies, pushed the thought away but it came right back. I was trying to flip it around, like, the cable ties had been in his car and not in Carmen's bag. Like, she hadn't come prepared but instead had randomly found them. He's the killer, Raych. He is. But it wasn't working for me.

'We're not leaving him,' she said. 'Help me get him in, and go up and check the street.'

We manhandled him in there. Dudehandled. It wasn't funny, it was fucked up. Carmen was stronger and hooked her fingers under his armpits from inside the car. I lifted under his legs and pushed, my breath panicky and tight.

The whole time I was thinking of the parents, the neighbours, the police, even with how dark it was. Whether the cops had come back like Carmen said. Maybe they were parked up on the street, impossible to see from down here. I was thinking of the media; hadn't they been following him too?

Where was everyone? Any second now we'd be flooded with sound and light.

But we got him in, lying across the back seat, and I chucked the bat in after him. He let out a groan as I did it, and I flinched.

I shouldered the door shut and stood there, hands on my knees trying to get my breath, but it was like it couldn't find its way in. I wiped sweat off my forehead with one arm because it was still that hot, even though Carmen was cool as an ice pick.

I've wondered these past days about her cool facade and when I'd see a crack in it. I hadn't yet, not at that stage. My eyes strayed over the car door handles she'd been touching, the top of the door I'd had hold of with my bare hand, the metal baseball bat lying across the dude's legs. She watched me clock these things.

'We can wipe it down, after,' she said. 'We can wipe down everything.'

After what?

But I didn't ask. I choked back my arguments, which is far from normal behaviour from me. I kept thinking, Wasn't this my plan? Didn't I want us to take him? But events were overtaking me so fast I had whiplash, and normal was back down the road someplace. I did as I was told and went up to check the street.

What I felt as I pushed up the slope at the side of the driveway was plummeting dread. The bottom half of me was exposed between the narrow branching trunks of the frangipani trees while the top half of me shoved through head height leaves and flowers. The flowers glowed in the moonlight like they were lit from within, like a million sick candles. The smell of them was in my face and my throat and I wasn't even thinking about spiders, which was a measure of the extremity of the situation. The dread wanted to pull me back down towards the house and that disembodied voice and whatever I'd missed in there. I turned over the door key in my pocket but that'd have to wait. *That* was on the other side of *this*, whatever this was.

There was a streetlight out and it was as dark at the top of the drive as the bottom. The wide verge and towering pines, the empty street. I hadn't seen anything on the way in, face to the floor in the back of Lock's car, but there were few parked cars on Broome Street and I could see right away Carmen was right – the unmarked police vehicle wasn't there.

I started back down to tell her, but she'd already turned the car, was already nudging it up the slope as I pulled open the passenger door and scrambled in. 'No one up there,' I said. 'But quick. They'll see the lights from inside the house.'

Not quick enough, as it turned out. Carmen took the right turn out of the drive onto the street and it was only as she straightened we saw the headlights behind. The dark-coloured vehicle drew level with the house, slowed for a moment like it might turn in but sped up again, closing the distance.

I thought it was a local, a fluke, a random nobody, but they stuck with us to the end of the block and around the first turn, down towards the beach.

It wasn't a random nobody. It was the cops.

Carmen was calm as she drove, two hands steady on the wheel and her shoulders back against the seat. As if she knew where she was going, as if she had a plan. As if she did this every night of the week. As if we weren't driving a suspected murderer's vehicle with an unmarked police car following us. With him and the weapon we'd used to knock him out, lying in the back.

The cops were still on our tail three turns later. So much for scaling down surveillance.

'Holy fuck, Carmen.' I was not calm. I was rigid with the

effort of keeping down in my seat. I was gripping my seat belt so it cut into my hand in the same place Lock's house keys had. She'd told me to keep low so it looked like there was only one person in the car, but get real, Carmen. She looks nothing like Lock. The police were not idiots.

'They know. They know we've got him in here,' I said.

Her eyes flickered to the rearview mirror. 'Do not. They'd pull us over if they did.'

'Why are they following us then?'

She shrugged.

Dark, empty residential streets. No traffic. The vibration of the engine. She got us back on Broome Street, heading north.

The car smelled super-clean – I remembered that from earlier. Suspiciously, forensically clean, like he'd had it valeted. Apart from the waft of his sweat from the back and some kind of medicated soap or shampoo. My stranger-danger radar was like, going *off*, knowing he was on the seat behind me. It took everything I had not to turn around.

Carmen braked too fast at a roundabout. The baseball bat rolled off the seat with a thunk.

'Carmen, I think I might throw up.'

'No.'

'Open a window. I need air.'

'There's aircon.'

'Not the same.'

The window my side slid open a crack as she turned down towards the ocean and Marine Parade.

'What are you doing? It's lit up like Christmas down there. They're going to see us. They're going to see it's not him driving the car.'

'Calm down, Rachel.' She checked the rearview mirror again. 'It's what they're expecting.'

I swallowed, and let a little of the fresh air into my lungs, breathing through my mouth. She was right. If it was him driving the car this is what he'd do. Drive blocks of the Cottesloe strip as the pubs and cafes emptied out and people started to drift home. But it wasn't the right night for it; it was a weeknight. It wasn't the right time in the evening.

And it wasn't the right people in the car.

She drove a long block of the strip past the Beach Hotel and the club. I squirmed each time she had to slow down, each time a streetlight passed over the top of us. I'd never noticed how many crosswalks there are along Marine Parade. How many car parks with cars pulling out in front of us, how many people on the footpath, even on a Tuesday night. Each time we had to stop the light was like a torch beam and I screwed up my eyes and told her to get the fuck going. I imagined some passer-by glancing down into the back seat, getting an eyeful of Lock's grey face.

His body had started to smell different and I wondered if he'd died. I was trying to decide if that was a good thing or not, if it might be a relief, when he groaned again, and I winced.

'Jesus, Carmen.'

But no one stopped us. No one bashed on a window or stepped out in front of the car. Carmen went as far as Eric Street and turned up towards the highway. I could tell because of the change in the streetlights, the hotel on the corner that's marked for demolition and change.

She crested the hill, turned along Broome Street and back around.

'Are they still following?'

She nodded. There was a little furrow in her forehead, the only hint this was testing her in any way.

'We can't do this all night,' I said.

'Agreed.'

'Sooner or later—'

'Shut up, Rachel.'

I zipped it. What else could I do? I couldn't see shit from where I was. I made myself as small as I could, watched the lights pass overhead, the dark starred sky in between, the pines. I listened to the vibrating hum of the engine and the rush of air in at my window, the occasional shout from outside on the street.

She drove a longer block this time, and still no one stopped us.

'Are they still behind us?'

No answer.

'Carmen. Where are we—'

'Shh.'

She turned right again. Uphill.

'Do you even have a plan?'

We went for longer, silent, until she turned again. 'Drive back to his place,' she said. 'Wait for them to give up.'

'We'll be trapped then, because I doubt that's going to happen. And his parents are in there.'

She said nothing.

'Or we hide in plain sight,' I said. 'Might work, in a car like this.'

She frowned. 'How?'

I told her what I meant and directed her. It was a long shot but all we had. I felt her make the turns until we were headed uphill again. 'You'll have to do it fast,' I said. 'Try to run the light. How far back are they?'

She shrugged. I felt her swerve the two roundabouts and keep driving the long hill. I lost my bearings after that until she said, 'Hold on for this part.'

I cricked my neck and looked up at her as we sped through the lights, pressed back into the seat. There was a car horn, and another, and a squeal of brakes.

'Fuck, Carmen—'

'Shut up, Rachel.' She pressed her foot down harder.

And then I heard it, the whine of a siren. The cop car behind us had run the light too. My heart dropped into a hole. But she didn't quit. She turned right and then left, right again. I hit my head on the handle of the door and swore.

And then we were bouncing along the track. I tasted dust and she said, 'Stay down.'

She turned again, parked. 'Lights off,' I said, though I was sure we were screwed. There was no sound but the whining gaining siren, the two of us breathing, my heart banging like a drum'n'bass track. No more groaning from Lock, and I wondered again if he'd died.

The siren grew louder until it was right on top of us. I shut my eyes, screwed them tight the same as I had on the floor of Lock's car. I waited for the knock on Carmen's window, the glare of torchlight, the shouted command.

But none of it came.

The siren died away, and when Carmen let out a breath and I did the same my lungs were bursting.

'You can sit up now,' she said.

I lifted my head, and there was the sign: *Cottesloe Car & Ute*

Hire. I clocked the line of white vehicles she'd parked us in the middle of. The deserted car yard, the precise angle she'd parked at.

She started up the car and put the lights back on, and we pulled out onto the street. No unmarked police car waited for us.

We drove, zigzagging residential streets, but I wasn't fully there. I was blinking at streetlights, marvelling at the escape we'd had. That we weren't in police custody. Not yet.

That was the first time we worked together as a team. The only time, maybe. I didn't know yet, what was to come.

Lock was still alive behind me. The feelings were complicated. I wasn't sure what I wanted.

And then Carmen slowed and pulled in by a set of garages. We'd turned in off another lane at the back of a block of units. She stopped the car and got out, pulled up the first garage door, drove us inside and pulled it down again. She did it all like she wasn't in a hurry. Like she'd planned it.

She switched the headlights off and in the blackness I tried to guess where we were. It took a few seconds to get it. We were in one of the garages behind the abandoned four-storey units across from the golf course. The beige brick building with the cracked concrete yard at the back, the double row of garage doors marked with seagull shit and unimaginative graffiti.

The building I'd first smashed up almost a year ago, three days after Piper went missing.

We sit there, in the pitch dark, the only sounds the engine ticking down and the three of us breathing.

And then Lock shifts on the back seat and, fuck the dark and the spiders, I unclick my seat belt and launch myself out of the car. Trip and fall hard onto concrete.

Ow.

The interior light from my open door makes a yellow pool in the space, like an old-style light globe suspended in a room, the corners fading out into blackness. I pick myself up and brush the dust off the knees of my combats, gritty and oily. 'Gross.'

Carmen looks out at me, her face pale under her dark angled fringe.

'I can't believe we did that.' Should I be saying thank you? 'What if there's a tracker on his car?'

'There isn't,' she says. 'They need a warrant for that.'

'Which they must have got. They searched his apartment.'

'They'd be here by now if there was one.'

Not a comfort, Carmen. But why were they watching his parents' place when Zee said they'd stopped?

The space smells of old car and engine oil, whatever's on the floor I've picked up on my hands, warm bricks from the heat of the day. It's oppressively hot, hotter than outside. No cracks for the breeze to make its way in, no windows, not that there's been a sea breeze tonight.

Carmen leans across and pulls the car door shut, extinguishing the light.

'Hey,' I say. 'Can we have the light back?'

She doesn't answer. My phone screen, thirteen per cent battery when I grab it out of my pocket, tells me it's 8.45 p.m. but by the silence it could be two in the morning. I haven't heard another car and I didn't see any house lights as we drove in here. There was only a crane, further up the hill to the east, outlined in stars like a giant praying mantis.

It's the construction sites on either side, making a wasteland of the place after dark.

Carmen opens her door and climbs out, the car's interior light blinking on again.

'Did you know I'd been here before?' I say. 'To this building. That I smashed those windows?'

She shrugs. 'I s'pose. You never said anything, about the glass yesterday, and it was all over the rooms at the back. Last year on the ward you smashed a lot of stuff.'

It's the longest bit of speech I've heard from her. I didn't know I'd made that big of an impression. It's not reassuring.

'Why have we come here?' I say. 'What's going on?'

'You want to ask him questions, don't you?' She tilts her head like a crow, like she did at Lock after she'd knocked him out.

'Okay. Yeah. Find out where he's got Genevieve Craigie.' I glance into the back of the car. 'She's depending on us. We're all she's got.'

It sounds lame even to me. Carmen looks at me deadpan, at my face and then my arm, the one with Piper's name repeated over and over. Or maybe I imagine it. Whether she believes me about Genevieve or not, hers is not a normal response to the situation.

But I haven't modelled one of those myself up to now. So maybe I need to cut her some slack. And she doesn't know about Piper. She can't know. She's given no sign of it.

She pushes shut her door and the light goes out.

I keep my distance, my glowing phone screen in my hand, and watch the car like Lock is about to come clawing out of it like a TV zombie. I used to love those shows before real life death rocked up on my doorstep.

'Can we have more light?' I say.

She says no; there's an overhead light that works but we aren't to use it. 'Let your eyes adjust to the dark.'

135

This makes me think of the nocturnal house at the zoo, the signs on the way in. I loved that as a kid, the magic of growing used to the dark, the creatures with eyes like frisbees. A memory comes, Piper and me holding hands in a crocodile line of year threes. Okay. Maybe I can do this.

I shove my phone back in my pocket and look away from the car, away from where the light was, into the corners, and try to do what Carmen says. The garage is bigger on the inside than I thought, with room for two cars side by side, though this side of it's empty. Thick cobwebs matt the bricks and there's part of a set of shelves coming away from one wall – there must be light coming in from somewhere. You'd expect there to be tools in a space like this, tins of old paint and wobbly stepladders, but there's nothing like that; it's been cleared out. I think of redbacks and white-tailed spiders. I've never seen a white-tailed spider and I wonder if it's obvious, the white tip, like something that glows in the dark.

Don't be a jerk, Raych, of course it's not. But how big are they and would I recognise one? I'm grossed out by what they do: a clotted lump of flesh comes away and leaves a hole in you. How long does that take, and does it hurt? I read somewhere about that having been debunked, an urban myth, but I won't be taking chances.

I'm distracting myself, but it's fair enough in the circs, which to cosmically understate things are more suboptimal by the second. I think back to Lock's parents' house and the traces we left there. My prints on the front door, my pen lost somewhere on the driveway, his house key in my pocket. What if there were security cameras we didn't see? Carmen is fallible; she hasn't thought of everything.

I register a scraping, scuffing sound that makes the hairs stand up on my arms, but when I turn it's only Carmen moving around the outside of the car. She's carrying something, and she sets it down with a scrape of metal on concrete.

A chair.

Metal-framed and straight-backed, in the middle of the space next to the car.

She opens the back passenger door, the nearest one where Lock's head is, and I step back as the light flickers on. I watch the stains under the chair, like Rorschach inkblots, emerge from the gloom. A bubble of nausea nudges at me.

They're random oil stains, I do know that. Like our garage at home. But there's something about them.

Carmen gets me to help, and I don't know, I'm on autopilot or fucking deranged or whatever, so I do.

We get him out of the car onto the chair. He doesn't struggle. We keep the car doors open while we do it, for the light. Carmen magics more cable ties from that backpack of hers. She cuts off the old ones with a small serrated knife and binds his wrists to the flat metal arms of the chair, his ankles to each of the front legs. She pulls out silver duct tape and binds his upper body to the chair back.

She's prepared. I watch her do all this in a kind of strung-out horror. I think back to her smile when she was bent over him in his driveway. I think further back, to my few days on the ward with her last year, but memories of that time don't come easy.

At one point I say, 'Carmen. You do know he needs medical attention. We have to call the cops. They can ask him about Genevieve.' But even I can hear how small my words are in the space, the lack of conviction in them, and she doesn't respond.

And the thing is, he's okay. Sure, his face is grey and slicked with sweat, his head lolls a bit now he's upright in the chair, but the blood from his ear has dried and his breathing is steady. His eyes, which were fast closed, are now open a crack – there's a glimmer of daylight there, of consciousness, a strip of something shining, and I take a step back from the chair when I see it.

They're actors, these serial killers; everyone knows that. They're experts at making you see what they want you to instead of what's really there.

'Careful,' I say to Carmen as she bends closer to him. 'Watch him.' But he's still. He doesn't even flex his arms against the ties, like he hasn't figured it out yet; how many oceans deep it is, the shit he's in.

I should be asking different questions. Hell yeah. Like, why is Carmen doing this? What does she want? Not to help me, that's for sure. Not to help find Genevieve either.

But it feels too late for that already, like we've entered a reality where different rules apply. And something happens to me in there. Not right away. It's the same as my eyes adjusting to the dark; once that happens there's no turning back.

We don't spend a lot of time with him. Not that first night.

We should do. We should push him hard, shake him, whatever it takes, while Genevieve is still alive. But we don't know enough. We don't know how urgent it is. We don't have the full picture.

We have all the time in the world.

Or so we think.

PART THREE

WEDNESDAY

8

Carmen

Like attracts like

Dawn and dusk are when big and small hunters hunt. It's the best time for camouflage, for the in-between light – like the countershading sharks have – and Carmen uses this now. The sun isn't over the back fence yet but it's somewhere, because there's light diluting the parts of sky she can see, making the stars less bright.

She used to do it all the time, walk before the start of the day and find whatever had washed up on the beach in the night. But after she found Christine's body she had to stop. She couldn't be sure no one had followed her that day and she still gets that feeling sometimes, even now. Plus the police are everywhere since the murders, on the beaches and along Marine Parade and Curtin Avenue, down as far as Fremantle and up past Scarborough, even out on the water in their boats. You never know when they're going to be there, waiting for the next thing to happen, the next development in the case.

Today, she leaves the house extra-early. The construction cranes are still and silent. The commuters and posties and schoolkids are all in their beds. Alexis is on a late shift and even Mr and Mrs G are asleep.

Still, she goes the long way around to the garages, crossing the railway line three times to make sure she's not followed, looping down to the stretch of Marine Parade at South Cottesloe, which is how come she sees the white tent on the beach.

It's the same tent they use every time. She doesn't even have to ask anyone – she knows what it is.

It's Mrs Craigie's dead body.

There's a kids' playground at South Cottesloe and a not-very-big car park, which is already full up with forensic vans and marked and unmarked police cars, even in the early almost-light. Carmen can only see the top of the tent from where she's hidden near the bottom of Deane Street on the opposite side of Marine Parade. The police tape flutters – dark, light, dark – in the breeze off the ocean. Even though she didn't like Mrs Craigie, she feels bad that South Cottesloe is the spot she ended up. No one ever goes there except to walk their dogs, and no one swims there except for the tourists who come in winter and don't realise it's not the best beach and it's not even warm enough yet. Already there's a straggle of journos and ran-domers behind the police tape, and the sand will be churned up with the footprints of everyone coming and going and doing their jobs.

It'll be on the morning news, and then Rachel will know too.

Carmen stays far enough away no one sees her, and then she loops back around to the garages. The morning doesn't smell of anything except the cool night and the ocean, which reminds her of finding Christine's body that time. The sand was smooth then and there were no other footprints except Carmen's, walking towards Christine and away again.

She hears the sharp, cut-short cry of something small getting got as she turns in off the laneway to the garages – a bird or a mouse – and thinks she spots the girl cat up on a fence. But the cat is hunting and melts away. It's silent when she gets to the back of the end garage where they have Neil – the one with the white bougainvillea and the nest of paper wasps – and she has a moment of panic like a hole opening up under her feet, scared something's happened to him. That he's died, or escaped on the first night, and he's not where they left him. Because when did he have time to kill Mrs Craigie? How long has she been out there, drifting dead in the ocean?

But when she goes inside she hears the breathing of him, and there's his smell, and her eyes adjust to the dark and he's there.

There's a back door into the garage where they have Neil; all the garages have them. They didn't leave at the same time last night – they mustn't do that – but Carmen showed Rachel the door when she let her out. They can't keep pulling that noisy garage door up and crashing it back down. The garages have been empty since they cleared out the residents and Carmen's never seen anyone, but once she heard movement in the apartments that wasn't the cat, and even with the construction noise next door, someone will hear. She's locked the big door now from the outside, with a padlock she found in Mr G's shed that's rusty and scratched, so no one will notice it.

The door at the back has a bolt on the outside that looks like it could fall off at any time. Carmen has padlocked that too. It might not be enough, but Neil can't get out because of the chair. And no one knows he's here.

There's light in the garage, leaking in, and when Carmen tips her head up she sees the light-coloured rectangle in the flat tin roof she didn't notice before: corrugated plastic clogged with dirt and gum leaves, filtering the light. The sun is up now.

Neil's asleep, which must be hard to do when you're tied upright to a chair. But they can't let him lie down. That wouldn't work. Carmen wouldn't want to move him anyhow. It was bad enough touching him last night.

She gets all the way up to him without him waking up.

She keeps back so he doesn't know she's there, and examines his face. The wounds from last night have scabbed over. They've only ever filmed him at a distance on the news but even in the weak light inside the garage everything shows up like the surface of the moon. Apart from the scabs and some lines around his mouth, his skin is smooth and pale. His eyes stay closed but Carmen knows they're pale grey, like the ocean on a cloudy day. He doesn't look like someone who works outdoors. He must keep his hat on all the time, like she does.

His beard isn't as neat now as it was on the news. Those lines around his mouth could be new. It's the stress of everything. Being a suspect in the case. It can't be easy, having that kind of attention on you when you're not used to it. Carmen knows what that's like, from last year.

She's not sure how she feels about it, Mrs Craigie being dead and him being inside here on the chair the whole time. But no one knows how long they spend out there in the ocean before they wash up on the beach, she reminds herself. The dead girls.

Up close, Neil is not as unmemorable as Carmen thought. Some people would say he's good-looking. She realises this with a shock that darts down inside her body to her toes.

She knows about those women and girls who write to serial killers. But what are they getting out of it? They're not meeting the person. He's not right there in front of them. They're not on the same level.

It's different with Carmen and Neil. It's not attraction – not *physical* – it's more complicated than that. And right now, she's still annoyed with him about *that night*.

He doesn't need anything yet. She rigged up a water container last night with Rachel's help. Carmen's pleased with it. It's got a tube tied to the frame of the chair that sticks up near his face. All he has to do is turn his head to drink from it, and they can keep his forearms tied to the armrests of the chair. She checks the cable ties and duct tape and how tight everything is. Tight, but not too tight. He hasn't struggled in the night.

They should gag him, Rachel said, but Carmen didn't want to. She didn't want to have to touch him again. Once the construction noise gets going no one will be able to hear him, and Carmen has a feeling he won't call for help. They'll do it tonight but only if they have to. Rachel told Carmen they should disguise their faces too, but that's pointless – Neil was staring at Rachel for a good minute before Carmen hit him last night. And anyhow, Carmen wants him to see her and recognise her.

The water container, one litre, is one of those collapsible expensive ones people use for bushwalking or running. It was Mrs

Craigie's, and Carmen stole it from the staffroom at school after that day Rosso asked her about, when Mrs Craigie was mean to her in a bullying way in front of the whole class out on the oval. That wasn't the only time, either. Carmen didn't know what she was going to use the container for when she took it, but it's perfect for Neil. Mrs Craigie doesn't need it any more, after all.

Neil hasn't drunk much, which is good, because there are practical considerations to do with that. Carmen has brought a bucket, for pee and other things, and put it down inside the back door. Rachel will make a big deal of this being gross, but what can you do? One of them needs to be practical.

There's sweat staining the neckline and under the arms of Neil's golf club uniform, and shining on the part of his neck she can see. The uniform is the dark blue polo shirt she remembers from *that night* with the logo for the golf club on the pocket. His eyes are still closed, his eyelids not moving. He could be pretending, after what happened with Rachel last night, but Carmen doesn't think so. He's breathing slow – a soft rasping sound – and there's a snail of drool on his bottom lip. She put something in the water to keep him calm – Mrs G's anxiety pills crushed into a powder.

Looking at him helplessly sat there, she gets the thrill again, down in her bones. She likes it here inside the garage, cut off from the bright light of the outside world. She likes that no one ever comes here.

She could wake him up and ask him everything she wants to know right now. It'd be easier without the distraction of Rachel, her strung-out loose cannon energy. She doesn't know what's stopping her. She wouldn't pretend it was about Mrs Craigie like Rachel did last night.

Carmen

Something happened to Rachel last night, once they had Neil in here, on the chair. Once he couldn't escape even if he wanted to. Carmen saw it in her eyes, how bright and glittering they were, like she was on something. How much it took Rachel by surprise.

Carmen knows what Rachel felt like because she's feeling it now. It's like being at the top of a rollercoaster, the moment before it plunges down and you can't stop it. Carmen's only done that one time, at the Royal Show, but she remembers it.

She wants to ask Neil things, things about *that night*. She wants to know why he stopped her killing Alexis. She wants to know what he meant when he said, 'Not her.' She wants him to recognise her because most of all, she wants him to see they're the same.

It's a lot.

Neil twitches his head and Carmen smiles. She won't ask him anything this morning, she'll wait until after school. He needs to wake up first. She'll wait until he recognises her. She wonders when he will, how long it will take and what will happen then.

Rachel was quiet at the beginning, with Neil. Like she was afraid of him, or afraid to start. But then she started and Carmen had a job to stop her.

Rachel sprang at Neil like a spider, or a cat. She knocked the chair over. Sounds were coming out of her that didn't make sense. She gouged both his cheeks with her nails. Carmen had to pull her off – it wasn't the right way to start. It was no good anyhow with him still knocked out. She told Rachel they'd have to wait and come back today.

It shouldn't have surprised her about Rachel. Not after last year. All the smashing and raging in the hospital. But that isn't going to work with Neil. He won't be fazed by it.

She doesn't need Rachel, anyhow. Not now they've got him in here.

Rachel apologised to Carmen before she left. Carmen's never heard her say sorry before. She said she wasn't ready, it won't happen again, she won't lose control like that.

But Carmen knows she will.

Usually, Carmen endures school on her particular version of autopilot, which keeps her under the radar. She knows how to make it look like she's paying attention, how to let instructions filter through while she thinks of other things. Sometimes her brain going offline feels like that, but school is different because she does it on purpose. It's like when you drive somewhere and can't remember how you got there, but you still obey all the rules of the road.

But today, the rules of the road don't apply and her autopilot isn't working. She worries about Neil all day – about someone finding him, or Rachel going there without her and trying to get inside. She worries about what she's going to find when she goes back this evening. She's told off four times for inattention during class and has to do an hour of detention, which even Carmen knows is an overreaction and unfair when everyone is distracted by the rumours about Mrs Craigie's dead body.

She's late home and there's no time to check the garages before dinner, or even the white tent on the beach. She listened to the news driving home from school but all it did was confirm Mrs Craigie is dead. At the dinner table, all of them – Mr and Mrs G and Alexis – ignore the giant elephant in the house of Mrs Craigie and what's happened to her. But that's what they're like in this family. Carmen's used to it.

Afterwards she has to help load the dishwasher and wash and dry the pots, and Mrs G has a talk with her about her attendance at school, which is an overreaction too, because it was only one day, yesterday, and that's nothing.

Everything takes too long and when Carmen leaves the kitchen, Leo, Alexis's fiancé, is right there like he's been listening at the door. It's a shock to see him – Leo keeps away from Carmen and that's how she likes it. Plus he never comes to the house during the week, only on a Sunday for lunch or dinner after Mr and Mrs G get back from church. He's in his AQWA uniform, which is nearly the same dark blue as Neil's, so he's come straight from a shift at work.

Leo doesn't say hello, good, but when Carmen steps around him, Alexis is there too behind his shoulder, looking hard at her phone screen. So they have been listening at the door, both of them.

She doesn't care. It was nothing important. But when she heads for the back of the house and her room, Leo and Alexis follow. Alexis avoids Carmen's room as a rule, so she knows this is something different. It's like there's a shadow falling across her back the whole way along the hallway, except there can't be because the two of them keep their distance. Still, it makes her mad, because she needs to get to the garages, so when she gets to her bedroom door she turns and leans against it and crosses her arms.

This is something Rachel would do, Carmen is sure, and she tries to keep that in mind. She hasn't got all night, and her backpack is inside her room, with things inside it she wouldn't want Alexis to see. Stolen things, and things she needs for later. 'What?' she says.

Even leaning back against her door, Carmen is as tall as Leo. He's sweating and pulling his collar away from his big neck because the aircon doesn't reach this end of the house. His face is pink and shiny, and his curly combed hair is damp at the ends. She sees him take a breath like he's trying to inflate himself before he says what he's come to say, even though Leo doesn't need inflating.

'Listen,' he says. 'Keep away from Lexie, all right? Stay out of her room. She might have qualms about calling the cops on you, getting the authorities involved, but I don't.'

Alexis is stood well back, with Leo between the two of them. She darts a look at Carmen over his shoulder, her eyes round like a mouse. For a second there's more to it, almost like an apology, before she breaks the contact and it's gone.

Carmen hasn't been in Alexis's room, not since *that night*. Leo's got nothing on her. 'I dunno what you mean,' she says.

He pushes his head forwards. 'Do you take me for a mug? You're on everybody's radar – your teachers, doctors, local shops and businesses. The *police*.' His eyes bulge on police. 'Stealing and lying. Making up burglarising men who don't exist. Assault.' This is all old news. Is burglarising even a word? And it was attempted murder, not assault. Carmen doesn't know why he's here saying it, apart from the fact Leo likes mansplaining people to themselves. Any second now he's going to say the word sociopathic. She tunes him out and waits. Shifts one hand behind her to the doorknob, keeps the other arm across her body.

'Out at strange hours, sneaking about – yes, you've been seen.' This sends a jolt through Carmen, because she's careful – *no one* sees her. She grips the doorknob so hard her hand goes numb.

She could open it and fall back into her room, but Leo might follow; he'd find her backpack. She looks at his nose, imagines snapping her head forwards and crunching it into his face. She can feel what it would be like, the breaking of bone and the wetness of blood in her hair. She doesn't like the thought of that second part. She doesn't want to do it.

'All of which verges on *sociopathic*,' Leo says. There it is. There's spit flying out of his mouth now. It's gross. Feral. That's what Rachel would call it. Rachel would headbutt him – she fully would. She'd already have done it and run. Carmen keeps her grip on the door. Leo says, 'If I had my way you'd be back in hospital.' He makes air quotes around hospital and at last he moves back and Carmen can breathe.

'Lexie needs to move on. She doesn't need you *lurking* outside her room, reminding her of that night, all right? So watch your step. Keep away from her.'

He turns and strides past Alexis, who follows him back along the hallway like a rubber dinghy tied behind a boat. She hasn't joined in, hasn't said one word to Carmen, and she's tripping to keep up with him, even in the flat shoes she wears for driving.

Alexis is always this way when Leo comes to the house. It's like she makes herself small for him, the opposite of how she is with everyone else. Carmen doesn't reckon she even knows she's doing it. You shouldn't marry someone if you're scared of them.

She hears the front door close, and the two cars start up and drive away – Leo's loud obnoxious one, and Alexis's silver electric hatchback, on their way to her 8 p.m. yoga class. He'll follow her there and wait outside, like he does every time.

You've been seen. Maybe Leo keeps track of Carmen the same way he keeps track of Alexis. Carmen's not scared of him but she'll have to be more careful. Some mornings when she wakes up, she's not certain herself where she's been.

She remembers Leo in the aftermath of *that night*. He was the one who was lurking. Not letting Alexis out of his sight and keeping Carmen from getting too close. He always had one hand on Alexis's back – steering or stroking with his bulked-up arms from the gym – or swamping her smaller hand with one of his. It seemed like he was more upset than Alexis was, but Carmen doesn't know what happened after that, because she was on the ward in the mental place the following day.

Carmen heard them talking late one evening two years ago, Mr and Mrs G, after Alexis had gone to bed. About Leo and Alexis and her *history*, as Mrs G called it. Another example of the kind of thing she says about Alexis behind her back. Alexis cheated on her first boyfriend at high school, and Leo found out years later and didn't like it even though it had nothing to do with him.

Leo's insecure. That's why he keeps track of Alexis the way he does. But why did he come today? It must have something to do with *that night*, after Carmen saw inside Alexis's room yesterday and reminded her of it. But Alexis doesn't know it was Neil in her room that night and Neil isn't someone who burglarises. She wouldn't have lied if she knew who he was.

Alexis should be more careful what she tells Leo. Because lying only works if you keep it up.

Carmen gives it ten minutes before she goes on foot to the garages.

Carmen has only got as far as crossing the railway line onto Curtin Avenue when she hears Alexis's toy car behind her.

She's memorised the non-sound of the little electric vehicle, how all you can hear is the turning of tyres on bitumen like a wheel going around without the hamster inside. She knows it exactly.

She speeds up and takes the cut-through to the next street, but when she gets to the end of the block Alexis is already there, stopped in the middle of Marine Parade like she's ripped through the turns like a maniac.

Carmen waits for one car to pass heading south, but Alexis stays where she is and Leo's car isn't behind her. So Carmen crosses in front through the beams of her headlights, wrenches open the passenger door and gets in.

'What are you doing, *Car*—?'

'Don't say that.' Carmen cuts her off. 'I don't like it.'

Alexis's mouth stays open like she doesn't know what shape to put it in. Her face is red and she's breathing hard, so Carmen guesses she has been driving fast.

'Stop following me,' Carmen says. 'Why are you?' She holds hard to her backpack, hugging it against her, heavy in her lap.

Alexis closes her mouth, sticky and sullen. 'I'm not.'

A car comes up behind them. Alexis freezes and checks the mirror but it's not Leo. She indicates, pulls over and parks, and crosses her arms over her chest. The car smells of her distinctive perfume and beauty products, and Carmen wishes she hadn't got in.

'I'm going to my class, Carmen. I'll be late.'

'Are not. Is the opposite direction.' Carmen turns in her seat but can't see Leo's car. 'Where is he?'

'I told him I'd left something at home.' She tries to deflect. 'You're on your way to that stretch of beach, aren't you? Where that … poor woman was found. You were going to *look*, like a vulture.'

Carmen notes the absence of the words *dead body*. A real vulture would do more than look, and it's not as if there's anything to see there except what she saw this morning. But she's already registered the change in Alexis, in the balance of things between them. Out the passenger window, she can see only dark. But she knows what's there: sand, ocean, the container ships, Wadjemup, sky.

'What do you want, Alexis?'

There's a gap before Alexis says it. Slow, like the words don't want to come out. 'I can offer you a deal.'

Now it's Carmen's turn to stare, as Alexis focuses ahead through the windscreen at the dark and the streetlights, the intermittent headlights and taillights of passing cars. They can't see the tent on the beach or the car park from here – it's too far. 'You don't talk to Leo about that night, *ever*. And I won't shop you,' Alexis says. 'I won't get you put back inside that place. That's the deal.'

This is giant, and strange. Carmen frowns. Why would she talk to Leo? She wouldn't want to. It's not much of a deal for Alexis. Doesn't she know Carmen tried to kill her? She must care a lot what Leo thinks.

'I can get Mum off your back too.' Alexis leans towards Carmen, gaining ground, or so she reckons. 'Maybe. About school. I can try. You can move out, get your own place.'

She still wants to get rid of Carmen, but it's not terrible. It's a crack in the usual way of things, and Carmen will take it. 'Okay,' she says. 'Deal.' She'd love to be a million miles from Alexis. She'd like Mrs G off her back too. It's not like she's letting

Alexis off the hook. It'll be easier then, when they're not living together, to kill her and not get caught.

But she's too quick. She should keep back what she knows about Neil for later but she doesn't. It's stupid. It's because she doesn't understand yet, the extent of things between Alexis and Leo. But there's never been any kind of truce between her and Alexis before, and she likes knowing something Alexis doesn't.

'Do you remember?' Carmen breathes. 'Who it was? In your room that night?'

Alexis goes still, her hands on the wheel. 'There was no one apart from you in my room that night.'

But Carmen can taste the lie, knows the texture of it; she's heard it too many times.

'I can tell you,' Carmen says. 'If you don't remember.'

Alexis twists around, and this time it's horror on her face. 'I don't want to know that!'

Carmen backtracks. 'I won't then. I don't have to.'

'No, you *won't*.' But she hasn't denied it this time, that there was someone. 'If you do, I'll say you lied again. Made the whole thing up!' Her voice is a squeak. She puts her hands back on the wheel, checks her mirrors and starts the engine. 'You know what? The deal's off.'

Carmen grips her backpack and frowns. 'Why?'

'I don't trust you, that's why. Get out of my car. I've changed my mind.' Her lip is back in its habitual curl. 'Get out!' she shrieks.

Carmen gets out. Anything to get that shrieking out of her brain.

Alexis pulls away, but before she does, she lowers the

passenger window and gives it her parting shot. Because, of course. Because she was always going to.

She mutters three words at Carmen and drives away, and Carmen watches the taillights of the little car disappear. She stands on the footpath, sensing the night smells coming up off the bitumen and the sand and further off, the ocean. She watches the dark flat water and pictures the bright lights of the forensic team, only a few blocks further up the beach. She half expects something to come back to her, from *that night*. A dark shape breaching the surface of her mind like a whale or a submarine or a shark. The full story. Because Alexis knows more than she's saying, maybe more than Carmen remembers. And Carmen's been so close to it, talking to her in the enclosed space of the car.

She did know. Alexis knew it was Neil all along. And now Carmen understands.

Alexis is afraid of Carmen, but she's more afraid of Leo. That's why she lied about *that night*. It must be. Because there was a man in her room and she couldn't risk Leo finding out.

Nothing else comes, and the water stays flat and dark. She shoulders her backpack and starts to walk, with Alexis's parting words keeping pace all the way to the garages.

'Like attracts like.'

She thought she was having a go at Carmen. But it's the opposite.

It's full dark when Carmen turns in off the lane, and the construction sites either side are silent. The girl cat slinks up against her leg in her jeans, which she's never done before, and once Carmen is over the shock of it, it's a good feeling. Then a car door slams at the end of the lane and the cat whips away into the night.

Carmen stops, imagining Alexis tracking her in the little silver car, but she doesn't hear anything more from the lane – no crunching footsteps, no talk. She remembers the things she found in Unit Seven, the sleeping bag and mattress and bag of clothes, the person squatting or camping out in there that turned out not to be Rachel. But the building when she looks past the row of garages is dark. No one has followed her. Good, because despite Leo's threats and Alexis's non-deal, Carmen is not going back inside the mental place.

There's no sound from inside the garage but there's an annoying digging and scraping from between the fence and the bougainvillea. It's Rachel, gouging the dirt with her sneaker over and over, impatient from waiting. The tension comes at Carmen in waves.

It's not a good way to start with Rachel, not after last night.

'There's a nest of wasps in that,' Carmen says in a whisper as she passes her.

Rachel swears and jumps away from the bougainvillea. 'Took your time,' she fires back. 'You saw the news, right? When did he do it, kill Genevieve? We have to talk about that, before we—'

But Carmen keeps moving, unlocks the padlock and steps inside, with Rachel still hissing something at her and breathing too close behind. And the girl cat slippery around her legs again like neither of them wants to miss out on what happens next.

Carmen would lock them both out if she could, but she can't. She needs time with Neil, to speed things up. She needs him to recognise her, to see her for who she is. No one else understands her, but he will.

For now, Neil is quiet. There's enough light through the rectangle of roof to see by – starlight, and the bulging moon somewhere. His eyelids are heavy, Carmen sees as she moves past the bucket she brought this morning and the bonnet of the car. He's drunk some more of the water.

No one has reported Neil missing. Or if they have, it wasn't on the news. Good, because they haven't finished with him yet.

She puts down her backpack as Rachel steps into the space and stops. Rachel teeters on the balls of her feet, riveted by him, tightening her fists and letting them go like she's squeezing a tennis ball – does she know she's doing it? She's got the same pent-up energy as last night. Carmen will have to let her go first.

Rachel's eyes are bigger and darker in the dim light than they were yesterday. In the daylight they're hazel, almost gold. 'What's the matter with him?' she says. 'Did you give him something?'

Carmen shrugs a yes. 'To keep him quiet,' she says.

Rachel swallows and takes a step closer. 'Right.' She shoots Carmen another look, licks her bottom lip where the ring is, a glint of metal. Her face says, 'What are we doing? What the fucking fucking hell?' Something like what Rachel would say. But out loud she says, 'Wake him up. I wanna talk to him. I wanna ask him about Genevieve.'

The girl cat is systematically sniffing each leg of the chair. Carmen steps aside so Rachel can get closer. 'Ask him,' she says. 'But, you know ...' She motions downwards with a flat palm. *Quieter.*

The best way to deal with Rachel, Carmen reckons, is to give her space. Let her do what she wants, get it over with, then get rid of her. And Rachel's small; it's not as if she can really hurt him. She wants to see what Rachel will ask, whether she'll keep up the lie about Mrs Craigie. She seems calmer now, apart from her eyes.

'Lock?' Rachel says. She scrunches her face and shakes her head. 'No, I can't call him that. Hey you,' she says, louder, kicks out at the toe of his work boot. 'Hey, mofo, wake the fuck up.'

His eyes open slowly, like shutters coming up, dark and glittery in the light. They blink twice and close again.

Rachel is motionless, staring back at him, her mouth part the way open. The next moment she's swiping at her face with the back of her wrist and turning away, into the corner where the light doesn't reach. 'Fuck.'

Carmen watches her go. Her attention is split now between the two of them – it reminds her of dogs she's seen on the beach when their owners walk in different directions. Running to keep up with one and then the other, wanting to herd them back together.

Rachel is talking to herself; Carmen can't hear what. She's shaking her head and sniffing and Carmen feels helpless for a moment, like there's no floor under her and she might fall through to somewhere else.

When she turns back to Neil, she spots it – his forearm flexed against the cable tie. His shoulders are slumped, his eyes still shut. It's a tiny movement between the hard plastic and the arm of the chair, barely more than a tightening of sinew over bone, but she catches it, and worries for a second if the ties will hold. He's not a big man, but his wrists and his hands are bony and square like they're too big for the rest of him. It's okay, she tells herself. Those ties will hold anything.

And then Rachel is back, stood in front of him. Carmen can't see her face in the light. 'So, you killed another one. Genevieve Craigie. Yeah, she had a name. When did you do it? Monday night?' Her voice is different, even from last night, a growl deep in her throat. 'Think you're so smart, don't you? Getting away with it every time. Well, that's all changed now. We know who you are, and you know why you're here, so let's not piss about.'

But the thing is, Rachel does piss about. That's what it seems like to Carmen, stood back in the shadows. She asks her questions, but they're not the ones Carmen knows she wants to ask. Rachel doesn't care about Mrs Craigie. It's obvious from the way she skirts the issue, around and around, wheeling in and away, like a seagull swooping at something it's not sure it wants to eat.

She asks, 'Where do you keep them? Where did you have Genevieve before you killed her? How come the cops haven't found the place?' And, 'How come no one's seen you at the bar or the club? Seen you take them, seen them in your car?' And, 'What would the profilers say? Was it something that happened when you were a kid?'

Neil looks past Rachel, blinks some more and says nothing. He knows she's not asking the right questions. He seems smaller tonight than he did this morning, except for his hands, and Carmen wonders how he does it, makes himself small for Rachel. He's slumped against the duct tape and his eyelids are heavy but he's acting, she knows he is, from the way he tested the ties on his wrists. He's alert, and Carmen can see he knows exactly what's happening to him. There are no questions in his eyes when he opens them and there should be. He's not going to fight or draw attention to himself.

Neil has his own agenda. And Rachel doesn't see it.

He's like one of those magic pictures that are two different things depending on which way you scrunch your eyes. One way he's a nobody – the careful face he shows when they interview him on the news – and the other way he's *The Shark* and capable of anything. But Carmen is a match for him. He's not as good an actor as he thinks he is.

She thinks back to Alexis. *Like attracts like.* And what he said that night. 'Not her.'

He was there for *her* that night, she understands now. For Carmen. He did see something in her, something better than killing Alexis. That's why he stopped her. 'Not her.' It's a relief that he did, instead of her not being able to do it.

They are the same, like Carmen thought.

It's a mixture of things, how it feels to realise this. A swimming sensation instead of the usual heaviness in her blood and her bones. She backs up against the nearest wall, steadier with the grit of it against her back.

Maybe Rachel's questions aren't the problem. Maybe he wants to talk to Carmen and no one else. Maybe he will only talk to a person like him.

'Ask him what you came to ask,' Carmen says. 'Or go home.' She sees a twitch of movement from Neil's eyes as she says it.

Rachel's head snaps around. 'What do you mean?'

Carmen shrugs. She can smell Neil's sweat, and the soap he uses, and the oily dusty garage. The girl cat is on her haunches in front of her, her spine straight and her tailed curled around her. The cat is impatient too, as if she knows why they're here. 'I know it's not about Mrs Craigie.' It's worth the risk. Rachel doesn't know the connection Carmen's found between the two of them, the significance of *that night* she found out at the library. She can't know.

'I am asking,' Rachel says.

But she's not.

The sea breeze comes up, sudden like a breaking wave. The big garage door behind Neil bangs like something's charged at it, and the cat streaks into a corner. The wind circles and buffets the garage like a pack of dogs, huffing and sniffing up under the edges of flat roof where Carmen didn't think there was space.

Rachel glances up at the roof, steps closer to Neil until her face is inches from his. She could kiss him, or headbutt him, like Carmen almost did to Leo today. She could claw his face like she did last night, or go for his eyes. Carmen feels the blood pushing hard in her ears, down into her legs. The changes to her heart rate and blood pressure. The garage feels exposed now, unsafe. Rachel needs to get on with it, but Carmen doesn't want to have to pull her off him like she did last night.

'Wake up!' Rachel says louder, over the sound of the wind. 'You're going to confess to what you did – to Genevieve, to all of them – then we're going to call the cops and we can all go home.' But there's no reaction from him. His head drops and his eyes are closed again.

'It's your fault he's not listening. You put too much in.' Rachel straightens up, her hands on her hips like Alexis. 'We can't ask him things if he's asleep.'

Carmen looks at how much he's drunk of the water. It's not much, not enough, but she can't explain this to Rachel. Carmen changes the water to keep her happy, but it's Rachel who's the problem. He'd wake up if she asked the right questions.

Carmen knows what Rachel wants to ask him about. Who.

This isn't about Mrs Craigie. That was a lie to get Carmen to help her. This is about her friend, Hana Piper Lee, the one whose name is written all up her arm. Carmen knows this because of what she looked up at the library.

Piper is the one they never found.

Why doesn't Rachel ask about her? Carmen thinks she knows. Rachel doesn't want to know the worst; that her friend, maybe her best friend in the world, is dead and not coming back.

But Carmen can see other things as she watches Rachel pace in front of Neil. You can't do something like this and walk away at the end like nothing has happened. Rachel's kidding herself if she thinks they can call the cops and go home. Can't she see they can't go back?

There's only one way out. Carmen's not going back inside the mental place, or somewhere worse. Either they get out of this garage and walk away, or he does. And why hasn't he given Carmen a sign? He's not properly asleep. He must have recognised her by now.

Rachel says, 'What if he's faking? We need him to wake up.' Maybe she's more on the ball than Carmen thought. She says, 'Where's your bag, that knife? The one you had last night,' and Carmen's not going to stop her.

And then Rachel is crouched by the car, unzipping Carmen's backpack, opening it wide. She's knocked over the bucket in her rush and it rolls on its side like an open mouth.

Carmen thinks back to the moment she hit him with the bat, how it felt in her fingers, the vibration and sound of it. How she knew they had to take him. She knows what's in her backpack. She chose to put those things in there. She *is* like Neil, whether he'll acknowledge her or not.

He's awake again now and not even looking at her. He's more awake than he's been all night and he's staring at Rachel. Rachel's left arm is stretched out straight where she's yanked open Carmen's backpack, and the square of moonlight falls on it through the roof exactly right. Neil's gaze is locked onto Rachel's arm of tattoos – the name Piper, written over and over. Rachel doesn't see it, but Carmen does, and then he looks from the name to Carmen and back again.

It's only for a moment – his eyes close again and his head tips forwards – but it's electric for Carmen. It's enough. Because she gets it, what Neil wanted for her *that night*.

Ever since Christine, Carmen has felt connected to the murders. Some days she's even thought she must be doing them and not remembering it, because of wanting Mrs Craigie to stop bullying her, and her jeans being wet a few times, and the shark's tooth she found snagged in Christine's rashie. Other things too, like those girls Maya and Mo, that she's tried not to think about: coincidences that might not be coincidences. Because her brain doesn't remember things in a joined-up way like a story, and because the murders are *big things*.

The rest of the time she thinks it can't be her, no way, because how would she get the bodies to wash up like that, in the exact places they do, when she can't even swim? She only took the aluminium dinghy out that one time to prove she could drive it. She wanted to see if she could get somewhere better, but she didn't even take it past the yacht club into the next bay.

But now she's remembering about Rachel's friend. What if 'Not her,' meant Carmen could do better? What if Neil's plans for Carmen meant killing another girl?

Because Piper's body never washed up anywhere. Carmen

only had *that night* – the next day she was in the hospital. But she was frustrated, the adrenaline overflowing, in the middle of trying to kill Alexis and not doing it. Neil would have seen that and taken advantage of it. Carmen could have gone out later without anyone knowing. She uses the door from her room into the backyard all the time.

And that, taking a girl and locking her in somewhere no one has found her. Maybe that's something a person like Carmen could do and not remember it.

It's a shock, thinking this. It's that feeling from the top of the rollercoaster, but far beyond what she expected. And what does it mean for them, Carmen and Rachel? Rachel would kill Carmen if she knew Piper's death was her fault.

There's a noise outside, a scraping against the big garage door. Carmen stands and listens but it's only the wind. Rachel has stopped now, her eyes huge and the backpack open in front of her like she's scared to go any further, scared to put a hand in there now she's seen what's inside.

'Give it to me,' Carmen says. 'I want to do it.'

9

Raych

The slippery dark

The wind was so loud outside I couldn't hear myself think. But why would I want to? The thoughts snapping and snarling around my head scared even me.

I was crouched in the shadows by the front wheel of Lock's car, in the garage. I hoped Carmen had a plan to get us out of there. She had to. I couldn't remember how we'd started. She was the one who'd wanted to do this. Wasn't she?

And why was I only thinking all this now I'd seen what was in her backpack? What was wrong with me?

The contents of Carmen's black backpack was the stuff of nightmares. Garden tools, knives, screwdrivers. An array of blades, their sharpened edges glinting in the low light. A coil of lightweight climbing rope, more of the thick black cable ties, and some kind of clamp.

Instruments of torture, basically.

How could I not have known who I was dealing with? I didn't know how long she'd had this stuff, how premeditated it was. She could have been collecting it for years or nicked the whole lot that afternoon from a single backyard shed. I couldn't believe she hadn't been clanking wherever she went, that she carried the bag around like it weighed nothing.

The opened-up bag looked like a shark's mouth with no teeth, but that was my mind fucking with me. I wasn't going to touch any of it. It wasn't like we were here to save anyone, not now Genevieve was dead. I felt some guilt about that, sure – it was the shortest interval of any of them, between him taking her and killing her – but I told myself what we'd done had made no difference. He could have killed her anytime from Sunday night until we'd taken him, but no one knew, did they? No one knew how long the bodies drifted before they washed up. And no one knew we had him in here.

I tried to close the bag but the zip stuck. My hands shook and then I wrenched it and the zip caught my thumb. 'Ow.' I sucked on the blood, could feel the drumming of my heart above the wind.

Carmen was agitated, I could see that. That wasn't normal for her. But for now, she was still in control. And I needed it to stay that way.

'Give it to me,' she said again.

'No, Carmen.' I swallowed. 'This is . . . No. We don't need to go that far.' I scrambled to my feet. 'Let me try with him again.'

But she was right there. She ignored the no, bent to the

bag and unzipped it again. I looked past her at Lock, slumped against the duct tape and the back of the chair. From this angle Carmen was huge and he was tiny. But he wasn't tiny, he was the monster who'd killed Piper. There were so many warring impulses in me it wasn't funny. I watched his jaw muscles twitch and his neck slowly straighten, how pale and fragile and skinny it looked against the dark of his beard. He turned his head in Carmen's direction and then mine, blinking. No eye contact. I remembered that from the news reports.

How was he a killer? That was my first moment of doubt.

'Carmen,' I said. 'Carmen!' I touched her shoulder and she shrugged me off like a bug. 'He's woken up.'

Lock cleared his throat and spoke for the first time, in that low grating voice I'd heard in his TV interviews. The voice he used for the journos with the distinctive hitch in it I'd always thought meant he was trying to disguise it, meant there was something hidden under his carefully constructed tone.

His speech was slurred, and first up we didn't catch it. He had to repeat himself.

'I . . . have to . . . urinate.'

Was it a trick, Lock needing a piss? Had he guessed what was in the bag from what was on my face?

Was he going to try something?

Whatever his motives, at that point it was a relief. To have something to distract Carmen from what was inside the back-pack. Even the cat was staring at Lock like it understood what he'd said. I took a step towards the bucket and as I did I nudged the backpack, still open, under the front part of the car with my foot.

'Okay,' I said. 'Let's do this thing.'

Carmen eyed me warily.

'Doesn't take a genius, does it?' I picked up the bucket. It was black plastic and smelled like garden dirt. 'I'm guessing that's what this is for?' I was speaking in this weird bright voice I'd never used in my life. It reminded me of one of the nurses on the ward.

I took the bucket over to the chair. 'Okay, mofo. You want to piss, you need to do what we say.' We couldn't untie him. That was obvious. I glanced back at Carmen. 'He can stand up, can't he, if we help him?'

But for all Carmen's practical nature, and Carmen is scarily practical, she hadn't moved.

His eyes were closed again. An act, maybe, because Carmen had changed his drinking water so it wasn't drugged any more. He had to be waking up by now. A mini bomb of fear exploded low down in my gut, an echo of all those serial killers I'd read about, the lurid true crime bios and docos and podcasts. Maybe it was a mistake to have left the knives in the bag. Maybe I could go back for one, a small one, the serrated one Carmen had used the night before. But no, that was a slippery slope, right there.

He was wearing a polo shirt and uniform pants, matching dark blue. A belt I was going to have to undo. There was queasiness as I contemplated it, but it was anatomy, human biology, nothing more. I don't do penises, but I could detach and unzip the dude.

'Carmen. I can't do this by myself.' After a beat she nodded. The chair was light, aluminium, and between us we did it. Wedged a shoulder under an armpit each and tilted until he was bent forwards with the chair on his back like a hermit crab.

He was helpless like that, swaying on his skinny legs, but I still didn't trust him. 'Watch him,' I said to her. I darted in and undid his belt and his zip. *There was no evidence of sexual assault. There was no evidence of sexual assault.* I repeated this to myself as I did it.

I picked up the bucket and thrust it at her. She looked blank so I gave it a shake. She could do this one thing. 'You must have thought this through,' I said. 'You'll have to hold it.'

Carmen's eyes slid to his crotch. Her face in that moment was like no face I'd ever seen. '*Hold* it?'

'The bucket, Carmen. You have to hold the bucket, is what I meant.'

Wrung out after the pissing ordeal, we retreated to the side of the garage furthest from the car. There was a bench against the wall there I hadn't spotted the night before. I checked it for redbacks using the torch on my phone – Carmen was distracted because she didn't comment on this – and we sat on the end furthest from Lock and his chair.

The sea breeze had died as quick as it came up. It was way too quiet. And Lock was awake.

He hadn't tried anything. We'd got him covered up and sat him back down, and Carmen left the bucket of piss on the far side of the car by the back door. She hadn't gone back for her bag but I'd seen her give it a look as she passed.

We could both see it from where we were sitting, lurking in the densest block of shadow under the car. The cat was under there next to it – a pair of gleaming green unblinking eyes.

There wasn't a whole lot of pee in the bucket. He wasn't drinking enough water and I didn't know why I cared. We had much bigger problems than this.

I still hadn't asked him about Piper. I knew why I couldn't do it – I'm not a total idiot, only a partial one. It was a gutless wonder thing, a big fuck-off one. I'd wanted to know the truth all these long months, got so close I could taste it, and now I'd bailed on myself. Where had I gone? Where was my rage? All I could find was fear. This panicky feeling ripped through me as I sat there, the same one I'd get at school when I hadn't studied for an exam and I was out of time, except magnified about a gazillion times. We'd had him in there for twenty-four hours and where had it got us?

That stuff I told myself about stepping up, not being gutless any more? It was a crock of pure BS. Piper was the brave one. It was the first thing I'd noticed about her.

I was still a wimp. I hadn't changed at all.

'I can't ask him. The thing I want to know,' I said to Carmen.

It bothered me, Lock sitting there, alert as fuck. I kept my voice low but I knew he could hear it. He was still slumped and silent but I'd seen him check out the inside of the space, clock his car there and blink. His awakeness was an alarm, sounding out its warning like a drumbeat through the floor.

Carmen was bothered by it too, I could tell, and Carmen's not bothered by a lot. She was like a coiled spring next to me, not her usual cool, aloof self. She was doing this thing where she'd stare intently at Lock then frown and shake her head like she'd made a mistake. Confused. Guilty, even. The rest of the time she stared at her boots or at her sick bag of tricks under the car.

I got it. At least I thought I did. She'd lost someone too – one of those girls – and it was complicated. It's always complicated. It was the first one, maybe – Christine, the water polo player. Everyone knows at least one of those girls, or knows someone who knows one of them. There was Genevieve too; she was Carmen's teacher.

It had to be one of them. I'd been so wrapped up in myself it hadn't occurred to me to question this. To question what she'd been doing there on the ward when I was admitted to the adolescent unit. Why else was she doing this now? It wasn't for me. She didn't know me. Three days on the same psych ward does not make a friendship, not even a flaky acquaintance.

It made me feel like a dick if I'm honest and a flood of guilt washed through me alongside the panic. Maybe Dad and Max were right to be so impatient with me. Haze and Zee too.

Carmen turned to me. 'I can ask him for you. If you want. Whatever it is.' Something in her tone made me think she'd figured it out. I guessed it wouldn't have been so hard. She didn't often make eye contact and it was striking, the hunger in her face at the thought of questioning him.

'What? No,' I said. 'No. I don't want you to ... no way.'

I thought she was thinking about what she had in the backpack and I didn't want to go there. It was like the longer I stayed in there with the two of them the longer the fucked-upness seeped into my pores.

She turned away, disappointed, and stared at Lock again. She hadn't asked him anything herself but I could see her mind working, her frown coming and going like weather. It was a big assumption I'd made about her knowing one of the dead girls. A pretty catastrophic one, as it turned out, but I didn't know that then.

She looked down at her boots, up at the roof and the back wall and then the car, everywhere except Lock in his chair. But I could feel the tension building. And then she stood up fast – there was an aftershock through the bench as she did – and went over to him. Three long strides.

'I need to know about that night,' she said to him. 'At the house. I need to know what happened, after.'

So that was a curveball.

His eyes widened but he hid it fast. Then he was shaking his head and blinking like he was confused or still drugged or acting the part, I couldn't tell.

'Don't you recognise me?' she said, louder. 'Don't you remember?'

'Are you . . . friends?' His voice was harsher, hesitant like he'd forgotten how to use it. The hitch in it more noticeable. He craned his neck past Carmen towards me. 'You don't . . . look like friends.'

'Why won't you talk to me?' she said.

'I am . . . talking to you. You're making . . . a big mistake.'

'No I'm not!' She stepped up closer. 'I need to know about that night, what I did. I need to know what you made me do.'

Her voice shook on the last part. This was her question, that was clear. It was what she'd come for, the crack in her composure I'd been waiting for and hadn't seen until then.

'I didn't,' he said. 'I don't . . . know you.' But why would she ask him that? What did she mean, *what you made me do?*

What had Carmen done?

Next thing I knew, I'd pushed past Carmen and was pacing in front of Lock again. I'd done all this stuff on the basis of one huge wrong assumption and I couldn't handle it, this agenda I didn't know about, this weird connection between the two of them. That night. What night? I'd seen her face as I passed her.

Blank with confusion and then incandescent with rage. I had this premonition Carmen wanted to go out in an amped-up blaze of glory and take Lock and me with her.

Had she actually lied? I thought back to the three times we'd met in the previous few days, the only times since last year – on the street, in the empty Pearse Street units and last of all outside his house. Had she engineered those meetings? But I'd lied too. I was the one who'd got into his car. I was the one who'd been hunting him for almost a year.

Fuck Carmen's blaze of glory. If anyone deserved that it was me.

Lock wasn't hers. He was mine.

I thought of Zee again, slipped on a patch of oil on the concrete floor and righted myself. One of those inky Rorschach stains near the chair. The last conversation I'd had with Zee was only the day before – Lock's alibi, the lack of evidence, her urging me to move on. But I'd get him to confess. She'd understand, wouldn't she, once I had that information? She'd put in a good word for me with the cops?

'Awake now, fucker?' I spat at Lock. 'You'd better be. You won't want to miss this.'

His head followed me now as I paced, every now and then darting a look at his car like he might magic himself back into it. He was like a spooky portrait on a wall, a spectator at a tennis match. Deep eye sockets and dark eyes. Short thick hair and dark beard. I hadn't looked at him head-on before then, I hadn't been able to do it.

'Is this ... about the driving?' he said. 'You're making ... a mistake.'

It threw me off for a second, the hitch in the low voice again, controlling his reactions, his response to what was happening to him. But I kept it together. 'We're way past that,' I said.

He had defined cheekbones – I remembered that from the TV footage. His pale skin looked soft in the weak light, almost luminous, weirdly delicate. He was young, late twenties or early thirties. Older than Carmen and me, but the right age for a killer of girls. He looked small in the garage and had the rounded shoulders I remembered, the bad posture, even taped into the chair. But it was all an act, I reminded myself. There was no real personality there behind the psychopath.

'Rachel.' I heard Carmen behind me. 'I want to talk to him.'

'Shut *up*, Carmen. He did it. He'll confess. Back the fuck off.' I spun on my heel to keep her behind me and kept pacing.

'I'm not ... a person of interest. This is a mistake,' he said, more strongly now. 'I told the police—'

'The cops don't believe you, Lock. No one does. That's why they've been watching you. That's why you're here.' I moved in so close I could see the pores on his nose but his eyes slid away. 'Know who I am?' He ignored that and looked down at his arms. Made a weak effort to pull against the ties as if he was only now figuring things out. 'Yeah you do. Not stupid, are you? Not as smart as you think, though. I mean, how did you end up in here, with us two?' A laugh came out of me, a horror-movie laugh, and he flinched. 'Does that scare you, Lock? Does it? It should. You should be shit-fucking-scared.'

For a second he cowered but I didn't buy that either. There's a look of alarm some men get when you get up in their face. Fear laced with disgust, a hardening around the eyes because you're straying outside your lane. He was trying to fight the disgust, but he wasn't winning. Close up I could see how big his wrists were against the cable ties, blocky and pale, with long dark hairs on them. His head looked too big for the rest of him too, like him being small had been a trick of the light. He wasn't the scared mouse he wanted me to think he was, that was for sure.

'Rachel,' Carmen said again behind my shoulder.

'Fuck *off*, Carmen. No, wait.' I spun to face her. 'Get it. Your bag. Get the biggest thing out, the sharpest thing. Bring it here.'

She backed away towards the car. Lock watched her go and changed tack. 'You're not ... friends, are you? How do you ... know each other?'

He said it to my back and it threw me off because how would he know that, how would he know anything about us? I spun to face him but he looked past me to Carmen and kept talking. 'One of you ... talked the other one ... into this. Am I right? One of you ... doesn't want to be here.'

There was a beat of quiet as I looked at Carmen and she looked back. No, screw him. 'Wanna know what she's got in the bag?' I said. 'You wait.'

But he went on, louder now. 'Do you know how many ... laws you've broken to bring me here? Deprivation ... of liberty, motor ... vehicle theft, grievous bodily ... harm. You might want to think about that.'

He reeled them off like a shopping list, like he knew what he was talking about, and all of a sudden the hitch in his voice pissed me off. The arrogance of it, the over-confidence of him thinking he could pull off the pretence and we'd buy it, we'd believe he was scared. It pissed me off too that he was making this about him when it *wasn't*. It was about Piper, and the other girls. It was about *us*, me and Carmen and all of us.

That's when it hit me. All those nights I'd gone out there and he hadn't taken me.

I was the scared girl, the gutless girl. I wasn't his type. I was the wrong kind of girl.

And he knew it.

I didn't like that. It made me feel helpless, less than the others, who had been something. And then it broke up out of me from my year of waiting. 'What did you do with her?' The words were ragged and I couldn't say her name. 'You know who I am. You *know*. She was the second one. Why did they never find her?'

He shook his head, speaking faster now. 'I'm not ... How would I know ... if she's dead? A mistake, I told you.'

But I'd seen him look. I'd seen his eyes linger on Piper's name written on my skin and I *knew*.

'No, it's not!' I said. 'Where is she?'

His eyes slid away and he ducked his head. 'No!' I grabbed his chin and the beard was rough under my fingers. I wrenched his head up. 'You don't get to do that. You look at me. You fucking look.' But he wouldn't.

And then Carmen was at my shoulder with this long-handled thing, a hooked scissor blade at the end of it. 'Get it around his finger,' I said. 'The middle one. That's the one I want.'

'I'm not ... who you think.' He was breathing quick as a rabbit now, wide awake, his big wrists twisting and pulling against the cable ties, and for a second I thought they wouldn't hold.

I was coming apart. It's no excuse I know, but ...

'You're going to tell me,' I said. 'You're going to tell me what you did.'

And Carmen? Carmen's Carmen. She went with it. She

tried to do what I asked and get the jaws of the thing around his finger, but his arms were writhing like eels and the handles were long and she was all elbows. 'Let me.' I tried to grab a hold but she brushed me off.

'I can do it.' She was all frowning concentration, the same as she'd been outside his house. 'Not that finger,' she said. 'It won't go.'

'It's the one I want.' I fixated on the finger and ignored the rest of him. A middle finger – it wasn't enough but it felt right. But she'd tied his wrist too tight to the chair.

'It won't go,' she said again.

The open jaws slipped off the arm of the chair. Scythed a red line where his little finger attached and he yelped. Blood oozed and Carmen lifted the blades back up. They were heavy. But I didn't want the little finger. It wasn't enough.

'Are you watching this, Lock? You going to confess now?'

But his eyes were closed again, his head lolling to the side. He'd stopped struggling. Had he passed out? The only sign of tension was in his thumbs, the way they stuck out at right angles from the cable ties and the arm of the chair. The square cut nails at the ends of them, the pale moons of his cuticles. 'Wake him up,' I said to Carmen. 'Get the thumb.' And she hooked the jaws around the nearest one.

Carmen eased back along the handles to where she had the best grip. I watched his grey face with its sheen of sweat and pushed away the excitement I felt, how much I wanted to hurt him. 'We're only giving him a fright, okay?' I said to her. 'Just until he feels it. We want him to confess. To tell me the truth.' I wasn't confident Carmen understood the concept of torture. I mean, it's not something most people put a lot of thought into.

But I must have jogged her arm, or she stumbled, or she'd already moved – I don't know. Or maybe she wanted to do it. Because I'd forgotten that flash of rage on her face from before. And there's leverage in those garden tools.

The handles closed, and the scissor jaws with them. They went through it like a piece of fruit. It was like it was happening on a screen, to three different people. The thumb bounced once in his lap like it was made of rubber, and slid to the floor in a slick of blood. It was his left one, and as it went I asked myself if he was left or right-handed because one day it would matter.

'Carmen. Fuck. You were only supposed to . . .'

I looked at where his thumb had been, up at his face, which was white now, down again to the slippery dark beneath the chair, the stains there that were growing as I watched them.

' . . . scare him.'

There was so much blood.

'I thought you wanted me to—'

'I was saying I *didn't* want you to.'

'That's not what it sounded like.'

'It was what I meant. You were only supposed to *threaten* to—'

'You should be more clear when you say things like that.'

'He didn't tell us anything. What the fuck are we going to—'

'I'll sort it, Rachel. You need to go home now.'

Back at home, I paced the rooms. I'd think the adrenaline had drained out of me and I'd slow to a stop like a flat battery, but then I'd get a flashback of Lock's thumb sliding off his lap, the bloody stump where it'd been, the blood under the chair and on his uniform pants, and the adrenaline would spike and I'd pace again. My room, across to Max's empty one, down the long hallway to the family room and TV room, then back again. At one point I could have sworn I was leaving a trail of bloody footprints between my room and the front door, that my own house was a crime scene and any second there was going to be a knock at the door. But when I turned to look, my heart stop-start and jittery, there was nothing there. I stared at the phone screen in my cramping hand but didn't call anyone.

Like, who do you call?

Carmen had made me leave and, gutless wonder that I am, I'd done what she said. She said she'd sort it, but what did that even mean? She'd wrapped it with a towel, the stump of his thumb, bound it tight with silver duct tape. That's all I saw before she marched me out the back door. But the towel was white and the blood kept coming, black in the dim light. His head was lolling like he'd passed out, and I knew it was bad.

Carmen hadn't looked that shocked. She took over like a medic in a war zone, like she was made for it. The only time she seemed fazed was at that noise we heard. Something scraped against the garage door from outside, followed by a crunch that sounded like a footstep, and I realised I'd heard both those things before, in the silence after the sea breeze had died.

It hadn't occurred to me until then that no one had reported him missing, not even his parents. That no one was looking for him, and how strange that was.

She told me to wait, went out to investigate and said there was no one there. She was only gone minutes but it felt like longer. Everything felt like longer. Then she got me out of there.

When the adrenaline finally ran down, I ended up on the couch in the TV room, scrolling muted channels to stop me flashing back to the inside of the garage. I felt like I did after smashing up Max's room last year, but that was like a kid's game now.

I called Dad. I mean, I didn't intend to, but my finger scrolled my contacts and tapped on his number and then it was happening. I panicked when I saw what I'd done, had no idea what I'd say to him, but the number wouldn't connect. So Dad was out of range. Nothing new there. Dad was always out of range when something monumental was going down. The phone screen told me it was 1 a.m. before I dropped it down the side of the couch and didn't go digging for it. I didn't know how it had got so late, where all the time had gone.

Carmen had got me out of there so fast that I started to wonder why. She'd given me the impression she needed to think, figure out what to do, but surely I needed to be a part of any decision she made.

I knew I should go back out there to the garages, that it wasn't safe to leave her. I was responsible. I was as responsible as she was. And what did I know about Carmen, really? There was that thing she'd said to him – *that night*. Like they had history I didn't know about.

What if she hurt him? What if she injured him badly, or worse? If she killed him, I'd lose everything. I'd never find out the truth. I wanted to go back and remind her of that but the coward in me had me pinned to the couch and I couldn't get up.

I got mad at her inside my head instead. She was just some nutcase I'd met in the loony bin. But I was a nutcase too, that was clear. I kept telling myself it'd be okay. He wasn't going to die from this. *Come on.* No one had ever died from losing a thumb. I dug out my phone to google it before I stopped myself. He had another thumb; he'd only lost fifty per cent of his thumbs. Plus he had eight fingers, ten toes, and other stuff – extremities, appendages, limbs. I mean, fuck, it could have been so much worse for him. Plus he was a serial killer. Why was I worried?

Through all of it something was nagging at me, something he'd said in there – but I couldn't get a hold of it. I was fruit-looping. My brain was toast. And he'd denied everything. He'd tried to play us off one against the other but it was half-hearted; it was hardly incriminating. The last thing I thought was, Carmen's not going to kill the dude. She wants something from him too. She knows him.

I'd tell her tomorrow. I'd tell her we had to let him go. Genevieve had died on our watch, it seemed to me, and I didn't want to be a part of it any more, whatever Carmen had going on. Maybe the cops would understand. I was the one with the mitigating circumstances, after all. Or I could lie and say it was all Carmen, that it had nothing to do with me.

But that was never true, and by the morning, everything was different.

THURSDAY

10

Raych

The second time I think we've killed him

I woke late, with the sun already snaking through the shutters.
I was on the couch in the TV room with not-enough-sleep
stinging my eyes and a rough corner of cushion chewing my
cheek. Passive solar house or not, it was already hot. For a long
happy moment I might have been anywhere in time. You know
those blissful seconds before the dread lands like a Qantas jet
on your face? That. The double whammy of Piper, followed by
last night's action in the garage.

The TV was still muted, stuck on the news channel I'd left
it on last night during my scrolling. It was the familiar night
footage of the Cottesloe strip that made me sit up so fast my
head spun, and the girl's smiling picture.

They're all the same, the pictures they use when someone is taken. The pictures the family gives the media when someone is more than likely dead, or soon will be.

This one was a posed studio shot – strawberry blonde hair in waves past her shoulders, a cream blouse with a high neck, a dude next to her who'd been cropped out of the frame. I didn't know her, but according to the story when I unmuted the sound, she'd left her Mosman Park home at 10.30 p.m. last night and never returned.

The scrolling headline at the bottom of the screen read: *Has Cottesloe killer 'The Shark' claimed a sixth victim? Fears grow for missing 23-year-old Mosman Park woman.*

There was no mention of her family or job or whether or not she was a swimmer. No mention of the Beach Hotel or the OVC either, but why else were they showing footage of the strip? My head was spinning, and at first I was panicky and confused, because why hadn't I been out there? How could I have missed a night? But I knew it couldn't be right, not so soon after Genevieve. And I remembered last night was a Wednesday, the wrong night for him.

Last of all, my sleep-bludgeoned brain got what was most wrong about the story, and the reason for my ballooning panic. Lock, tied to a chair in a garage in Cottesloe with his left thumb missing at the time a new girl goes missing.

Lock did not take this girl.

Scenes from last night flashed before me like a grainy true crime documentary. Lock, his voice catching, proclaiming his innocence. Lock cowering away from me. Lock's blood running like oil down one leg of the chair.

I'd thought he was manipulating us, faking his fear, keeping his rage under wraps. I've always thought that, right back to his first interviews with the media.

But what if he wasn't? What if he was just scared?

Had we done what we'd done, and it wasn't even him? Had we done it to an innocent man?

I was up and out of there, storming towards the garages before my brain had time to absorb the full impact of the news, or talk myself out of going. I wasn't even smart enough to take a detour. The humid heat was brutal, and between that and the dread my feet were like dream-feet, the footpath along Broome Street heading nowhere. The exact cause of the dread could have been way too many things. Because, like, Jesus fuck, Carmen and me might've cut the thumb off an innocent man. We'd kidnapped the dude, FFS. Or the dread could have been because the real killer was still out there. Or because of the missing Mosman Park girl and whether she was already dead.

Or it could have been a forewarning of worse to come, because something was wrong about this day, even more wrong than all of that. It took me two blocks to figure it out because the sky was banded with cloud and the pines along Broome Street blocked the view. It was only as I got up to Pearse Street and the view opened out I saw the smear of smoke against the sky and realised I'd been smelling it since I'd left the house. There'd been nothing on the news about bushfires, but the dread was congealing, shrinking to a single focus as I reached the end of the laneway and dragged to a stop. A fire truck was emerging, taking up the width of the lane.

Okay, it'd be the empty units or a construction site or

someone's house that backed onto the laneway further down. It wouldn't be the garages. Why would I even think that?

The truck pulled forward and indicated – they were leaving, they were done. But down behind it was a smaller vehicle, the crew stretching red and yellow *Do Not Cross* tape across the lane, and the driver of the big truck had seen me and stopped.

'No access this way. There's been a fire at a premises down there.'

I tried to compose my face, which I've always been shit at. 'Oh. Yeah?' I managed to say. 'A house?'

There was a woman in the passenger seat and two more crew in the back, bulked up in those full-on uniforms they wear. They were all eyeballing me like it was a weird question. Either that or they could hear the shake in my voice.

'Set of garages,' the woman firey said, and my vision swum. It took everything I'd got to keep my shit together and ask the next thing.

'Was there ...' I swallowed. 'Was anyone ... ?'

...burned to a fucking crisp. I was going to chuck up or pass out. I needed them to leave, but I needed to know.

The two in the front gave each other a look. 'No access,' the driver said again. 'Fire's been dealt with.'

Run along now, is what he meant. I craned my neck but all I could see past the end of the two vehicles was the fluttering tape in the flat light. He looked like he'd say more but his colleague cut across him. 'Do you live down there?' she said, concern on her face.

I shook my head, tried to say no but my tongue was stuck to the roof of my mouth and wouldn't do it. I pointed back down the street instead and her face wiped, the concern gone.

'It's for law enforcement now,' she said.

'The site'll be hot for some time in this heat,' the driver said, keen to get in the last word. 'No access until the tape comes down.' He kept his gaze on me as the truck pulled away.

There was a Land Cruiser parked on the verge of the corner house and I chucked my guts up behind the back tyre. It took a while, which amazed me because I couldn't remember when I'd last eaten. When I was done I looked each way along Broome Street, slipped into the laneway and ducked under the first strands of tape. The tape that said, when I got close enough to read it: *No Entry: Department of Fire and Emergency Services.*

There was another double strand of criss-crossing tape a few metres down. Of course there was. This one was blue and white and I knew what it said without getting close. POLICE, and the Crime Stoppers phone number. I kept this side of it, tucked in behind a wheelie bin on the south side of the laneway. There were more vehicles down there, an unmarked van and sedan, one marked police hatchback. I couldn't see the fronts of the garages on this side, only the end of the row opposite and part of the cracked concrete yard, the suited-up CSIs tracking through pools of black water.

The mix of smoke and steam was heavy in the windless morning and the smell was nothing like a bushfire – it was oily and dirty and coated the inside of my nose and mouth until I retched. The CSI activity was focused on the end garage where we'd had Lock, I could see that much. The bougainvillea was destroyed, the end wall blackened and smoking. The police presence could surely only mean one thing: a suspicious fire and a dead body.

Maybe it wasn't that bad. Maybe he'd got out. But I grabbed

the handle of the wheelie bin, went up on tiptoe and I saw it –
the end of a body bag, zipped shut and stretched out on the hot
ground.

It wasn't lost on me either, what I was looking at: this side
of the double row of garages destroyed by fire while the row
opposite was untouched.

Where the fuck was Carmen?

Is this what she'd meant by *I'll sort it*?

There was no one at Carmen's house, no cars in the drive or the
carport, not even hers. She'd given me her address, grudgingly,
before shoving me out of the garage the night before. The place
looked empty, curtains drawn, and I didn't try the doorbell.
When I checked my phone I saw it was already after 10 a.m. A
school day, a work day.

A normal day.

Would Carmen have gone to school? Could she have done
that, after last night? After whatever had gone down at the
garages this morning?

What had she done? Had she killed him? I could taste the
fire, even here across the highway in Mossie Park. It was in my
hair and my clothes and stuck in my throat.

I called Zee. No answer. I called Dad again. Unobtainable.
I even tried Max, which was stupid, and got her voicemail.
I didn't leave messages. I hyperventilated for five minutes on
Carmen's front verge, but weirdly that got me nowhere. There
were so many questions I should have asked the fireys but I only
thought of them now. What time did the fire start? How did it
start? Who called it in?

Somehow I got a grip, went home and checked the news. The

missing girl hadn't come home. They hadn't released her name. It still made no sense to me, the super-short interval between Genevieve and this one. There was a press conference scheduled for this afternoon, 5 p.m., on the grass terraces above the beach. That was a whole six hours away but it reminded me there was way worse news than the fire.

Another killer was out there. We'd tortured an innocent man and now he was dead.

I couldn't handle it, how wrong I'd been. Not only that I'd fixated on the wrong guy – we both had, and look what happened – but that I had no idea who the real perpetrator was. I felt him like a spectre, waiting to fall on us all, hiding in plain sight.

Out of options, I got in my car and staked out Carmen's house. It's one of the older ones – 50s style and a little run down, with a high brick wall and a clipped and watered front verge. I parked under a pine tree two houses down, but the car grew hotter by the second, the smell of warm leather and heating metal. Carmen's place was a ghost town; I could practically see the tumbleweeds from across the street. Even so, my car is not inconspicuous. I hunkered down in my seat and wondered if her street had neighbourhood watch.

I knew which school Carmen went to, but school was too public. I'd wait until the press conference, come back here overnight if I had to.

Fabrication. The word came at me out of nowhere as I huddled there. A word from our time on the ward, although I tried not to remember those few days.

They'd been talking about her, the couple Carmen lives with. The parents. I couldn't remember their names, or maybe I never knew them. Carmen had been asleep or appeared to be; had her face turned to the wall as they spoke in low voices. *Fabrication. Lies. A tendency to fantasise.* Had they been accusing her? Trying to understand her? Either way, Carmen's habit of making stuff up was alive and well, even then. I pushed away the other memory, the strongest one of our time there, the darkest one, and I raked over the last few days instead. The times we'd met, the seeds she'd planted. It wasn't hard. I'd wanted to believe Lock was the dude. Hell, everyone believed it.

The police believed it too.

What had happened to me in that garage? I was supposed to be the bait. I was supposed to be the one who found out the truth about Piper or died trying. That's how I've always thought it would go down. I've imagined it so many times I don't know what to do with this version of me, the one that's capable of what we did in that garage.

I'd wanted to hurt him. I couldn't kid myself I hadn't.

But Carmen was the one who'd encouraged me. She was the one who'd said we had to take him. And until I'd proven otherwise, she was the one who'd killed him.

The grass terraces were a terrible spot for a press conference. Too close to the crimes – where the girls went missing and the bodies washed back up. Too hot, and the light too bright for the cameras, or anyone else for that matter. It blazed at us off the sand, off the day's flat calm ocean, off cafe windows and car windscreens, even in the shade under the pines.

I was there before anyone else, lurking by the wall of the tea-rooms, a cap pulled down low, a baggy shirt and a pair of Dad's 90s wraparound sunglasses for disguise. There was a crow above me in one of the bigger trees, my personal portable shadow, lifting its wings and fidgeting like it was waiting for the action to kick off. I scanned the arriving crowd for Carmen and Zee, the two leading edges of my paranoia.

Would Carmen come to this? It wasn't her style but surely she'd want to find out what the cops knew. I couldn't see Zee; I went to call her again and stopped myself. Wait, Raych. Watch and listen.

The parents stood out as broken people from the moment they arrived. I spotted them as they climbed out of the marked cop car that had brought them and there was a long, unreal second before I recognised them.

Carmen's adoptive parents. What the fuck?

I couldn't breathe, couldn't move, could barely watch as they shuffled into position. They looked old enough to be grandparents, brittle hair and faces – that's what this shit does to families – but I still knew them from last year. Jared was with them, and another of the Polaris task force detectives, a woman – most likely family liaison. The questions spun in my head and I batted them away one by one. All except the biggest. Who was missing?

It couldn't be Carmen. It wasn't her picture on the news, it wasn't the right age for her. But what if the news report was wrong?

They said the name and it wasn't her. My arms goosebumped up as I heard it. Alexis Glasser. I hadn't recognised her from her picture because she'd never come to visit Carmen on the ward. The older sister. The bitch. And no, that didn't make it better.

Was I relieved it wasn't Carmen? Sure I was. Was I? Fuck, I didn't know.

At least I didn't feel bad for not talking to the cops. I'd never met Alexis Glasser.

The usual stuff happened. An official statement. What time Alexis had left the house and where she was going: 10.30 p.m., on her way to meet her fiancé at the Italian cafe down on the strip. She never arrived. I scanned the faces but the fiancé wasn't there.

Neither was Carmen.

There was an appeal from the parents and I couldn't watch that part. I turned my head away and stared at the ocean, tried to let their words wash past me, my teeth gritted and my eyes half-closed like a dog waiting to get hit in the face.

'Alexis, if you're listening, please let us know you're all right. If anyone has seen our daughter or has information for the police, no matter how small it seems, please come forward or telephone. Alexis, we love you. We want you home. Please. Come home.'

The mother was rigid and didn't cry but the father broke ranks at the end. 'Let her go, you mongrel!' He choked up as his wife turned away from him. The family liaison officer steered them back towards the car.

Jared said more words and repeated the Crime Stoppers number but I wasn't listening. I was scanning the crowd again for Carmen, and then I saw Zee up on the street, leaning against the first of the marked cop cars. She was wearing her aviators, the lenses pale enough I could see her eyes, and for a second she stared right back. My heartrate spiked but she didn't make a move – my disguise was working. But why hadn't she returned my call from earlier? She was keeping a low profile maybe, didn't want to spook me. All that did was make me shit-scared I was the reason she was there, that she knew something about the last few days.

I should go to her. Tell her everything and it would be over. The end of the fear lodged in my throat along with the taste of the fire. Does that go away when you cop the consequences of something?

I was about to do it. Rip the cap off my head and Dad's bad sunglasses off my face and yell out to her. But Zee melted away as the knot of people with the parents approached. And then I saw Carmen.

A tall pale human with a dark cap and curtain of hair trying hard to blend in and not succeeding. Another person keeping a low profile. She saw me too, and then she was gone, away through the people and pines towards the largest of the Marine Parade car parks.

If she had her car with her I wouldn't catch her.

As I pushed through the thinning crowd, I heard the first questions from the press: 'Regarding the Pearse Street garage fire this morning. Can you confirm the existence of a fatality at that location?'

'That's under investigation,' Jared said.

Another journo, a dude this time. 'Will you respond to rumours surveillance on the suspect Neil Fraser Lock was downscaled before this latest abduction?'

'Mr Lock is no longer a person of interest in this inquiry.'

I felt Jared's words like they were aimed at my back. They made no sense at all. Missing at the time of the latest abduction, Lock had to be top of their list. Unless they already suspected he was dead.

'No more questions. Thanks everyone,' was Jared's parting shot.

How long until they knew? That the fire was deliberate. That the body in the fire was Lock.

That Carmen and me were the ones who put him there.

*

Carmen was on foot and I was faster than her. I caught up to her halfway up Napier Street.

'Going to the press conference?' I yelled out. 'That was one dumbass move if you reckoned I wouldn't see you there.'

She kept walking, cut into the bush reserve.

'Where's your car parked?' I said. 'You know what, I'm sick of you not answering me when I ask you something. Carmen?'

Nothing. She wove between stands of trees but I was right on her tail.

'Carmen! You owe me a shitload of explanation here. If you don't stop and talk to me I'm going right back down there and straight to the cops about last night.'

That got through. She slowed to a stop but didn't turn around.

'Too right.' I wheeled around in front of her. 'Okay, where was I? Oh yeah, going to the cops because guess what, we kidnapped a dude and cut his thumb off and I'm buggered if the place where we did it hasn't burned to the ground! With him inside. Lucky it didn't spread to half the suburb. I mean, what the fuck, Carmen?'

Her face was so closed up it might as well have been painted over, but her eyes were all over the shop. I knew something was getting past the wall she puts up.

'Did you know your sister was missing, last night?'

'She's not my sister.'

'That's not an answer!' I took a step forward and she flinched. I'd never seen Carmen like this. I mean, I'd wondered before about her cool calm exterior, if that's all it was, but I'd never seen her scared. Then the word came back to me. *Fabrication.* Don't trust her, Raych.

'Just tell me,' I said. 'Did you do it or not? Did you set that fire and burn down the garages with him inside?' I dropped my voice for the next bit. 'Did you kill him first? Or ... fuck, was he still alive? I mean, they're investigating it. They can find out that stuff.'

A light in her eyes switched off and she turned and walked away.

'No, Carmen. No way can you shut me out of this.' But she was faster now, striding out uphill, and I had trouble keeping up, my breath coming hard. 'He's innocent, you know that right? Because of your sister going missing, the timing of it.'

'She's not my sister.'

'Not the point! I came to find you today to say we had to stop, we had to let him go, and look what's happened now.'

She lowered her head and walked faster, taking a sand track back towards the street.

'Did you even hear me? We did this to an innocent dude. Do you not get that?'

But she strode on, her right hand gripped around something in the pocket of her jeans. I got this horrible sick idea she'd got his thumb in there, wrapped in clingwrap or something, that she'd saved it from the fire. That it was the only bit of him left.

'What have you got in your pocket?'

She always had something in that right-hand pocket of her jeans. It's the place her hand goes to like she's checking something is safe. It's what Max does with her phone. I put on a sprint, caught up and yanked on her arm so it came out of the pocket. 'What the hell is—'

It was a flat square tin. Maybe it'd had cough lollies in it once but it was worn back to the metal. She was looking down at it like it was an unexploded bomb.

'Open it,' I said, pointing. 'You owe me this.' If it was his thumb in there, I was going to the cops. 'Carmen,' I said.

She turned her head away as she opened it, reminding me of that dog not wanting to get hit in the face, but then I remembered that dog was me.

What was in the tin was a collection of sharks' teeth, and I snatched back my hand. A variety of sizes. Some of them were white, some of them dirty yellow-brown. All of them lethally serrated and shaped like you'd imagine. They were, in the circs, not as bad as a dead man's thumb, but not far off that either.

I stepped away from Carmen and the tin, ran my tongue over my lip ring, put a hand on my heart and tried to calm myself down. I thought of the places the bodies had been found, the state they'd been in every time. The injury detail I'd read on a true crime blog and regretted it as soon as I had. The serrated tooth-like lacerations, the catastrophic blood loss.

Every dead body that's washed up has been the same. This latest, Carmen's adoptive sister, would be too when she was found.

Carmen was staring back down the hill towards the pines and the ocean and I followed her gaze. I'd so often seen her looking out that way, towards the horizon and the ships. There was a stream of traffic along Marine Parade, people heading away from the press conference, normal people doing normal stuff. Apart from the ones who never would again like Alexis's parents, in that space between knowing and not knowing what had happened to their daughter.

What was Carmen doing with a tin full of these teeth? Why did she carry them everywhere?

Did she know something about her sister going missing?

When I looked again, she was gone.

Back at home, I was no longer pacing, but drifting. The time for pacing, for decisive action, for anything like rational thought had gone and I didn't know what to do instead. I didn't reckon I could even go to the cops now, not until I knew what Carmen had done.

Had I been too brutal, back there? I hadn't exactly come at it with concern for her family. Adopted or not, this latest disappearance was close to home.

But what if it was no coincidence Alexis was the latest missing girl?

I pulled out my notebook and started to write, the pen flying and jerking across the page. Carmen hated Alexis, who bullied her. She knew Lock, she had history with him. She was a liar who'd spent far longer on the psych ward than I had. She was tall, she was strong, and when pushed, like today, she could be fast too. She could disappear like smoke, like that little cat that might have been the only living thing in the world she actually liked.

Had Carmen killed Lock to cover up more than what we'd done in that garage? What else was she hiding?

Did Carmen have something to do with the murders?

11

Carmen

Carmen is different

Carmen waits between two tea trees holding her breath. The leaves prick at her face and her arms through her T-shirt, and the smell is up her nose and in her hair, like the fire smell was this morning when she woke up in her room. She's only a few metres from where Rachel last saw her, but as long as she doesn't sneeze she knows she won't give herself away, knows Rachel's impatience will work to her advantage.

Rachel swings this way and that. 'Fuck. Carmen? Fuck.' She's wearing a disguise – a man's daggy sunglasses and a cap squishing down her bright hair – but Carmen knew it was her as soon as she saw her down at the press conference. Rachel has a distinctive gait: tipped forwards like she's leaning into the wind, always rushing, always going after someone or something. Now she's going after Carmen with her assumptions and accusations when she doesn't know anything.

Rachel has seen Carmen's tin of sharks' teeth, that's all, the same as Alexis did. Big deal. Carmen should have been more careful, but she's distracted – after the things that happened last night in the garage, after waking up this morning to what was in her room and not having any way to explain it. And then Alexis being gone and the house in upheaval, Mr and Mrs G fighting and then talking to that detective Rosso and his sidekick in the front lounge room.

The detectives didn't ask Carmen any questions but as soon as anyone sees inside her room they will. Rosso will want to talk to her again. He might get a warrant this time because Alexis going missing is a *big thing* and the fire in the garages has made everything get complicated very fast.

The forgetting episodes are happening all the time now, every single day. Almost anything can trigger her brain to do what it does: her senses peeling away from her so she does things without knowing it, like they're happening to someone else. And after, when she looks back, there are only moments of memory left, like islands in a hazy flowing stream.

She knew as soon as she woke up in her room this morning it had happened again, and the timing of that is bad.

Carmen is different, she knows that. She walks a line most people don't even think about, but she only needs to stay on the right side of it. It was okay, up until last night. Or maybe it was one of the other nights. Either way, she was handling it and now she isn't.

She wishes she could have gone to school today. Mr Ayele

always lets her go in the music room on a Thursday and she'd like to have seen his face one more time. Drumming is the only time Carmen feels like she might be different to what she's always thought. Drumming would have helped her today. But it's too late for that now. It's too late for school, and normal things.

She thinks back to Neil in the garage. *I don't know you.* Not even acknowledging Carmen or admitting the truth. How it made her feel. Pretending not to recognise her when she knows he did recognise her, after he looked at Piper's name written on Rachel's arm like that.

Neil is a disappointment. He was a typical man, after all. Carmen thought she was the same as him but she's not.

She shouldn't have done it, cut off his thumb with the tree loppers, but she was so mad. That's why she did it. That, plus Rachel's clumsy interference when she wouldn't do it herself and couldn't even decide which finger she wanted chopped off. Rachel's like a bull in a china shop for someone so small. Carmen had to get her out of the garage after that.

When Rachel doesn't see Carmen, she swears again and stamps a foot, storms away up the hill towards the tennis club. 'What have you *done?*' She shrieks the last part like a seagull. 'I *will* find you.'

Only when I want you to, Carmen thinks. Rachel is becoming a problem. Almost as much of one as Alexis, and that's saying something.

She looks at where Rachel was a minute ago, towards the blue stripe of horizon and the lighthouse on Wadjemup and the container ships. There are no whitecaps this afternoon – there haven't been all week, the ocean silky and still every day like glass someone has breathed on – but there are five ships, hulking and motionless on the flat water. If you're observant like Carmen you can distinguish individual ones, even from a distance. They're different shapes, and some of them have giant letters and numbers written on the side. The stranded one is still there.

Carmen knows the Crime Stoppers number off by heart now and she's called it four times, each time to tell them something different. That's not counting the call she made to triple zero after she found Christine's body. They want her to give her name when she calls but she can't, because of Rosso, so what she tells them gets lumped in with thousands of other jigsaw bits of information from people all over the city, maybe even all over the state by now. She uses a different payphone every time. There aren't many left that still work but she knows where they are. She's even told Crime Stoppers about the container ships. Of course she has. Because of that day when Neil opened the door of his parents' house to talk to the journos, and how they got up so close you could see the pictures on the wall inside the hallway. Carmen notices things like that – you only need to be observant.

It feels worse than not telling them at all when they don't listen.

Rachel's yelling has got fainter and fainter and now she's gone, which is a relief. Carmen steps out from between the prickly tea trees and starts the walk back to her car.

Of course Carmen didn't set fire to the garages with Neil still inside, despite what she found in her room this morning. What would be the point of that when he hadn't answered her question about *that night*?

But she thinks she knows who did.

*

The Shark

There's a redback spider that lives inside the hollow arm of one of the metal garden chairs outside Alexis's room. Carmen has only seen it at night – the red is always brighter at night, luminous, like someone has painted it on – but it's not there now. There's only a gecko high up on the bricks next to the patio doors. Usually it calms her, seeing these things, but tonight it's not working.

There's someone watching and following her. They've been doing it since she found Christine's body, maybe even before that. She thought it wasn't a real person, that it was her brain making her paranoid because of the murder case. Then she thought it was Alexis, or Leo. Except it can't be Alexis, not now, and Leo works at AQWA five days a week. But the feeling of eyes on Carmen's back, of someone on the footpath outside school or invisible in a crowd on the street, is there every day.

Carmen stands at the side of the house, outside Alexis's room. She didn't want to run into Mrs G so she's parked a block away and come straight here through the back gate and backyard.

Mrs G doesn't know Carmen didn't go to school today. You'd think she wouldn't mind about that now but she might. Mrs G is in denial about Alexis going missing. Her face is pink and tight and she's been in the kitchen all day, cleaning and cooking. This morning she said Alexis wasn't one of *those girls* and that she'd be coming back. That's why she and Mr G have been fighting. Carmen doesn't know what *those girls* means but she can guess, because of the things Mrs G says about Alexis when she thinks no one's listening.

Carmen can still smell the fire from this morning, even here outside Alexis's room. But it's been a hot, windless day. It makes sense for the heavy scratchy smoke to have lingered, stuck in the bricks and the early evening air, and the drooping leaves on the salmon gum over the fence.

There are food smells on top of the fire ones, coming out of the kitchen. Mrs G is making an early dinner before her Thursday evening bridge game as if nothing has changed. The food smells aren't terrible but Carmen won't be going in for dinner. She knows she can't keep on living here, not even with someone out there watching her. She took two hundred dollars from the grocery money this morning while Mrs G was talking to the detectives.

Mr G would give Carmen money if she asked him, she knows he would – he's the best one in the house. But it's too late even for that. He'd only want to know how she is, and he'd ask her with that look on his face that makes Carmen feel bad for doing the things she does and never telling him the truth about anything.

Carmen's only here for one last look at Alexis's room before she runs. One last attempt to remember *that night*, what happened after the police left and everyone went back to bed. Whether Carmen left the house and where she went next, which is the answer to everything, because of Rachel's friend Piper and her missing dead body.

But it's no good. She's been stood here for twenty minutes, not moving, staring at the outside of the patio doors. She can't remember later that night, only what happened inside Alexis's room. Neil was there and then he wasn't. His smell was left, plus the memory of his voice and the dark blue polo shirt. Carmen had one hand holding up the lamp and the other at Alexis's throat. She wasn't touching her skin, only twisting her pyjama top tight like a noose. She remembers the scratchy feel of it.

It's hard to believe she won't hear the little electric car squeak to a stop in the driveway out front like it always has. The handbrake makes that sound whenever Alexis pulls up and parks, like a rabbit or mouse. But the car is missing along with Alexis, so Carmen knows she won't.

She hears the other car pull up in the drive instead as she's stood there, the one she's been expecting. As the two doors open and the two sets of feet clump up the path to the front door, she's already backing away.

She turns the corner of the house and stops outside the door to her room, the one that opens onto the backyard. She can see Mr G's shed near the back fence; there are redbacks in there too. Carmen wonders when he'll notice the things she took from it. She hasn't taken them all from there; she's been careful. There are things she found in neighbours' sheds and garages, even the storeroom at the yacht club and the maintenance shed at school.

She hovers on the threshold of her room, not wanting to go in. Not wanting to go in ever again. The fire smell is so much worse here, and the other one, from this morning.

Petrol.

The door in front of her is open, and Carmen's room is like a crime scene in a TV drama.

Her backpack is heavy and so are her legs and arms. Her blood is moving slow, creeping along her veins and through her muscles like it's losing the will to keep going. It'll have to speed up soon, because she hears the doorbell, Mrs G calling her name, and the word *police*. Carmen hears it all, even from back here at the other end of the house; she's been waiting for it.

Carmen

The things she knows: Alexis followed her to the garages. The things she remembers: the smell of petrol. The clink of the silvery padlock keys. Alexis's big mouth saying something, but Carmen can't remember what.

And when she woke up, this is what her room was like:

The green jerry can on its side in the corner near the door. Her clothes in a black garbage bag next to it, smudged with dirt and ash and reeking of petrol. Both padlock keys missing, but when she opened the door to the yard, there they were on the step where someone had dropped them.

The stink of petrol and burned things is overpowering and she's surprised Mrs G hasn't come to investigate.

Or maybe she has. The footsteps are inside the house now, in the hallway, getting closer. Carmen hugs her backpack to her chest and steps back from the doorway.

The annoying fact is that if she was going to make a fire, she would not have used this exact can of petrol Mr G keeps in his shed for emergencies, or road trips, or other contingencies that never seem to arise. She'd have used one from somewhere else, like any sensible person. She'd have been more careful.

But it's not as if it will help to tell Rosso the truth – that Alexis has done this on purpose to get rid of Carmen and Neil at the same time. It doesn't matter what Carmen thinks, because she can't remember enough in a joined-up way to explain it. And if you can't remember things in a joined-up way, no one believes you, especially not Rosso.

Carmen takes a last look at her room. She won't set foot in it again. It's for Rosso and his young woman sidekick and her notebook now, and crime scene investigators in white suits. The door opens from the hallway and his bulk fills the frame.

The Shark

Carmen shrinks back into the darkening backyard, away from the light inside her room and the rest of the house, the sound of the radio and the food smells in the kitchen.

And she turns and runs.

PART FOUR

FRIDAY

12

Raych

Unlocked

Friday morning I woke from a dark gnarly dream of the inside of the garage. Lock was there, his scared pale face floating above the chair. He was writing me a message on the floor with the bloody stump of his thumb but I couldn't read what it said. The roof was burning and I knew Piper was in there with us but I paced the walls and couldn't find her.

Jesus. I slapped the dream out of my head and planted my feet on the floor but the image of the dark garage lingered. One more day. Not even that. The anniversary and the move. Tomorrow.

I didn't know WTF I was going to do now. Everything had turned on its head. I made coffee in the upstairs kitchen and clicked the radio on for the news, with my hands shaking and the dread pulling at me. Carmen hadn't been in the dream. Did that mean something? Yeah, like, I wanted to erase her from my consciousness but I couldn't, because I was implicated in whatever she'd done. There was this sense of time running out and at the same time something I was missing, something from our night in that garage.

I wondered if Carmen's sister was still a missing person. If there was any news from the fire.

There was a voicemail from Dad when I checked my phone. Had he remembered the anniversary? I listened, and that was a no. No gold stars for Dad this century. Another change of plan from him instead, his shift extended by two days. But the movers were still booked and he wanted Max and me on a flight to Port Hedland the next evening. He'd have someone meet us off the flight.

Not happening, Dad. I didn't call him back. He'd be out of range again by now anyway, conveniently unobtainable whenever everything was going to shit.

A bunch of missed calls from Haze and Zee – the string of calls and messages that had started yesterday after the press conference – and I kept the phone on silent and shoved it back in my pocket. I assumed Zee's calls meant she'd recognised me there. It could have been something worse but if it was I didn't want to know.

I was squinting out at the side balcony when I heard the news – hot white light off the ocean and metal and glass, my hip against the high-gloss kitchen units. The coffee machine was burbling away and I didn't even get to drink it.

The task force had a new suspect.

I spun around and cranked the volume. Listened with my elbows pressed too hard into the kitchen bench. The guy worked at AQWA, the aquarium up at Hillarys Boat Harbour. A caretaker and tour guide. The AQWA connection bothered me when I first heard it, but I couldn't figure out why. They were calling him a person of interest, not a suspect, the same way they had with Lock, and giving nothing away. But he was helping the police in relation to this latest disappearance. Alexis Glasser. Carmen's adoptive sister was still missing.

There was nothing about the Pearse Street fire or the person who'd died in it, and I was about to click off the radio when the appeal for Carmen came on. *Last seen at her home in Mosman Park. Concern for her welfare. Potential witness to a suspicious fire in Cottesloe.*

Fuck. So the news was out. They didn't mention the dead man in the fire or Carmen's connection to missing Alexis, but 'witness' was a crock of BS for a start. Maybe they hadn't identified Lock's body yet. That couldn't be easy after a fire, right? And DNA isn't quick, not like it is on TV. I slid down the kitchen units to the floor and stuck my head in my hands.

How long until they caught her? And what was she going to tell them?

How long before they wanted to talk to me too?

Knowing Carmen, I wasn't likely to find her if she didn't want to be found. But neither was I going to sit home waiting for the cops to rock up.

I texted her but she didn't reply. I called her and it went to voicemail and her weird 'this is a wrong number' recorded message, which has to have been designed to put people off ever contacting her again. She'd never picked up before so I don't know why I expected her to now.

I felt like an insensitive jerk ringing the doorbell of a house with two daughters missing, even if one of them was Carmen, but what can you do? It wasn't until I was standing on the doorstep that I panicked, because what if the family liaison officer answered the door? But it was the brittle woman from the press conference who pulled it open, pale pink skin and eyes too big for her narrow face. The mother. I was tongue-tied as soon as I saw her, thinking of Piper's mum in the days after she went missing, all the other parents of all the other girls. But I got a grip and asked if there was news.

'Sorry,' I said. 'I know this is ... but I'm a mate of Carmen's.' Lie. 'I'm worried about her.' True, and not the half of it. I tried to look sad and apologetic but I don't reckon I pulled it off.

'We don't know anything,' Mrs Glasser said, and went to shut the door on me.

'No, wait.' I put my foot in the door. She looked down at my sneaker and back up at my face. She pushed against it, confused, her pale fingers hooked around the side of the door. 'I lent her something. A book,' I said. 'For school. I need it back. Can I see her room?'

Jesus, Raych. The skin around her eyes twitched and her lips tightened. She glanced over her shoulder at someone behind her in the hallway but I couldn't see who. 'You may not. The police are here. Now go away.' She lifted her clunky heeled shoe, the one I could see through the gap in the door, and stamped on the toe of my Converse.

Fuck. I ripped my foot away as the door slammed and I was left there, hopping and rubbing at the top of my sneaker. Was that weird? Yeah, that was weird. *We don't know anything.* Not, *We haven't heard anything* or, *There's no news.* She didn't ask me who I was, nothing. I mean, she didn't know me. I might have been able to help.

They knew something. Were they harbouring Carmen, protecting her? I didn't think they had that kind of relationship. I was sure the woman was still there, on the other side of the door. I felt her watching and waiting for me to leave.

I looked up around the porch for a security camera but if it was there I couldn't see it. I felt like waving – *Yep, still here! I know you're hiding something.* I thought back to Carmen and Lock in the garage. Carmen and Lock knowing each other. Lock burned to death. I could smell the fire again but it was my brain fucking with me.

I felt like a neon sign on the doorstep, my skin crackling with unanswered questions, but Carmen's place was a dead end.

I only stopped at home to dump my car in the drive, but as I climbed out a tall shadow detached itself from inside the porch. My heart gave a lurch – Carmen? But I saw the bike propped against Dad's boat, and when she stepped into the light it was Haze.

'Hey, Raych.' Her plait was dark dripping wet like she'd this minute stepped out of a pool or come off the beach. I hadn't seen her since Fight Back Club on Monday.

'Oh. Hey.' I frowned at her bike against the boat. 'Dad said he'd sold that.'

'Huh?'

'The boat. Dude should have picked it up already. Yesterday, he said.'

Neither of us mentioned the house move this time – a no-go area. 'Okay. So, should I shift my bike?' She didn't do it, though.

She grabbed the end of her plait and wrung it, darkening the driveway with water. It was a weird humid day again, swathes of cloud across the sun that trapped the heat and made it hard to breathe.

I shrugged. 'Doesn't matter.'

You're not staying, is what I meant. There was an awkward moment. Those awkward moments I was getting to be an expert at. Too close to before, when I'd have bounced past Haze and flung open the front door, or she'd already have been inside, chatting up a storm with Max or Dad.

'I'm not going in,' I said, chucking a look at the porch.

'Right.' She nodded, slow. The light was behind her and I couldn't see her face. Worried, most likely. 'I've been calling you about tomorrow, I guess.'

The anniversary and my non-plans for it. 'Yeah. I figured that.'

'But you didn't pick up?'

'No, I guess not.' I locked my car. She watched me do it like she was wondering where I was off to without it. But it was none of her business. I flipped the keys around on my finger, watching the shadow on the driveway, the flash of sun off the keyring. 'I don't want to do anything for it. Tomorrow.'

Her head snapped up. 'Raych. Seriously?' She dropped her plait and let it swing. Took a step closer until I could see the shock on her face. 'You have to do something.'

'I don't *have* to.'

'A vigil.'

'I hate that fucking word. So lame and sad. What does it even mean?'

'It's a period of—'

'I don't want to know, Haze.'

'Fine. Not that, then. A celebration. Something.'

'Oh yeah. So much to celebrate.' I fumbled my keys and dropped them, bent and picked them up. Pushed my sunglasses up my face where they'd slipped down. 'Look, sorry. Sorry for . . .' I shook my head, blew a puff of air at my fringe that kept flopping into my eyes in the heat. 'But I'm not doing anything for it. It doesn't matter.'

'How can you say that?' She looked like she might cry, which I was so not up for.

'You go ahead, if you want.' I buried my hands in my pockets. Felt Lock's house key stab at my palm. I'd forgotten that was in there.

'She wouldn't have wanted you like this,' Haze said. 'To be like this. She would've—'

'You have no clue what she'd have wanted.'

'I don't know what you've got going on, but—'

'I need to be somewhere, Haze.'

' . . . but whatever it is, you have to stop. This . . .' She flapped a hand at me, the street, the house. 'Dumping all your friends, being secretive and aggressive and weird—'

'I'm not—'

'Roaming the streets? Smashing shit up? This isn't you, Raych. Not the friend I had.'

'Yeah?' I kicked the toe of my sneaker into the drive. 'Well, maybe I was never that friend.'

She nodded. 'Right. Okay. I guess not. Well, some of us are going to do something for Piper. Come if you want. I'll message you the details.'

'Fine.'

'I mean it. Please come.' She took a step closer. A last ditch at being kind when I'd told her where to go, which was just so Haze.

I crossed my arms and looked away. Bit down on my lip and waited for her to leave.

'Right.' She strode over to her bike, spun the pedal and got on. 'You know this isn't about Piper, right? Whatever it is you're doing?' She cricked her neck like the weight of her hair was bothering her. 'That's why you don't want to do anything for her tomorrow.'

She threw me one last look as she went. 'Maybe it's to do with your mum. Or something else, I have no idea. But this is about you, Raych, not Piper. It's all about you.'

It felt like my heart was going to storm out of my chest as I stalked to the garages. Haze was wrong. This *was* about Piper – it had always been about her – but if Haze kept pushing and pushing I was going to end up back on the ward. I was going to end up ... I didn't know what, but it wouldn't be good.

I needed to put everything into *this*, not some lame vigil. Into finding Carmen and figuring out the truth. That was a real thing I could do for Piper, but Haze wouldn't get that.

The fire service tape was still across the lane but the police tape had come down and the place was quiet. No more vehicles or CSIs or fire investigators, or whoever had been here yesterday. That was quick, it seemed to me, but what do I know? When I ducked under the tape there was no one to see.

The site was still warm when I got to the edge of the concrete yard, but it was a brutally hot day. I clocked the charred stump of the bougainvillea at the base of the end wall. Those things are indestructible – I'd bet good money it'll grow back. But the row of double garages on the right-hand side was a blackened shell – the metal pull-down doors buckled, the corrugated roofs fallen in. Most of the water had evaporated but there were black sumpy pools in sections of the collapsed roof and on the concrete in front of me. The smell was as full-on as yesterday.

I checked both ways down the lane. Still deserted.

Dried-out things crunched and snapped under my sneakers like tiny bones, too loud in the quiet. I took it slow, tried not to imagine what they were. I didn't know what I was looking for, what had pulled me back here.

I hung back from the interior of the garage. It had to be dangerous, right? That fallen-in roof. But I couldn't help myself and crept closer. I was looking for his car, I realised. They'd have taken it, though. With the body. It was evidence.

But the buckled garage door was still there. They'd have had to shift that to get the car out. I eased past the end of it into the fallen-in space, the yellowy light making abstract shapes on the floor. There was no sign of a burnt-out car.

My head got hot as I stood there, the sun having a go despite the cloud, the taste of the fire making my stomach jumpy. Suddenly I didn't want to be there, didn't want to think about what had happened in the place or what I'd been treading on.

As if to prove the point I stepped back onto something hard that reminded me of Mrs Glasser stamping on my sneaker. It felt like a rock or a bit of rubble, but when I shifted my foot it glinted through a layer of wet black dust. Sweat ran past my eye and I rubbed it away. I scraped the sole of my sneaker across what was there, toed it out from under a twisted bit of metal.

It took time to understand what I was looking at. It wasn't like

I saw it and everything fell into place, or I saw it and my blood ran cold. It's not like it is in the movies. I stood there staring at it for a good minute, trying to make it make sense.

What I'd found was the padlock from the big garage door. It was rusty, that padlock, but some of the rust had scraped off down to the metal on one side.

Okay, so it came off. I mean, the fireys had been in there and so had the police. The big garage door was wrecked. Maybe they'd taken it off to get access, to get the car out. But no. I nudged it again with my foot, flipped the thing over until I could see it clearly. It wasn't locked. It hadn't fallen off the door as it burned. It hadn't been cut off with bolt-cutters.

The padlock had been unlocked. And one person had the key.

Carmen.

I was still trying to get my head around the unlocked padlock at my feet when my phone vibrated in my pocket. It was Zee, and I knew she'd be calling about tomorrow. But my brain hurt and I couldn't hide from her for ever, so I gave in and took the call.

'I'm not doing anything for it.' I moved across the laneway into a fingernail of shade.

'Sure you are. We'll do it at the surf club. The girls and I can set it up.' She was talking fast, overcompensating for my failure or for something else I didn't know about yet. 'All you need do is show.'

'No, Zee. I don't want to. I've told Haze.'

There was a pause and then, 'Meet me, hon. Twelve noon. The usual place.'

'Can't. I have to pack.' Bullshit, but it might get her off my back.

'I have something for you. So quit your packing and meet me. Thirty minutes.'

I took my time heading there, didn't know if it was a trap. But I got there and didn't see any lurking police vehicles or detectives. I sat and glared at the low cloud and silvery ocean, the long curves and angles of the sundial. The water was flat and there was no breath of wind anywhere, the smell of the dune scrub heavy in the heat.

Seeing that padlock, the fact it had been unlocked and not cut off with bolt-cutters, reminded me again of the key to the Frangipani House in my pocket. Carmen never noticed I'd taken it, never said a thing about it the whole time we were in the garage with him. She'd left his keys in the ignition of his car and they'd hung there for the duration. My fingers kept going to the house key now, running over the teeth then the smooth rounded end and back down the other side. I needed to get rid of it.

I kept trying to convince myself there was an innocent explanation for the padlock. Like, Carmen had given the police the key. Or there was a copy at the Glasser house. But I wasn't getting there. Because the fireys had been first on the scene. They'd have cut it off. It wouldn't have been lying there unlocked like no one had even seen it.

Zee was twenty minutes late and I felt like I was coming down with something – half burning up and sweaty, half chilled with goosebumps – but I knew I wasn't sick. At least, not in that way. There was this dragging fear with me every second now like something dead in the water. Before the padlock it had been, *Fuck, Carmen killed Lock?* Now it was, *Fuck, Carmen let Lock out?*

But there was a *body*. There were police. So . . . what? She'd driven the car out and left him in there? Why would she do that?

Zee settled next to me, cutting off my thoughts. Close but not too close. No police escort, thank fuck. 'All right, Valenti?'

'Hey.'

She gave me the once-over then squinted at the horizon through her aviators. 'How are you doing?'

You'd think Zee of all people would know better. I wish people would stop asking me that. 'Awesome. Apart from you leaving a tsunami of missed calls on my phone.'

'Oh, you saw those.'

'Yeah. And I'm guessing you didn't leave me a string of calls to ask me how I am about tomorrow.'

Zee sighed and I felt her energy come in to land next to me. 'No.'

'So? Spill. I don't have long.'

She kept her eyes on the horizon. Chewed her cheek.

'Zee?'

'I'm only telling you this because of tomorrow, you got me? I shouldn't be, so you need to sit on it until it's public.'

'O-kay.'

'This new suspect,' she said.

'The AQWA dude? That's where he works, right?' That fact was still bothering me but I guessed it made sense, his connection with the ocean. She nodded.

'And?' My heart dangled like bait on a hook. 'Jesus. You can't—'

'He's . . . talking. Leo Barros.'

I didn't know what to think about it, not at first. It wasn't like my world flipped. 'About Piper? What's he said?'

'Nothing yet. Don't get ahead of yourself.'

'Fuck, Zee. How can I not? You ask me to meet you. You tell me this, and then you backtrack? Whatever you tell me, it's not like I can do anything about it.'

'No. There's not. And Lock is out of the picture. Parents and son in temporary accommodation.' The way she said it stopped me, like she knew something. She arched an eyebrow above her sunglasses, and I felt the steel of her gaze before she looked away. Her arms were folded and her long legs crossed tight like a corkscrew.

'He's confessing. Barros,' she said. 'That's all I've got for now. The times and dates are right. I wanted you to have something, but be patient, hon. Jared and the task force, they're confident.'

Patient? Was she serious? My heart was storming again, whole weather systems battling it out inside me. My head was still full of the garage, the missing car, the unlocked padlock, and Carmen. There were so many questions I wanted to fire at Zee but I couldn't risk any of them. Except for the last, which I figured I could get away with.

'The two missing sisters, too? Has he said where they are?'

'No. But he's in a relationship with Alexis Glasser. They're engaged.'

'Okay.' Another massive curveball connected to Carmen.

'And there's evidence. Details he knows about the case that haven't been released. Personal items belonging to two of the victims. *Not* Piper, hon,' she said when she saw my face. 'But like I say, the team's confident.'

What if he's faking? I wanted to ask but I didn't. He can't be faking, Raych! He knows things. He has trophies. He knows Alexis.

'And those two, the two sisters and that garage fire.' Zee frowned and shook her head. 'Something's not right there.'

My mouth went dry. 'Like what?'

She checked her watch. 'Got to go.' She gave me a look. 'You sure about tomorrow? Call Haze back, yeah? Say the word and I'll be there.'

I clamped my jaw. 'No, Zee. I want to be alone tomorrow.' It came out short and brutal. 'Tell me what you mean, about the sisters. What's not right? You mean the arson case?'

She was on her feet now, harassed and a bit hurt. I was on a roll, pissing off the few friends I had left. 'That's under investigation. That was a fatality. It was reported.'

'I know.' My arm snaked out and I grabbed her wrist. 'Have they identified him? The dead man? Is that what you mean?'

She blinked. Looked down at my hand and I let go her arm. 'Man?'

The dragging fear resurfaced. I should have stopped right there but I couldn't. 'The dead man in the garage fire.'

'There was no dead man, hon. The fatality in that fire was female.'

Zee headed off after I told her for the third time I didn't need her tomorrow and adlibbed that I'd misheard the news on the arson dead body. On both counts I think she bought it, at least for now. She explained to me the body in the garage was only partially burned and had a female pelvis, not a male one. No ID so far, and I knew DNA identification would only happen if the victim was on file.

Somehow I made it home, on full autopilot the whole way. I ended up back on the couch in the TV room, numb and reeling.

The events of the past few days and hours, implications and revelations and ramifications, pinballed around my head.

I should have felt safe. There was a suspect in custody. But I didn't feel safe. I didn't believe in this new suspect, Leo Barros. Lock wasn't dead. Lock was alive. Carmen hadn't killed him.

Who the fuck had died in the fire? The only reasonable deduction was Alexis, but what was she doing there? I'd seen Carmen since the fire, since I'd seen that zipped-up body bag outside the garage. Carmen had the padlock key. She'd gone back for Lock and let him out. She must have done. He'd driven his car away.

Why would she let him out? She was worried about his injury, or he manipulated his way around her. But what had happened after that? Did he burn down the garages or did she?

I thought back to that night, how I was pinned to the couch with shock then too and couldn't move. I knew it hadn't been right, Carmen getting me out of there so fast. And then I got what it was that had been bugging me for the last two days, the thing Lock had said that I couldn't remember afterwards. *How would I know if she's dead?* A weird thing to say when I'd asked him about Piper and why they never found her. I'd forgotten it in all the drama but it wasn't a straight denial. Had he been telling me she was still alive? Or messing with my head so we'd let him go?

And if Lock was the innocent man he said he was, and he was now free again, why hadn't he reported us to the cops over what we'd done to him? The serial killer suspect we abducted and questioned. The dude whose thumb we cut off with a garden tool, FFS. He couldn't be innocent, whatever Zee said. Someone had burned down the garages. Carmen was missing and Alexis was dead.

Who was he going to come for next?

I was suddenly hyper-aware of the empty house at my back, of the too many, too big rooms and endless corridors. Of hiding places and entrance points, the security alarm I never arm when I'm at home. I got a flash of that nightmare corridor in *The Shining* and I jumped up off the couch and started to pace again. Out of the TV room and down towards my room and Max's.

Max was back from camp today but staying at Kylie's tonight. That was what she'd said. She was safe. But here was not safe. Here, my skin prickled and pulsed, thinking about where Lock was now and how soon he was going to come. I needed to make sure Max stayed away.

She picked up after two rings. 'Why are you calling me? You never call me.'

'I'm … checking in.' I tried to sound like it was no big deal. 'Are you okay?'

'Like, yeah? We're driving back.' I could hear the car engine in the background, a thump of music. 'Coming into the city now. What's going on, Raych?'

I scuffed my sneaker on the floor in the doorway to her room. 'Are you at Kylie's the whole weekend?'

'We're swimming and you're not talking us out of it. None of you are – not Dad, not Ky's mum—'

'I'm not calling to talk you out of it. Swim. You've trained for it.' It was the best place for them. The safest place. Out on the water in the Rottnest Channel. 'I'll come and cheer you at the start.'

'It's early, you know.' I heard the frown in her voice. 'Before 7 a.m.'

'Fine. I will. But . . . stay at Kylie's all weekend, okay?' A plan was forming but I hadn't got a hold of it yet.

'Why? What's going on? Have you packed up your stuff?'

I could feel it at my back, the accusing mess of my room; the strewn clothes and open drawers, the towers of books.

'I'll see you tomorrow,' I said. 'I'll see you at the race.'

But I didn't know if I would. Because you know what happens when I get scared? I get reckless. It was Friday night – the very last Friday before Piper's anniversary tomorrow. It all made sense to me in the moment. Tonight was an extension of all of the last year, an extension of my obsession with him. Yeah, I admit it. It's an obsession.

I had unfinished business with Lock's parents' house, for a start, and his key in my pocket. There would be something I'd missed there, a hole in the police investigation. I had the entire night ahead of me and a room full of shit-hot clothes and shoes. I wasn't sitting there waiting for him to come and get me. I was going to do what I'd been doing for the whole of the last year.

I was going out after him.

13

Raych

Freshwater Bay

In my room, I chose an outfit and changed for a night on the strip, went all-out with the effort to impress – face, hair, heels, dress. Another Friday, another Cott summer night out. And at midnight, as the hour and the day turned over, the anniversary.

Piper's anniversary was the culmination of everything, the opportunity I'd been waiting for. I didn't know how I hadn't seen it that way before.

Tomorrow, one way or another, it would all be over.

I found myself outside Carmen's back gate, wearing my sneakers and carrying my heels in my hand. It was early – the sun only now setting, the night too young to be hunting Lock just yet.

And I wanted to know if Carmen had helped him willingly or if she'd been coerced. I wanted to know if she'd been helping him all along.

I needed to get a handle on her, even if it was too late.

It was hot and humid and airless like it had been all week, the cloud cover persistent like it wanted to build up and storm. Sweat pricked at me as I peered over the gate into the yard. I could smell the fire again.

Carmen's backyard was lawn and a brick path, long and narrow with a shed at the bottom. No pool. I remembered her telling me where her room was, practically in the backyard was what she'd said. There was what looked like a converted sleepout, a set of steps up to a fly-screened door. The windows were curtained like this morning. No lights on and no police vehicles out front.

I listened and heard nothing. If they caught me I'd spin a story about that book I wanted to get back. There'd been nothing more about Carmen on the news tonight when I checked. No report of Alexis's death either, no ID on the body in the fire. The gate wasn't locked and neither was the back door. I crossed the yard and scrambled inside, got down on the floor out of sight.

Jesus. That smell, worse inside than out. It was darker than I expected, too dark to see. I lit up the torch on my phone and checked the place out at a crawl. It was Carmen's room, I knew right away from what was lined up on the windowsill. Dead, abandoned things – bird skulls and bones and sea urchins and a whole blowfish, puffed-up and perfectly preserved.

No razor-sharp teeth.

The room was a meeting of chaos and control, exactly like

she is. Cheap carpet and furniture, uncluttered and neat. A bedside table, a desk and chair, a single wardrobe. On the desk an older model laptop, on the bedside table a digital alarm clock and lamp. It was complicated, what I felt as I took it all in, the mismatch I was sure would be obvious if I checked out the rest of the house. Carmen on the outside of the family who'd adopted her.

The only thing not lacking in her room was books. At one end of the narrow room, furthest from the single bed, were two bookcases filled with hardbacks. It was only when I shuffled closer and used the torch I could see they were all library books. At least a hundred, overdue or stolen, and I wondered where from.

The books were non-fiction: biology and nature, wildlife, natural history. Why had the Glassers let Carmen steal all these books? I glanced up at the window but the backyard was still empty, the sunset billowing orange. No sound from further inside the house.

I crawled the other way and found Carmen's phone, its screen black and empty. Pushed to the back of the bedside table, exactly square with the corner. Underneath it was a business card – Detective Jared Rosso, his direct line and mobile numbers. I wondered what that meant, if Carmen had been playing both sides, the cops and Lock, but I couldn't see it. On the back of the card she'd scrawled two words: *Ships* and *Orca*. As in, killer whale. I didn't know what that meant either, but I pocketed the card and her phone. This family didn't need it. The cops didn't either.

There was a wall of pictures above her bed, I saw when I lifted the torch beam. Cut out of magazines and newspapers,

Blu-tacked to the wall in a grid. I played the light over them, looked again at the book titles: *Apex Predators, Deep Water Hunters, Sharks of the Indian and Pacific Oceans.*

Each photo on the wall above Carmen's bed was of a great white shark, breaching.

Okay, it was weird. But this was Carmen – that's what I told myself. Sharks, killer whales, dead things on the windowsill. Another link with the new AQWA suspect. It was only when I turned to go that my phone lit up the floor by the wardrobe and recent events fell into place.

The black garbage bag open at the top, full of discarded fire-damaged clothing. A used can of petrol on its side. Ash trodden into the carpet.

The smell of burned things made sense now. Why wasn't this room a crime scene? Where was the tape that should have sealed shut the door? What was this family playing at?

I looked down at myself for a long moment. At my fingers around my phone, the heels I'd change into when I got to the club, my sneakers on my feet. I'd left fibres here, DNA, traces of sand and dirt from the Frangipani House and garages, from everywhere I'd been in the last week. Flakes of skin and strands of hair floated from me like dust motes in the shaky light from my phone.

I'd set a trap and caught myself, or Carmen had. Accomplished nothing but confirm the worst about her – that she set the fire and killed her sister. I scrambled up and got out. Pulled the gate shut behind me and took off down the footpath, zigzagged streets towards home. It was dark now and I checked over my shoulder every block. But, chill. No one followed me.

Carmen's phone was almost fully charged when I pulled it

out of my pocket, a string of missed calls on the home screen from a number I didn't recognise, passcode protected so there was nothing more to see.

Someone's looking for you, Carmen. Someone who's not me.

The Beach Hotel and the Ocean View Club were heaving. The main room at the club radiated hot bodies and sweat, deodorant and suntan lotion, the shit we all put in our hair. I drank water on ice that looked like vodka with a slice of lime. I avoided Haze and the tight knots of ex-mates, the girls I'd hooked up with before Piper – the ones I knew from school and the ones I didn't, but everyone knows everyone here. I tried not to think about Carmen, where she was now, those freaky fucking fruitloop pictures on her bedroom wall.

I'd wait for midnight. I'd hover on the street in my usual style. If I didn't see him I'd head for his house.

As it happened, I wasn't there long at all. I was vaping on the balcony, the music was Fletcher singing loud about getting the last laugh, when someone tapped me on the shoulder and I spilled half my drink.

'You looking for Max?' It was Haze. I thought she was going to have another shot at me about tomorrow, but it wasn't that.

'No.' I frowned at her. Max wasn't there, she's underage. But my heart pushed up into my throat like it knew something I didn't. 'She's staying at yours tonight,' I said.

'She was just down there.' Haze nodded towards Marine Parade, the steps of the club. 'She looked a bit lost, I guess. I went down but couldn't see her. Ky's at home; she said they had a fight.'

I mumbled thanks and bumped my way back through the

crowd. Hustled out through the main door and onto the steps. No Max. I asked the few people leaving and the crowd queueing to get in if they'd seen her, but they were chatting or vaping or looking at their phones and their faces stayed blank. I called her phone and it went to voicemail, left a message for her to call me. I called Kylie's phone too and got the same.

It was late to be out, with the early start they had. Why right here, Max? Had she been looking for me? There was nothing from her on my phone. I didn't like this, here on the steps. The last place Piper was ever seen.

Across the street was dark flat ocean and towering pines. The beach stretched widescreen, the cloud peeled away in a curtain. The stars looked like a blood spatter pattern in luminol and I shivered despite the clammy heat. *Come on*, Raych. Max would be back at Kylie's already. Those two fought and fixed it all the time.

But the security camera pointed directly at me, on the spot Piper last stood. *I'll be right back. It's all G, Raych! Don't go away.* I lifted my chin and glared at it. What good did you do? I thought back to that image, the one seared into my brain, the one that was circulated and debated for months. The blurry figure standing too close to her. The cap and short dark hair turned away from the camera like he knew how to avoid it.

Was it Lock, the man on camera? And why had she gone with him? What had she left the party for in the first place?

It was only then, as I stared up at the angled head of the camera, with Carmen's stolen phone heavy in my pocket, that I realised the figure on camera could have been a girl. A tall, big-boned girl, near enough the same height and build as Lock, with her dark hair and angled fringe tucked up under a cap.

Why hadn't anyone else seen that? And why had I only thought of it now? The idea solidified as I stood there on the steps. Carmen, on that security camera.

I thought of her strangeness, her tin of serrated teeth, those freaky breaching shark pictures. The fire in the garage, her dead sister. Had Carmen been helping Lock all along? Did she make up a convincing lie while he waited around the corner with the car? Is that how they did it?

I pulled out my phone to call Zee, call the cops, call pretty much anyone who'd pick up, but as I did I realised the insanity of it. Carmen and me had tortured Lock. Carmen had burned down the garages. I'd broken into Lock's house and car.

I still had his key in my pocket, FFS.

The music dimmed as bodies from the club and the bar washed past me down the steps to waiting cars. Two girls from school said goodbye as I frowned at my blank black phone screen.

It was well past midnight now. Race day. Anniversary day. I'd expected to feel *something*, but not this numbness and dread. I still had my heels in my hand. I'd never changed into them. I looked across at the beach and the ocean through the pines, the pulse of the lighthouse on Rottnest Island, and I knew I wasn't done yet.

He kills close to home. Ditches the bodies practically on his doorstep. He's a homebody like Carmen.

I knew where I was going next.

I stopped at home to change and dump my shoes. Tripped over Max's bag on the doorstep and swore as our security light clicked on.

WTF? The bigger of Max's two rucksacks, dumped there

with a wet towel on top like she couldn't be arsed taking it indoors. Dirty clothes and a pair of her sneakers inside when I unzipped it. If she thought I was doing her washing from camp she was dreaming.

It was off, though. Not like her. And what, she'd left it here on her way out, or decided not to stay at Kylie's after they had the fight? But what was she doing there, on the steps of the club? I called her again but it was late, and they had an early start. No surprises she didn't pick up.

I left Max's rucksack in her room and didn't realise the other thing until I was on my way out again, back in my combats. The boat. Dad's boat was gone from the drive. So the dude Dad had mentioned, whoever he was, had come and picked it up.

I didn't know what these things meant. Not then. Max's bag. The missing boat. I was too focused on Carmen and Lock and the key in my pocket.

I wasn't thinking. I didn't know what else had changed, how it all fitted together.

The trap closing shut.

It was deep dark at the bottom of the driveway of the Frangipani House. There was no breeze and except for the almost-full moon it was exactly like it had been three nights ago. It was only me that was different.

And I was different. Different in relation to Lock and to Carmen, and other things. I hadn't wanted to smash anything since our time in the garage with him; it helped to have a project. I didn't want to die any more. I wanted to live through my next meeting with him. I had Carmen to thank for that although it cost me something to admit it.

What makes me so special, that she'd help me but hurt a bunch of other girls? It made no sense.

There was no sign of the pen I'd dropped on Tuesday. I'd thought it might still be here but it wasn't. I checked back up the driveway: no lights and not a sound except the white noise of crickets. A single car passed and kept going.

The house had the same pull it had three days ago. There was something here for me. Something I'd seen without knowing what it meant, or in those few words I'd heard from his father. I headed up the porch steps, pitch black. Pulled Lock's key out of my pocket.

Despite my numbness and dread, I didn't hesitate this time. Didn't make a big fucking deal of it even though it was one. I unlocked the door, stepped inside and shut it behind me. I leaned hard against that door as if I was safe, the shine of polished floorboards in front of me, a red answerphone light blinking on a table. Lock was with his parents in temporary accommodation, that's what Zee had told me. But I wasn't safe, I knew that, and if Piper was ever here, she sure as shit wasn't either.

No smell of Anzac biscuits now, only polished wood and my own sweat, the ticking of a big clock in the dark where I couldn't see it. I resisted the urge to call out, switched on my phone torch and inched along the hallway.

On the wall was a gallery of framed black and white photographs. Local landmarks, one of lightning and the Wadjemup lighthouse, a row of container ships on the horizon. Carmen was always looking out at those ships. I pulled Jared's card out of my pocket, read what she'd written there. *Ships.* Is that what she meant?

I stopped between two pictures. A bunch of yachts and motor launches moored in a bay on the river; a close-up of a young couple with a toddler on the deck of one of them. Lock and his parents. It was the name of the boat that lifted the hairs on my arms.

Orca 2.

The boat in *Jaws*. *Orca*. I can't be the only person my age who remembers it. Carmen had written that name down too. I checked along the line of pictures but these were the only two. An old boat. If it belonged to his parents, maybe they still had it. It might mean nothing but I wondered if the cops had searched it. The picture was Freshwater Bay, near Piper's place. I recognised the peppermint trees, and the boatsheds at the far end.

I backed up to the table and stopped. My pen was there by the cordless phone, the blinking red light. I swiped it up, my heart thudding, expecting someone to shout my name, to loom out of the dark. But they didn't. The light blinked in time with the clock at the end of the hallway, the thump of my heartbeat. It reminded me of the flashing red beacons on the river, guiding boats along the deep channels at night. Is that what he does to get them into the water? Take them downriver from one of the yacht clubs. But how does he get them there? Where does he keep them before that?

Not here. Another house. A basement or shed.

I had to get down there. To Freshwater Bay. I searched the rest of the house in a rush – the living areas on the upper floor, the bedrooms downstairs. Tidy rooms and vacuumed carpets. Barely any personal items, like they'd taken everything with them. I knocked on walls and floors, didn't find my fantasy of a locked basement or secret room, but I did find the study.

Not much bigger than a cupboard. A bare desk and a lamp, a locked filing cabinet, and a murder board.

Okay, it wasn't a murder board. That was my mind fucking with me. There was nothing on it but a bunch of red drawing pins and a load of pinholes. But it bothered me. I backed out of the room and wiped the door handles, everything I'd touched. I let myself out the back door, listened as it clicked shut behind me and I could breathe again.

I was like, *come on*, Raych, no way was that a murder board. But where was the stuff that had been on it? Had the cops taken it? And did they know about the boat in Freshwater Bay?

I saw the cat as I hovered outside the back door. It was in a stand-off with another cat, one outside and one inside the glass of the bedroom window. Lock's parents had a cat, or he did, and someone had been coming in to feed it; there were food and water bowls upstairs in the kitchen. The cat outside the window was smaller and lost interest, sniffing along the boundary like it was hunting. The moon was well up, flooding the backyard and striping her silver, and I realised it was Carmen's cat. Okay, not Carmen's cat, but the little cat she was with when I found her that day at the empty units. It made me think the cat had followed me the whole way from Carmen's place. But if she had, I hadn't seen her.

The yard sloped down to a back fence and a stand of gums. There was a Hills Hoist clothesline and a fenced-off above-ground pool, everything silvery in the light. The driveway looped around the side of the house to a set of double gates onto a side street. The cat disappeared underneath and I slipped between the gates and followed her.

She was gone when I got out onto the street. There was a garage opposite, a tangle of vines heavy on its roof and a FOR SALE sign that could have been for the garage or the neighbour's house. 'Cat?' I whispered. 'Where'd you go?'

The place and the moonlight had me thinking about Lock's impossible crimes. Lock's alibi for the night Genevieve Craigie died, the route to the river from here. Had the task force searched the neighbours' places? Did they have to get a warrant every time?

I knew the way to Freshwater Bay. I took off down the footpath and the cat materialised out of the shadows and kept pace with me. We crossed the railway line and highway at Salvado Street – no traffic – then zigzagged blocks towards the river. She stuck with me the whole way. I took a left past Freshwaters Cafe and the yacht club, and I didn't register the empty boat trailer at the boat ramp as we passed it, not the first time.

We came out into Freshwater Bay, full of boats and moonlight, and at last I got what had been bugging me all week about the moon. Each of the bodies had washed up at the full moon. At least, Maya and Mo had. No one had noticed this. No one had mentioned it, but it stopped me in my tracks, because Genevieve Craigie was different.

He killed her early. He was spooked by the surveillance, or something else.

Was it us, Carmen and me? Had we done that? The thought knotted my gut.

I started to walk again, my skin hot and then cold like it didn't know what to do with this new information. We were so close to Piper's old place now and I wanted to keep going all the way to her door. But this bay of boats was the one in the photo. One of them had to be *Orca 2*.

The cat had vanished but I walked the shoreline, past the end of Piper's street, two more blocks to where the moorings stopped. I strained my eyes at the boats but it was no good, the bay was full and I could only read the names on the nearest.

I turned and walked back. There was a pelican asleep on the roof of one of the boatsheds. The cat had reappeared on the narrow jetty there, was waiting outside the second shed, and I wondered if the police had searched those too. I took the jetty to the first, the cat watching me the whole time. I wasn't expecting to find anything.

The door to the boatshed was locked but I took out a pane of the front window with the bottom of my sneaker and a tinkle of glass. The door opened into thick dark, the lap of water on wood, what you'd expect. I knew right away it wasn't empty, but it took time for my eyes to adjust, for my brain to catch up with what was there.

Dad's boat. The boat he'd sold earlier in the week, rocking in the middle of the space.

My skin prickled as I stood there. It was the thickness of dark maybe, despite the moonlight filtering in through the front windows and gaps in the wood. The contrast between that and the pale bloated bulk of Dad's boat. The boatshed was a u-shape, planked platforms on three sides, a back door the width of the building that opened onto the river. It was shut now but they'd have opened it to get the boat inside.

They. Who was they? Who'd bought Dad's boat? What was it doing here?

I took a step into the space, watched where I was putting my feet. I knew it was Dad's boat from the Save Exmouth Gulf sticker in the windscreen – I'd put it there, after all. It was his trailer I'd seen back there at the boat ramp too, but I still couldn't make the pieces fit.

I clicked the torch on my phone and ran it over the space. I was reminded of the garage, Carmen's room, the Frangipani House – and none of them in a good way. *Orca 2* out there in the bay. Max's stuff on our doorstep.

Most of all, I didn't like Dad's boat in here. I was missing something, I knew that. And then the torch beam ran over a metal bin against the wall. It caught a flash of red and I flicked it back.

The bin was full of papers and as I rifled through them I felt it at my shoulder, the cold dark thing I didn't know yet, the last piece of the puzzle. The papers were news clippings, printouts, articles about shark fatalities going back decades. The corners were holed from drawing pins, and as soon as I saw that, even before I caught sight of the stray red pins at the bottom of the bin, I knew. I knew that's where they'd come from – Lock's parents' house, the murder board that wasn't a murder board.

It was the most-repeated story that made it all connect, and the picture of the boat *Orca 2*. Teenager Roman Smith, attacked on his paddleboard on the river at North Fremantle by a bull shark. Anyone who's local knows about that day, even more than twenty years later. His girlfriend, a state swim champion, gave him first aid at the scene, but he died of blood loss before the paramedics arrived.

They'd been there, Lock and his parents. They'd helped pull the boy out. Lock would have been six years old at the time.

I knew it then, that Lock *had* killed all those girls. That what had happened to Roman Smith on the river waited in his head for years like a fuse that only needed to be lit. That his parents had lied for him. What parent wouldn't do that for their child?

I heard the noise as I crouched there, skimming the articles by torchlight. A thud like something heavy, falling, someone kicking a wall or a door. The sound came from the boat – muffled by water – and I knew what it was right away.

As it slid into place – Dad's boat here in the bay, Max's bag left on our doorstep, Max on the steps of the club tonight – I'd already sprung to my feet and turned for the boat, my foot skidding on the wet planking as I did.

'Max?' My voice was weird, loud and echoing in the watery space. 'Max, is that you?'

She was here, on Dad's boat. Lock had taken her, but I would get her back.

I clambered on board, slipping and stumbling. The deck so familiar – the stink of fish, plus that sunblock Dad always uses. It was empty but I couldn't see enough in the dark. Why hadn't Max replied? The steps to the cabin yawned in front but I heard the thud again and spun around.

The storage box along the stern. I froze when I clocked it in the torch beam because it was big enough for a body. But *come on*, Raych, get a grip. She was in there. She'd made that thud. I heaved it open.

Empty.

'Max?' I turned for the steps then, but there was another sound, on the jetty outside the door. He was out there – he was coming – and all I could think was, *Hide!* I threw myself in the box as the door to the boatshed opened, banged my knee hard on the way down. The lid closed on me but I didn't know if I'd been quick enough. Didn't know if he'd seen me.

I should have taken the steps. I should have gone down there first. I should have called Jared, or Zee, as soon as I'd seen Dad's boat. It didn't matter any more, what Carmen and me had done. I tried to do it even then, cramped into the space with my knee blazing pain, but I couldn't get Jared's card or my phone out of my pocket.

There were footsteps out there, wet splashing sounds I knew in my gut weren't water, rough fast breathing I figured out was mine. I smelled the petrol and thought, Fuck, Carmen and Lock are out there together – they're going to burn the boatshed like they burned the garages.

It all happened so quick. I heard the *whump* as it went up, as the petrol caught, like a bonfire. It sounded exactly like you'd think. And then one of them stepped onto the boat – I felt the lurch as they did – and started the engine.

I tried to tell myself it was right. It was what I'd wanted, that I'd save her, but I couldn't make it work. There was the sound of the big door sliding open, the gurgle and grind of the engine reversing. And then we were on the move.

Out onto the river to where he'd taken Piper and all the other girls.

14

Carmen

Carmen can't go back

Carmen hides out at the boathouse. No one comes here at night. She has her water bottle and backpack and she sleeps on a fake leather bench seat that was ripped out of a car and has seen better days. She might be losing the plot in other ways, because of what her brain's been doing, and she can't remember when she last ate something, but she didn't park her car nearby or anything stupid like that. She walked, like she always does.

She watches the river foreshore and street from one of the small front windows, the parts of both she can see. It's dark and the window is thick with dirt and cobwebs but there's an almost full moon out and things show up. Every now and then a car passing or someone walking their dog. There's loud music and shouts and barbeque smells from over at the yacht club building, the clubhouse spraying out noise and light, but inside here is the opposite of the clubhouse. The opposite of the daytime and the wide dry sky full of seagulls and corellas and the tops of trees. The opposite of the fire at the garages and the sharp smell of petrol in Carmen's room.

Inside the boathouse, the surface of everything is slick with dark and cool and wet. It smells and sounds like wood and water, seaweed and dead brown jellyfish, those huge ones that even when they're alive make girls squeal on school trips to the river, which is idiotic.

Carmen misses the girl cat, but the cat wouldn't like the water. She's never missed anything before, not even her mum or dad – the situation has always been too complicated for that. But there's a pelican that roosts on top of the boathouse, cormorants and black swans on the river, a rat or a possum in the roof, plus the jellyfish and mice and spiders – it's not as if she's on her own.

She watches from the back of the boathouse when she's not watching the front. There's a big door there, and the aluminium dinghy tethered to a post. When she looks at the dinghy, she wants to get in it and go and never come back. But she can't do that. Not yet. She only took it out that one time, and it was dark. Or maybe it was two times. Some things, the longer she thinks about them the more confused they get, like a film with the frames moved around so the order is different to how it started out.

Tonight, one side of the big door is open to the river and the boats on their moorings. She knows which one is Neil's boat, *Orca 2*, because she's seen him go out to it before, on the other nights she's been here. She'll be able to see if he gets on board.

She knew about the boat because of the picture in his parents' hallway, next to the photo of the container ships she saw that time on the news. Anyhow, now he's been here and talked to her it's not even a secret any more.

It's been a week of making deals with people, which is not something Carmen's used to. It makes sense that Neil is the one who's been following her ever since she found Christine's body. She's given up calling the Crime Stoppers number now – it's too late for that.

Neil's hand was properly bandaged up with his arm in a sling when he came, like he'd been to hospital, but Carmen thinks that can't be right. He didn't look too bad, not considering the things that have happened to him. He didn't say much, but Carmen doesn't mind that. He only said what he wants her to do, which she would have done anyhow even if he hadn't said it.

She's not doing it because she *has* to. He can think that if he wants.

After the music at the clubhouse is switched off, it's an hour before the lights go out and the yacht club is quiet. With no wind, there's not even the usual clinking sound of the yachts. There's only the soft scrape of the pelican up there on the roof, the noisy frogs on the foreshore and the whine of a single mosquito. Then, annoyingly, she sees Rachel arrive on foot from the direction of the cafe and boat ramp. Rachel can't have followed Carmen because she goes straight past, but she must know by now that Neil didn't die in the fire. She must know he's the killer and she was right about him the whole time.

But Rachel doesn't know everything.

She turns north along the foreshore and beach, away from the boathouses and yacht club, stopping every few steps to look at the boats in the bay. Is she searching for Neil's boat? She took his house key off his keyring that time, after all. She's probably been in there and seen the pictures. *Orca 2* hasn't moved since last night because Carmen would have seen it.

If Neil has any sense, he'll want to get back at them, Carmen and Rachel, for what happened inside the garage. He'll want to keep them quiet. There was no sign of that when he came and talked to her, but it's what Carmen would do if she was him. She needs to be careful.

Because she needs to know about *that night*, about Rachel's friend Piper. About Mrs Craigie and the other girls. She needs to know what she's really like – what she's capable of, one way or the other – before the end.

All day Carmen has listened on the radio to the news from the police that they're looking for her. She has an old plastic radio Mr G gave her with one of those telescoping antennas no one uses these days because everything is digital. The radio sounds crackly and falls over unless she props it up against something, but it works.

The arson squad are investigating the fire. On the news it says they're concerned for Carmen's welfare but she knows they can't be. Because she ran instead of staying to talk to the detectives, and Rosso and maybe the arson squad will have spoken to Mrs G and seen Carmen's room by now. And because the body in the fire was a woman and not a man. Alexis didn't burn down the garages.

Carmen's been waiting to hear the sound of sirens in the distance, or worse, right outside the door that leads to the jetty and foreshore.

But no one has come so far except Neil, and now Rachel.

What's most annoying about the situation is that after all these years of imagining and longing and inventively planning to kill Alexis, and after Neil stopped her *that night* when she was in the middle of doing it, Carmen isn't the one who did it. She wasn't even there when it happened. Or if she was, she can't remember it.

She'd have liked to be able to confess to killing Alexis. To draw a line under that one thing at least so it made sense. But the police wouldn't have believed her.

Neil must have done it after Alexis took Carmen's keys and let him out.

This makes Carmen mad. As mad as she was inside the garage. As mad as she's ever been. Neil made her do something to Rachel's friend *that night* and he won't even admit it. And now he's killed Alexis, the thing Carmen has wanted to do for her whole entire life. She had to pretend she wasn't angry when he came and talked to her, which luckily she's good at.

It's another example of men muscling in on things they're better off leaving alone, which has been a big part of the problem all along. And then there's Leo, the most recent unbelievable development in the murder case.

Leo is a suspect and the media are calling him AQWA man because he works at AQWA, which isn't funny or even original. When Carmen first heard it, she thought about Neil's dark coloured polo shirt, because the golf course uniform and the AQWA uniform are the same colour. That must be how they got them mixed up. But it's a mistake, she knows it is.

Carmen can't imagine Leo killing anyone. He's mean and insecure and a bully like Mrs Craigie, but that's all. He'll have been mansplaining sociopaths and serial killers to the female detectives on the case. They'll be relieved when they figure out it's not him and they can let him go.

Sometimes when Carmen thinks about *that night* and tries to remember it, she wonders if Neil forced her to hurt Rachel's friend when she didn't want to do it. Sometimes she even thinks she might not be the psychopathic killer she's always thought she was.

But then she decides she must be, because of the other things she's started to remember.

How that girl Mo with the buzzcut who worked in the surf shop in Claremont would follow Carmen around the shop each time she went in there. She'd look down on Carmen from under her dark eyebrows, like what did Carmen think she was doing in there, it wasn't as if any of the clothes would suit her, and was she going to take something? Even though she never had, not from there. How the last time it happened Mo followed Carmen home in her car for no reason and parked across the street from the Glasser house. Mr G had to come out and tell her to go away.

How the next girl, Maya, took Carmen's parking spot that day in Subiaco when she'd been waiting ages for it, and she and her friend laughed when Carmen got out of her car and said something. How afterwards, when she'd found another spot and parked and later gone back to her car, someone had scratched *WEIRD* in spidery letters on the driver's door, right through the paint to the metal.

How each time one of them went missing, something like that had happened the week before. Things those girls said and did to make it clear to Carmen they knew she was different, that she wasn't from around here and didn't fit. Even the way they looked at her made her feel small and bad and wrong. Made her think about her mum not wanting her, and why.

What if she had killed them, and made it look like a shark?

She grips the tin of teeth in her pocket so hard her hand cramps, and she pulls it out and sticks it in her armpit. Carmen loves sharks. She loves the moment of breach, that instant when all the trawling and sensing and waiting explodes into unstoppable force.

If she was killing those girls to get back at them, that's the way she'd want to do it.

Rachel has turned around further along the bay and is walking back this way towards the boathouses. She keeps coming along the foreshore, around the curve of the bay, stopping and starting. Neil said Rachel wouldn't find out her sister is missing until tomorrow morning, but she's here now, so Carmen will have to improvise.

The boathouse is an in-between place. Between water and solid ground, air and sky. Before, Carmen liked this about it, but now it feels too much like her brain when she can't rely on it, and the situation with Neil. The wooden posts under the walkway disappear into the dark salty water and the whole thing laps and shifts like it would break apart in a storm. Once in the daylight she saw what she thought was a bull shark under the water in the big doorway, but it turned out to be a long strip of plastic rubbish.

At night, like now, light leaks in from the river, the slick sheen of reflected city lights and navigation beacons, the purple haze of sky and stars, but the water is always moving so what

light there is is unreliable. When she presses her forehead to the
cool window glass she can feel the big open door at her back,
how easy it would be for the river and all the things that live in
it to surge inside and swamp everything and carry it out into
the night and then the ocean.

Maybe it would be better if it did.

Rachel has stopped walking. She's got all the way to the end
of the first jetty and is staring at something Carmen can't see.
She opens the door of the first boathouse and goes inside.

Carmen waits. It's too long and she can't see what's happening. She checks the big door at the back but can't see anything
there either. Then she sees the moving growing fire glow at
the front windows of the boathouse next door and she takes a
step back.

There's a stretched-out moment when she stops breathing and
doesn't know what to do. Whether Rachel's still in there and if
she should go over there and get her – because without Rachel
the plan with Neil won't work.

And then Rachel's dad's boat drives out from the boathouse
next door onto the river. It's the boat she's seen parked in
Rachel's driveway, the same one Neil told her about. It drives
away and disappears, and for a long time nothing happens.

Then, as Carmen watches from the front window, something
long and slow and black humps and froths through the water
under the jetty, and Carmen thinks the bull shark is here and
was real the whole time, that it wasn't a piece of rubbish.

But the thing gets bigger and stands up and it's Rachel.

There's a little scrappy beach there, between the jetties and
below the foreshore, and Rachel hauls herself onto it, wet and
gasping. She spends minutes crouched there, breathing fast.

And then she peels the seaweed off her arms, slicks her hair back off her face, and she stands and faces the river and sways. She pulls her phone out of her pocket and stamps her foot, looks out to the river and screams, and Carmen has to go out there and get her after all.

She opens the door and the night rushes in, plus something slippery that turns out to be the girl cat. Carmen has to call 'Rachel' three times until she snakes her head around and hears her, climbs up onto the jetty and picks her way to the door.

Rachel's eyes are wild, as wild as Carmen's seen them. But when Carmen throws a towel at her and tells her it's for her phone, she snatches it up and sits on the fake leather seat and stays. 'Hellish cold in the river.' Rachel coughs and wipes the back of her arm across her mouth. 'The fire, next door. What happened to it? Did it stop?'

Carmen shrugs. She doesn't know what happened to it either.

She watches Rachel scan the dark space inside the boat-house – the cobwebbed windows and sliding black water, the silvery shape of the tethered dinghy. 'Why are you here, Carmen?'

'Hiding,' Carmen says.

'I thought it was you. The fire in there.' Rachel's eyes narrow. 'What happened in that garage after I left? Did you let him out? I have to know.'

Carmen says nothing, and Rachel swears and shakes her head. 'I'm not going to give up,' she says. 'This is serious now.' Which is idiotic, because when hasn't it been?

'What happened on the boat?' Carmen says.

'Why should I tell you? You don't tell me anything.'

There's a moment of nothing but the two of them breathing,

the push and pull of water. Carmen thinks back to the first night, watching Rachel in the Beach Hotel, a part of the crowd except not a part of it, not ever again. She feels the wood shift under her, a sudden doubt about Rachel and her sister, about what Neil has asked her to do.

'I dunno what happened at the garage,' she says. 'Sometimes I don't remember things.'

Rachel weighs Carmen up and stares her down. She doesn't believe it, Carmen can tell. And then her body shakes, top to bottom like a wet dog. 'It's the end of the road, Carmen. My sister . . .' She glares at her phone screen, still dead. 'I fucked up. Had a panic attack on Dad's boat. Max was right there, I heard her, but then . . . We need to call the cops.'

But Carmen thinks about Neil and his boat and all the dead girls, the question of who has really killed them. About loose ends and wanting to disappear in the dinghy and whether Rachel is a problem or not. She pushes away her doubts about Rachel's sister and says, 'No, Rachel. No police. You need to stay calm.'

Rachel is a loose end, and so is Neil. Neil is not calling the shots and making the rules like he thinks he is, and Rachel doesn't need to know everything.

Carmen tells her what they have to do.

SATURDAY

15

Raych

The anniversary

It's chaos down at the race start, with swimmers and officials and spectators ramming the grass terraces and beach. I get there not long after sunrise, pushing between bodies, scanning the crowd. The churned-up sand is streaked with shadows, the early light bringing up the blue of the water.

I told Carmen I needed to get something from the house, but what I needed was time out. From her telling me what to do, from scribbling yesterday's action in my notebook, from pacing the slippery walkway inside the boatshed while we waited for Lock to make his move. I hoped I'd come here and find it had all been a dream, that I was wrong and Max was never on Dad's boat, that none of what Carmen told me last night is true. But each time the klaxon sounds for the swimmers I flinch. And Max is not here.

I called Haze first thing, but all she could tell me is Kylie and Max were gone before she woke up, that she hadn't seen them and as far as she knew they were swimming today. I wanted to tell her about Lock, and Max, and Dad's boat, but Carmen was watching me the whole time, and she'd made it clear: no police. And then Haze started in on me about Piper's day today and I hung up on her.

Waking this morning, I had the longest moment of not remembering where or when I was. Not the anniversary today or the last few cosmically fucked up days. For those seconds it was like the year never was. Max wasn't gone and neither was Piper. It was Saturday. There'd be a party tonight. Maybe we'd get another shot at it, at that kiss and what came after. I had butterflies in my stomach thinking about it, FFS. Then came the squeak of my skin against fake leather and I realised where I was: on my side on that wrecked car seat in the boatshed while Carmen kept watch for Lock.

Orca 2 hadn't moved and Dad's boat was moored next to it. I didn't believe her at first, that it hadn't gone anywhere, but she was right. They were both there at first light.

I will never admit to anyone except Carmen – and I only told her in the shock of the moment – that I jumped off Dad's boat last night. Lock was at the helm when I got out of that storage box. He had his back to me, his arm in a sling, but then everything seized – breath, muscles, heart – and the side of the boat was right there. The next thing I knew, I was in the water.

No one else can ever know how I've let Max down. But I can still fix this.

Carmen told me she'd spoken to Lock – all those missed calls on her phone. To get Max back alive we have to meet him face to face. And no police. He can see for miles, she said, from where he's taken Max – he'll see if the cops come, if anyone comes except us, and then she'll die. So what choice do we have?

In my heart I know he wants a reckoning with us, but I want that reckoning too.

Last night I told Carmen about the shark attack articles and we figured that's what the fire was for, to destroy them. I thought they'd burned the whole boatshed, but the only damage in there was a teardrop scorch mark up one wall. Carmen went over to the yacht club and stole a phone from the lost property, put my SIM in it and got it working. Why did it matter? I said to her. I didn't give a fuck about my phone. But hers was still working after its dunking in the river and she said I needed to have mine. We had to be able to keep in touch.

She promised she'll message me when his boat moves and I have to believe she's good for it. I watch until the girls' teams are all off the beach. No Kylie, no Max – but I knew that, didn't I, as soon as I got here. Because all this – the support boats waiting out on the water, the swimmers rushing the shallows each time the klaxon sounds – is one big diversion. It's the perfect day for him. The leaders are already out of sight, swimmers and paddlers and boats moving off towards Rottnest. I yank out the phone and call Max again, get the same straight-to-voicemail as I get every time. Panic flutters at the edges of my vision as I fight my way back up the terraces to the street.

The new phone vibrates in my pocket. When I pull it out it says number withheld. 'Max! Is that you?'

'Ah, no. Rachel Valenti?'

I don't recognise the caller, can barely hear above the traffic and the music on the beach. I head for my car, hold the phone hard against my ear. 'Who is this?'

'Detective Rosso, Rachel. How you doing?'

Jared. Fuck. A spike of hope and fear punches up from my gut. Because whatever Carmen says, he's right there.

'Rachel? Can you hear me?' he says.

'Um ... Yep, I'm here. Why are you—?'

'I need to speak with you.' I get to my car and freeze. 'You at home? I can send a vehicle,' he says.

I unlock the driver door. 'What's this about?'

'Where are you please? You want to make your own way?' Jared's clipped style doesn't go down so well with the public. I've not been on the end of it until now.

'What about?' I say again.

Tell him, Raych! Tell him what's happened and where to look. I've got my mouth open to do it when he says, 'You know a Carmen Chase?'

That's all it takes. Carmen wins: no police. I open the car door and slide in. The seat hot, the steering wheel hotter. 'No, I don't think so, Jared.' I start the engine. The klaxon sounds again from the beach.

'This is not optional, Rachel.'

Fuck it. Stick to the plan. I check the rearview, look down at the phone screen. Jared's still talking, asking me again where I am. The message from Carmen comes in as I sit there. *Rachel. You need to come now.*

I hang up on Jared, dump the phone on the seat and drive.

*

I race home. No marked car waiting outside for me, only the empty driveway, the space left by Dad's boat. I clatter inside and into the kitchen. Carmen will wait for me. She won't go on her own.

The phone buzzes in my pocket. Two texts from Zee, plus more missed calls from Jared's number withheld. Zee's messages say, *Leo Barros released. Don't want you to be alone today. Where are you? Call me!* No surprises there. I switch it off.

What do I need? I scan the kitchen bench – kettle, toaster, Dad's knife block. Why didn't I come here first? I yank the biggest of Dad's kitchen knives out of the block – one of the sashimi knives with a ten-inch blade. I look at the length of it, the shine of it, feel the weight of it in my hand. Good, but I can do better. Carmen's probably got a stack of knives just like it.

I hit the garage on the way out of the house instead and grab the biggest of Dad's fishing knives. Don't kid yourself – size does matter.

It's insurance, that's all it is. Carmen will have that backpack with her.

I made a deal with Carmen. She has her own agenda, I get that, but I don't have to trust her. We're going after Lock. We're going to get Max back and take him down.

At least I think we are.

The crowd down at Freshwater Bay is small for a Saturday morning. A handful of people on the cafe terrace and a couple walking a black dog on the foreshore. Everyone is out the other side today, looking in the opposite direction towards Rotto. I take the back way through the yacht club to the boatsheds, slide unnoticed between trees and boats and vehicles to the jetty and in through the door.

Carmen's at the back, at the big open door facing the river, her backpack at her feet. She swings around when she hears me. 'Took your time, Rachel.'

'When did he go?'

She frowns at her phone screen. 'Twenty-two minutes.'

'And he's going where you said?'

She nods but looks away, back out at the bay. 'Course. He took a dinghy out to the boat and left it on the mooring.'

The ships. But why risk going in daylight? Even with the crowds heading to the island today. What's made him do it? I think of Genevieve Craigie again, the full moon and him killing her early.

'Why now?' I say. 'Why didn't he go while it was dark?'

She grips the frame of the big door. Tucks a slippery strand of hair behind her ear. 'How should I know?'

I make my way around the decking towards her. The water underneath it is spangled with light from gaps in the wood. It makes me think of last night – the boat and the water, salty and churned with weed – and I pull my eyes away. I've got Dad's knife held awkward across my body, under the loose hem of my top so Carmen can't see it. I wish I'd brought a bag, something to hide the long blade in and protect it. I'm going to end up stabbing something I don't intend to stab.

All those warnings Zee gives us in Fight Back Club come back to me – never arm yourself with anything you don't want turned against you. Never arm yourself, full stop.

Never approach a serial killer without arming yourself. That's one of mine. But I should have brought something different, something practical. The Maglite from next to my bed. The can of pepper spray I ordered online.

'What's that under your shirt?' Carmen says.

'Nothing.' She keeps staring so I set my jaw and show her the knife. 'This.'

Her eyes darken.

'For him,' I say, clarifying, but I see her clock the lie. Her nostrils flare and I feel the change between us, the curdle of fear that says I've jinxed it by bringing the knife. That I should have trusted her.

She picks up her backpack. 'Would you use it?'

What's that supposed to mean? 'Yeah, I'd use it.'

She lifts her chin and meets my glare. 'You reckon?'

That pisses me off. It makes me want to prove it to her. I could confront her; tell her I don't trust her. Tell her I saw the padlock and I don't believe her about the garage. Ask her what happened to her sister.

But it's too late for any of that now; I should have made her tell me it all last night.

Maybe she's right and I won't be able to use it, won't be able to do what I need to do, but I have to try. I point the knife at her and the tip of it shakes. 'Just get in the dinghy,' I say. 'Show me the way. All we're doing is wasting time.'

The sun's relentless off the water and the tin of the dinghy, even from behind my sunglasses. Sharp salty spray and the petrol stink of the outboard motor. The river's flat calm and windless and the clouds are back, sliding across the sun.

We pass the spot where both boats were moored this morning – Dad's boat and *Orca 2* – now empty.

'We're going where he's taken her, right?' I say. 'That's what he said?'

Carmen's hand tightens on the strap of her backpack as she nods. 'Told you.'

'So who's driving the other boat?'

She shrugs like it's no big deal when of course it is. I always knew he had an accomplice. Didn't I tell that to Zee that time?

'Carmen?'

But she frowns away from me, directs me downriver. She looks exhausted in the daylight, deep purple shadows around her eyes where she hasn't slept. I've got her in the bow, perched as far away from me as she can get. She's not wearing the black baseball cap and I wonder if she lost it somewhere. The sun's behind her head and the breeze floats her dark hair around her face like she's a character in a Stephen King novel, which maybe she is. But I told her to stick up front and so far she has, with the backpack on one shoulder and the empty mid-section of the boat in between us.

I can't tell who's calling the shots here – me with the knife or Carmen with her backpack. It's one thing coming up with a plan like this in the dead of night. It's different now, in the daylight. How can I trust what she says about Max when I don't know what happened to her sister? Whether she's made other trips in this dinghy. How she knows Lock.

Last night she said I'd got it wrong, I'd misheard her in the garage, of course she doesn't know him. She looked right at me as she said it but I knew it was a lie. I scan the bottom of the tinny looking for streaks and scabs of dried blood, think of Tom Ripley beating his best mate to death with an oar. There's only a thin wash of clear salt water over drifts of sand but Carmen could have cleaned it, or someone else has. I don't know whose it is or whether we've stolen it.

It's quiet out, my theory of everyone heading over to Rotto holding true. The usual landmarks slide past I remember from river trips with Dad – the Dalkeith mansions across the river, Point Walter, the Bicton Baths, and then we get close to Freo and I see the bridges up ahead. I grip the tiller, the vibration of the engine shaking the bones in my fingers, up my arm to my teeth. We pass the water police on our right, their powerful patrol boat moored and waiting, and I yank Dad's knife down out of sight. I wish I hadn't turned off the phone but if I pull it out Carmen will see me. She seems unbothered by the knife, an impenetrable look on her face, but a good half of me wants the cops to see it and come after us. For everything to be taken out of my hands.

Mate, whatever plans I made and trashed, this is not how I imagined spending Piper's anniversary. The guilt is sucking at me, a brutal bruising undertow trying to take me down. Max would be swimming now, or safe at Kylie's, if I hadn't done the insane things I've done. I'm rigid against the hard seat, my muscles tensed and ready, but for what?

Because I know, with each navigation beacon we pass, each turn of the river, as we get nearer to Lock and to Max, I'm getting nearer to Piper too. The closest I've been to her at any point in the last year. I don't like it, this intersection of the three of them. Knowing whatever Max is going through is my fault.

We cruise under the bridges, the shade sliding cool and dark over the top of us, and I shiver at the place Roman Smith got pulled off his paddleboard by the bull shark. After that it's a straight run through the harbour to the lighthouses and open water. There are people there, tiny from where I'm perched in the dinghy, strolling or working the docks, doing Saturday like it's any other Saturday, and there's a point as we approach the South Mole lighthouse when I want to aim the dinghy at the docks, scream out to someone to help me, anything, because I've made a giant fuck-off mistake and should have called the water police myself, should have told Jared the truth when I had the chance. But Carmen watches me like she guesses what I'm thinking, and then the people and the two lighthouses are gone in smears of colour, and we're out on the ocean and I'm still holding course and there's no going back.

'Head for Wadjemup.' She doesn't look at me. 'Rottnest. Keep it straight.' It's the first thing she's said since directing me downriver to here. She hasn't turned her head once to check where we are, that I'm steering us right. She must have done this trip before.

There are waves now, smacking the little boat and slowing us down. I throttle up and hear the whine of the engine respond. The dinghy looked a decent size in the boatshed but it's tiny out here on the swell. What I wouldn't give for Dad now, Dad and his shiny monster boat I've hated for so long. Rotto is a low smudge, looming clearer with every wave that approaches and falls behind, every lurch upwards that makes Carmen blot out the sun for a second before we crash back down.

The island is swarming with white boats, tiny dots in an Impressionist painting, the race crowd cheering the incoming swimmers. I get a falling sensation as I see them, a déjà vu lurch of panic, because Max and Kylie should be there. Of course Lock has set out today. No one will notice another boat out here. Everyone's looking the other way.

Between us and the island, the line of shipping at Gage Roads. The container ships that are always there, the same ones in the photos in Lock's hallway. We're approaching the nearest when Carmen talks again. 'There's a ship there. Black paint, straight ahead. See it?'

'The first one?' They're spaced apart, not in the straight line they always look to be from the beach.

'Past that,' she says. 'The one with the rust patch.'

I nod. A cargo ship, empty, no containers. The one she told me about. The anchor chain at one end drops vertical into the water. The smell is rusty metal and diesel fumes, the paint black and flaking, towering above as we get close. I strain my gaze upwards. 'Are you sure?' If there are people up there, they're invisible, but they'll have seen us coming.

For the first time Carmen turns and looks ahead. She's different now, sitting straighter, every line of her alert. 'Go around the other side,' she says.

It takes an age to turn around the back of it. My hands are slippery, one on the knife and the other on the tiller. The hull is like a cliff face and the engine whine bounces back off it and throbs in my head. There's a tall structure at the back that must be cabins and the bridge, isn't that what they call it? This is a working vessel, there'll be a crew. But somehow I know the ship is empty. It *feels* empty, like a ghost ship.

I know what this ship is. I'm blanketed with dread now. I'm back in Lock's hallway with the photos and the red blinking answerphone. This is the place. So much space to keep a girl, and no one in any direction to hear you scream.

We round the corner to the far side, and there's Lock's boat, waiting. A different colour to the boat in the movie – a sea green hull, the deck painted white – but the name in black letters across the stern: *Orca 2.*

'Carmen? What the fuck?'

Dad's boat isn't here.

'Get closer,' she says.

'Where's Dad's boat? Where's Max?'

Orca 2 looks empty. Engine off. No one on deck. Carmen doesn't answer, but frowns hard at the knife in my hand, up at the ship and back again at *Orca 2.* Calculating.

'Where's Max, Carmen?' I say again.

She doesn't look at me. 'Not here. Safe.'

It takes a second to land. 'Safe? What are you saying?' She's not sure about it, I can tell. Maybe she was once, but something has changed and now she's not.

'You told me she'd be here with him.' I grip the knife so hard my vision swims. 'You said this was a rescue.'

'No, Rachel—'

'You made me think it.'

'So you'd come.'

I'm out of words, drifting and numb. I pull out the phone and switch it on, knowing there won't be a signal. Carmen watches me do it, her face closed and blank and exhausted.

'He doesn't want your sister, Rachel. Of course not. He wants you. He wants both of us.'

PART FIVE

SATURDAY, later

16

Raych

The ship

We're in full sun on this side of the ship. It's well into afternoon now and the heat rebounds off every surface. With the engine throttled down and the dinghy tipping on the swell, seasickness rams my throat like someone has flicked a switch. Carmen has made me tie a line to the back of *Orca 2* to secure the dinghy. Okay, like, she didn't *make* me, but what can I do? I wanted this. I agreed to the plan. She just didn't tell me all the facts.

Engine off, it's too quiet. Slapping water, and somewhere a seagull I can't see. Dad's knife is pretty much the only thing I've got going for me. I hang onto it like a lifeline. Carmen hugs her backpack to her body like she's thinking the same thing.

'Where is she then?' I ask for the zillionth time. 'Safe where?'

But all Carmen does is shrug, her face unreadable as she stares at me.

'What?' I say.

'You don't have to come.'

'Yes, I do.'

'You should stay with the dinghy. In case.'

'In case what?'

Her gaze slides along the knife blade. 'I can do it. I can sort it. You stay behind.' But I hear the doubt again, so different to her usual vibe.

'What's changed, Carmen? You said he wanted both of us.'

'He's seen you now,' she says. 'He knows you've come.'

My head snaps up and around. The dread churns in my gut but I can't see anyone.

'I'm not staying behind,' I say. 'I don't trust you. Have you not got that yet?'

She goes first. *Orca 2* is not small, almost the size of Dad's boat. It only looks that way next to the hulking ship. I watch Carmen lever her long body out of the wobbling dinghy and onto the deck, the backpack clamped over one shoulder, her baggy jeans and boots and long-sleeved T so wrong for the ocean and the day, but it's not like I can talk.

I follow her, close as I can. Lock's boat is run down, paint peeling but seaworthy. The deck is empty and stinks of something that turns my stomach. There's the glassed-in helm, empty too, and stairs to a deck below. 'Shouldn't we check that?' But she's already crossed to where the boat is moored to the container ship, tied at the bottom of a ladder. A rope ladder, flat against the ship's hull like a limp flag, running up to a set of metal steps. She's across the shifting gap and climbing, quicker and lighter than I'd expect of her, like she's on a mission. Which she is, but I don't know what it is yet.

I bang down the steps to the lower deck. Fling open doors. The smell is worse, choking and feral, but there's no one here. I climb back up and crane my neck to the ship above. No one there either except Carmen, already on the stairway slanting up the side of the ship. In the other direction, Rottnest Island, still swarming with boats but too far to help us. I look at the knife in my sweating hand, the sun off the blade. The shape of it is seared on my eyelids when I shut them, even through my sunglasses.

Lock is up there. The only person who can tell me where Max is. If he kills her I'll never forgive myself. And if I don't go up there, I will never ever know. I'll never get the chance to find out what happened to Piper or do something about it. My chance will be lost.

I put the blade of Dad's knife between my teeth, like Lara Croft or Indiana Jones, FFS, reach for the rope and start to climb.

It's nothing special, being up on the deck of this massive ship. It's like being on the top floor of the abandoned units on Pearse Street. You wouldn't sell tickets to it. That's what I tell myself to try to calm me the fuck down.

It doesn't work. My vision shimmers, like swallows are darting at the edges of it. The smell is oily diesel mixed with the heaviness of salt. I should be pounding the deck, ripping open doors, scouring cabin after cabin for Max. But where to start?

Carmen was gone by the time I reached the top and pulled Dad's knife out of my teeth, and I don't know if that's better or worse than I was expecting. I mean, she wasn't waiting to snatch the knife or push me overboard, but there are so many times she could have done something like that and didn't. Going back as far as hospital. That day when she found me.

She could have done worse by me, all those times. But I don't know what she expects of me here. Why didn't she wait? Has she gone to find Lock? Are they watching me together from a spot I can't see?

Come on, Raych. I flex my fingers, raw and painful from the salt-stiffened rope. The dinghy looks like a toy from here. It's not normal, being on a ship of this size anchored off the coast with no visible crew. Stranded, Carmen told me, after storm damage. I look across at the city, the tiny cluster of skyscraper shapes like someone's cut them out of paper. And nearer, on the coast, the Dingo Flour sign, that hopeful red dog with its ears pricked. Reassuring things.

I don't look the other way, to the horizon and Rottnest. I keep one eye on the deck while I check the phone. Still no signal. I keep it on silent, shove it back in my pocket.

Everything on deck is orange-red metal, stained and flaking paint. The ship is barely rolling, my seasickness gone, but the heat is intense in the breathless air. There are six floors of decks at this end with the bridge at the top, stairways and railings and satellite dishes, and one of those giant ship chimneys, painted red. Rectangular portholes with nothing but dark inside, until I see a shape move behind one of them and I miss my step.

FFS. Pull it together. A second storey window. I fix my gaze on it as I climb the steps but the sun flashes off the glass and I can't see inside. There's a thick metal door propped open when I get up there, a rectangle of waiting dark. A door opened by Carmen, or Lock before her?

I take off my sunnies and hook them through the pocket of my combats. Hold the knife ahead of me and step through into a corridor, narrow and dim. A laminated neon poster tells me how to stay safe at sea. Yeah, right. The diesel smell is stronger here, layered with old cigarette smoke and sweat, and there's something else too, a pheromonal trail that sets my blood running. The doors either side are shut and locked when I try them. Halfway along is the only open door.

'You should have stayed with the boat.'

Carmen.

I force myself to keep walking. It's a cabin, cramped and bare, the sun throwing a bright square onto dirty carpet. There's a set of bunks against one wall, a door open into a tiny bathroom, a wooden desk and chair under the porthole window. Carmen's in the corner behind the bunks, bending to pick something up off the carpet. There's no one else in the room.

'You could have waited for me,' I say. It comes out as a whine. I step inside and catch that smell again, the one underneath the others, and I get what it is.

Lock's coal tar soap.

My breathing flutters like a trapped bird. I will not have a panic attack in here. Not going to happen, not after last night. I count breaths and keep the stale air moving in and out as Carmen straightens and turns towards me. Her face is pale and closed, the purple shadows deeper than they looked outside in the sun, and she's got something in her hand. She holds her palm out flat, the way they say you should feed sugar to a horse so it won't bite you. First up I think it's one of the teeth from that freaky tin of hers, but it's glinting silver in the sunlight.

'What is it?' My throat is dry, my voice hoarse. I want to turn and run, from Lock's smell in this cabin, from Carmen, from whatever answers I might find on this ship. But my muscles are jammed and won't move. I lean towards her until I can see what's in her palm.

Piper's flying fish pendant.

It's like a dream, too much. Like I'm back in his parents' house where I expected to find something like this. I reach out to take it but my hand is shaking too hard and I drop it. 'Keep *back*.' I wave the knife and fall to my knees, scrape at the grimy carpet without taking my eyes off Carmen until my fingers catch the pendant and pick it up. 'You don't get to touch this.'

The flying fish is pewter, Native American. Piper wore it on a chain, but I scan the carpet and the chain's not here.

Carmen doesn't answer, only swings her head towards the door behind me, her eyes wide with what she's seen there, her chin and the fall of her hair carving two arcs through the air.

I'm still on my knees when the door bangs shut.

You imagine a cabin door closing on a ship like this would make an echoing clang like you've been slammed into a dungeon. But no, it's an ordinary door, the sound of the lock turning an ordinary sound. The handle as you wrench at it with sweaty slippery useless hands an ordinary door handle.

One that's locked from outside and won't budge.

I can't compute Piper's pendant in my fist so I put it in the *too hard, not now* basket. Except for the fact she was here. But I knew that already, didn't I? Carmen told me this is where he'd come. He brought them here, all of them, before he killed them. And now we're here too.

Carmen stands silent in the corner by the window, too still.

'You saw him. You could have done something. Why didn't you stop him?'

The door opens inwards, he'd have reached inside to close it. It's not like I can batter it open but that doesn't stop me trying. I lift the chair above my head as she watches, bash it at the door handle again and again. Dull thuds jarring my arms, splinters flying off the chair legs. 'Hey! Let us OUT! You fucking fruitloop.' I kick at the base of the door with my sneakers. Drop the chair and grip the handle, brace my foot against the wall, put all my weight into it. But the door doesn't shift.

'Fuck!' I give it one last kick and swipe the sweat from my eyes. Flex my hands and grab up the knife from the carpet. Carmen watches every move. 'What are you looking at?' I growl at her. 'This is your fault. You knew it was a trap. I don't know exactly what you've done, how you've helped him—'

'I haven't *helped* him—' She looks furious, offended.

'I found the padlock, Carmen. At the garages.'

She opens her mouth but says nothing.

'You already admitted last night's plan was a trick to get me here.'

'It's what you would have done, Rachel. To keep her safe. An exchange. Us for her.'

'But I don't know if she's safe, do I? We don't know where she is.'

She hunches her shoulders and looks away, out the window. The view is the port side of the empty deck.

'How long, Carmen? How long have you been helping him?'

'I haven't—'

'You *have*. That was you on the CCTV, outside the Beach

277

Hotel. The night Piper went.' I step towards her. 'Wasn't it? Don't shrug or say nothing. And don't lie. I'll know if you lie.'

Everything slows down except the freight train of my heart. She must be able to hear it. I think she's going to admit it and I don't know what I'll do when she does, what I'll do with the knife. And then things speed up again and she shakes her head. 'No.' But it's too quick and she looks confused now, less sure than she was a second ago.

'Do you help him take them? The girls.'

'*No.*'

'Why should I believe you? Who's to say you weren't out there helping him while I was asleep in the boatshed?'

'I wasn't.' She frowns at the floor. I take in the shadows on her face again, livid in the light. It's then I hear the cry. A yell cut short. She does too – her head snaps up.

Max? I run to the window. 'That was her.' I say it but I can't be sure. 'Was it?' Nothing to see but the stretch of bare deck and blue horizon. Carmen stares too.

She shakes her head again, paler than she was. She's like she was in the garage with Lock. Holding it together, but barely.

'We have to get out. How do we get out?'

'You can't. You can't do anything,' she says. 'But if you give me that knife—'

I push out a laugh. 'Are you joking?' I keep one eye on her, pick up the chair and swing it at the smeared window, but the glass is hardened or reinforced because it doesn't crack. I try twice more but it's hopeless, bouncing back so I barely keep my feet, and I can't hold the knife and the chair at the same time.

The horizon tilts, a slip of movement as the ship rolls. I kick the chair away and grip the knife again, press my forehead against the warm glass. 'Right.' I step back and rub my eyes. 'Get over here.' I point at Carmen with the blade. She doesn't flinch but does what I say. She watches the knife.

I make her sit on the chair in the glare of full sun where I can see her, and I take the bare mattress on the bottom bunk. There's a pillow, no pillowcase, a folded dark blue blanket that matches the stained carpet. I don't hear anything more from outside and I don't let myself think about what that means, or where Max is. Don't let myself look at the carpet stains, or think about Piper's pendant buried in my pocket or what happened to the broken chain.

I pull out the phone and punch out a text to Zee, tell her where we are and press send. It doesn't go – no signal. Maybe it'll come back. Maybe it'll send later.

Do we have a later?

Carmen watches everything I do, or is it the knife she's watching? How long's she been doing that? Since the dinghy, maybe even before. But is she looking because she's scared of it, or because she wants it for herself?

'You're going to help me,' I say. 'I've played my part here, I fully admit that. But not like you. You got me in here. So what now?'

She hugs her backpack to her chest with one arm, the other hand curled around the seat of the chair. Her neck is twisted away from me to stare out the window, her dark fringe falling over one eye. 'I didn't. I told you not to come.'

'So? That was a lie too. You found that pendant!'

She swivels her head to look at me, the first time since we got in here. Her teeth are gritted like they're the only thing holding her together. 'I didn't know that was here.'

'Yeah, I believe you,' I say. 'Heaps wouldn't, but this is a special occasion.'

'Well, you should.'

'Well, I *don't*. That was sarcasm.' I slide my hand into my pocket and press my fingertips to the flying fish. 'Do you know what today is? It's my girlfriend's anniversary.'

Carmen's eye widens in response, the one I can see that's not hidden under her hair. But she looks away and says nothing.

'Do you know what that means? She's DEAD. That's what it means. She's fucking dead. Because of you. I don't want my sister to die too.'

This time, she doesn't deny it.

I think it might be the first time I know it's true: Piper is dead. Gone and not coming back. And now, today, on her anniversary, Max will die too. Might be dying right this second or already dead. And these things are because of me. Because I've fucked up. Because I didn't go to the cops when I could have. Because I didn't kill Lock when I had the chance.

But also, they're because of Carmen.

'Why aren't we out there with Max or whoever that girl is? Why are we in here? What does he want, Carmen?'

She makes that impatient huffing sound. I haven't heard it for a while. 'He's waiting,' she says at last.

'Waiting for what?'

'Waiting for dark.'

I don't know how it happens. I'm at the window to the left of the desk, scanning for movement on deck. Carmen's in the chair, well back from the desk where I put her. My hand is cramping, maybe that's what does it. Or I loosen my grip, rest my hand on the desk. Or I micro sleep. How the fuck should I know?

But one second I have the knife and the next I'm scrabbling on the desk for it. It's right here. No, it's on the floor. I drop to my knees. It's here somewhere. It's right here.

It's . . .

Carmen has the knife.

The light has changed, sunset gold. She's in the same spot like she hasn't moved. But she has. Obviously. And fast. She looks awake. More awake than I've seen her in days. Lit from within, feverish almost. Her skin reminds me of the flowers at the Frangipani House and my stomach twists. Raych, you dickhead.

Dad's knife looks bigger in her hands than it felt in mine.

'That's a good knife,' I say. She doesn't react. 'It's Dad's best fishing knife. He keeps it sharp. I mean, it's a hunting knife, but he prefers it to a filleting knife. It's big, for a hunting knife.' I'm babbling but I can't stop. 'He says he likes the weight of it but I reckon it's vanity. I reckon it's the look of it – the length of the blade and the double edge at the tip. It makes him feel more of a dude.'

Her head swivels to stare at me, slowly. For a second the look in her eyes is feral, like an animal. Dead, no emotion, but intense like she can see right inside me. I don't mean to my thoughts; I mean to my organs and blood. And then the look is gone, replaced by her usual frown, and I think maybe I imagined it.

She goes back to staring out the window. Patient, the way I've never been patient. Like she's waiting, the same as him. I don't like that knife in her hands. I don't like the way the light tints the blade pink like rare steak. I can tell she wants me to stop talking but I'm nervous, okay? I'm not sure I can. Why is my brain working slower than my mouth when I need it to be the opposite?

'When you said he was waiting, does that mean ...? Will he come and let us out? When it's dark. Is that what you meant?'

She shrugs. 'I told you. I told you to stay behind. To stay with the boat.'

'What changed, then? Why did you bring me here?'

But she won't say more. I back into the bunk and sit on the edge of the mattress. 'What are you going to do with it? Dad's knife?' She's not looking at it any more. Not now she's got it. 'Because listen ... we could do something with it. To him, I mean. Lock.'

She doesn't answer, but shakes her head like it's too late for that. Stares out at the ship and the sunset.

'Ambush him,' I say. 'When he comes. I don't even mind if you keep the knife. You can take it. Dad won't care. He can—'

'Shut up, Rachel,' she says. 'I'm talking now.'

'Okay.' I whisper it and hug my knees. I'm that gutless girl again, locked in a room with a psychopathic killer, except not the one I was expecting.

She keeps her eyes on the deck. Her knuckles holding the knife are stretched and bright. 'This is how it started.'

If she's about to confess, I'm not ready. Her face does this thing sometimes, like she's recalibrating. Little shifts in her expression – her frown, her mouth, the width of her eyes. You have to watch for it. It's quick. She's doing it now.

She tells me she found the first body on the beach at Leighton. 'Christine. I got there first,' she says. 'You remember?'

No. But I nod, frozen to my spot on the bunk.

'It was early,' she says. 'Still dark. Except for the sand which never goes dark. Cold, they said on the news. I was shivering, after. I don't notice the cold as a rule.' She rubs her nose with the arm holding the knife, lowers it again.

'I saw it a way off. It was big. A dead dolphin, I reckoned. A shark even. I'd never seen a dead shark. I wanted to. I wanted to see its teeth. But when I come up to it, it wasn't a shark.'

She describes the body, exactly as they did on the crime forums online. The rash vest and bikini bottoms Christine was wearing. The injuries and blood loss. 'Like she had none left,' she says.

'What, she was—?'

'Don't talk, Rachel. It was a shark got her. You could tell. Plus, I saw one of its teeth. There was a tooth in her.' Her face is smoothed out and her eyes are wide and honestly, she's like a kid who's seen Santa. She's sounding a little crazy so I don't contradict her. I don't say anything. Everyone knows by now Christine Watkins wasn't taken by a shark.

Carmen swallows, staring down at her hands. 'I took it,' she says. 'The tooth. I wanted it. I had to dig it out.'

I wince, the image too graphic. I have to ask, even if I don't want to know, and this time she doesn't shut me up. 'Is that where you found them, the teeth you have in that tin?' I swallow. 'On the bodies of dead girls?'

She shakes her head, impatient. 'No, Rachel. The tin's different. It was one tooth. It was caught in a rip in her rashie. It was half in her, from the shark.'

'Okay. But what about—'

'I had to take it. But someone saw.'

I'm at the edge of the bunk now, leaning towards her. 'Someone saw? Who saw?'

'I'm different. I don't react the same as some people, but I wanted it.' It's like she's talking to herself.

'That's okay, Carmen,' I say. 'It's okay to be different. Who saw you?'

'He must have. He's been following me. I thought it was Alexis, because she does that sometimes, but it was him.' She traces a finger along the blade of the knife. 'I called them from the phone on the highway, the ambulance and the police, even though I knew she was dead. I didn't give my name because I took the tooth.'

'Carmen. Rewind. Are you telling me Lock saw you? He was still there when you found her? Because that's not your fault. Anyone could have found her. He's the one that killed her.'

'No, Rachel.' She rolls her eyes like I'm thick.

'What then?'

'That's what I'm trying to explain to you. I took the tooth. That's what started it. It's my fault.' She puts her thumbnail between her teeth and bites down on it. 'It wasn't the same every time, but. I didn't even know Christine; I'd never seen her before. That's how I know she was different. That's how I know it was a shark.' She looks at me round-eyed like I should get it, but I don't.

'I never meant to kill anyone except Alexis. He made me do it, made me do the other things. But I'm gunna fix it. That's why we're here.'

I've been writing in my notebook, getting everything down because what else is there to do here? But it's full dark now except for the distant blinking lights of the two lighthouses at Wadjemup and Bathurst, and a red blush along the horizon that disappears as I watch it. The moon will be full but we can't see it from here. Carmen's in shadow and I can't see the knife, only her head and shoulders in profile against what's left of the light. I should be scared but I'm not now; something has flipped. Maybe I've been so goddamn scared for so long it's run out. Or maybe I'm saving it for later. Let's face it, the worst is yet to come.

Carmen says Lock was watching when she found Christine Watkins's body. If that's true, then she didn't help him, she interrupted him. I don't get why she feels responsible.

She keeps talking about *that night*, saying he made her do something and it's her fault. But I don't know what night she means and when I try and get more out of her she gets agitated and won't answer.

I could be losing the plot or it's some freaky reverse psychology on Carmen's part, but when someone tells you repeatedly they're responsible for something you end up thinking they can't be. I'm starting to think she didn't help him at all. I mean, she's had that knife for a good few hours now and hasn't used it.

Plus, she saved my life, didn't she, back on the ward. Who knew you could cause such unprecedented damage with a set of plastic cutlery?

I don't say any of this, hell no I don't. I'm not going to argue the point with her. She thinks she's connected to Lock's crimes somehow, I get that. That's why she's here. I just don't know what she plans to do.

'Carmen?' I whisper. 'We can still help Max. Still get ourselves out.'

She shifts position, maybe a nod.

'When he comes, I'll go to the door first. You stay behind me,

The Shark

close enough he can't see the knife. When he opens the door, I'll get out the way.'

'No, Rachel,' she says. 'That's not gunna work.'

'But you can't use the knife on him. We need to find out where Max is.'

She doesn't answer.

'Or you could give me the knife back?' I say. 'You've got what's in your bag.'

I can't see her at all now. Too dark.

She doesn't give me the knife back.

We sit in the dark. My mind is pinballing thoughts. It feels like an hour before he comes, but at last there's a sound. The echo of a door banging on the level below. The metallic clang of footsteps up the external stairs.

I hear her unzip the backpack. She's still got the knife. I slip off the bunk so I'm ready. My legs are wobbly but hold me up. The footsteps come closer, along the corridor outside.

I'm at the door. Carmen hasn't moved yet. There's the sound of a key turning in the lock. His smell. I can smell him. My heart's going like one of those drills they use to dig up the road.

She's behind me, silent and quick. I feel her coiled ready, her cold breath on my neck. It's only at the last moment I get what she plans to do.

I'm gunna fix it. That's why we're here.

She didn't want the cops involved. She wanted the knife. She told me to stay behind, in the dinghy.

She wants to kill Lock.

'Carmen? You can't—'

The door opens, washing us with light. He's there. Lock's there with the light behind him, looking past me to her. I can't

286

see his face but he's different. There's something different about
him. He's ...

Fuck. We—

There's a shift in the air behind me. A sound like a magpie,
swooping. A sound the same as when Carmen hit Lock with
the bat.

A push. A flash of pain and dark at the back of my skull.

Then nothing.

17

Carmen

The Shark

He is strong, stronger than you'd think to look at him, but so is Carmen. And for now at least, she does what he says. Her brain is working overtime recalibrating, figuring out how she got things so wrong and what to do about it. For the first time since she started with Rachel, since the whole raft of events connected with the murders, a shaft of fear spears down and settles inside her. It makes it hard to move, but she does move, because she has to.

They carry Rachel together, out of the cabin and along the corridor to the outside staircase. Down the steps to the deck, which is hard, because they're almost the same height and he goes down the steps first. Carmen grips Rachel's ankles and he has the top half of her, his big hands under her armpits with the tips of his fingers in his black neoprene gloves showing up in the low light. He knows Carmen is here to help him but it's strange with everything swapped around. The same as when Rachel helped Carmen in the driveway outside his house, but the opposite.

Carmen hit Rachel with a wrench wrapped in one of Mrs G's hand towels. She's not sure she hit with the right amount of hard – it's not something she does every day, even if now she's done it twice in one week. Rachel's still breathing, slow and regular, her head heavy and her silky hair hanging down. She could even be asleep.

Rachel shouldn't have come, but she's here now so she might as well be useful.

He gives instructions in his distinctive grating voice – deeper and rougher than Carmen remembered it – without using too many words, the same way she would if she was the one telling him what to do. Which she'd like to be, and will be, soon.

She can't see enough of his face under the hood of his wetsuit. He had his arm in the sling, the left one, but he took it out to lift Rachel. His eyes are glittery and bright like the eyes of a lizard or a bird and always moving, and except for the first moment, Carmen avoids looking at them. When Rachel was laid out flat at her feet in the doorway, then Carmen looked at him. Only at him, because Rachel didn't matter. He said, 'Here we are at last, Carmen. The final act.'

She didn't like it, him saying her name like that. But she said, 'I want to see how you do it,' and his eyes crinkled at the corners. Some people smile with their mouth and not their eyes. He did it the other way around but it wasn't a real smile. Still, she convinced him, because he's a man and thinks she's only a girl. She gave him her tin of teeth, held it out and he took it, with his head tipped to one side like a butcherbird. Carmen knows she does that with her head sometimes too. The tin was the only thing she could think of, the best thing she has, apart from giving him Rachel. He opened it and looked at the teeth and put it in his pocket. She'll get it back, after.

She hopes it's enough. She knows now, what went wrong in the garage.

After that, he told Carmen to do what he said and leave her backpack in the cabin, which she didn't want to do but she did.

They take Rachel across the uneven deck in the dark. There's no sign of pain in his face or the way he moves, strong and quick. There's not a lot of breeze, the night as hot as the day in a way that'd have most people, including Rachel, complaining. Carmen likes it out here on the deck away from the land; it's how she thought it would be. The air is like the ocean, breathing, and she likes the water being underneath and all around them for miles, deep as well as wide and full of the things she likes. Bigger things hunting smaller things and all a part of the trophic cascades that make everything work the way it should.

They start down the metal steps at the side of the ship. She's not sure what it might do to the blood in Rachel's brain, going down head first like that after Carmen hit her on the back of her skull. The steps don't reach all the way to the water and Carmen doesn't know what they'll do at the bottom. There's no way they can carry Rachel and climb down the short section of rope ladder. But she doesn't say anything to him. They work without talking as if they've done it before. She still doesn't know if they have or not, but now is not the time to find out.

There's no railing on the bottom step, which is wide. When he reaches it he twists to look down at the deck of *Orca 2* below. Carmen can already smell the boat – diesel fumes and fish blood. For a moment she thinks he's already killed the girl. But no, she knows how he'll want to do it.

Carmen saw him move the girl from Rachel's dad's boat onto *Orca 2* this morning while it was still dark. She was alive, with a long ponytail of hair swinging against the sky as he lifted her. The next time Carmen looked, Rachel's dad's boat had been driven away. Of course, she couldn't tell Rachel any of that.

'Put her down,' he says now. 'On the step.' Carmen doesn't, not at first. She waits. He hasn't let go and if she pushes hard, he'll fall; there'll be no way he can stop it. But Rachel will fall too, and Carmen won't be able to tell him why she's done it and make him tell her what she needs to know about *that night*, which is a thing she's been looking forward to.

She doesn't push him. She lowers Rachel's feet to the metal steps instead and lets go. There's so little light down here near the water – only the liquid skin of the ocean, moving, and the smell of it. He pulls Rachel to the edge of the step and for a moment Carmen's mouth opens, because he's going to roll Rachel off the edge into the black water.

He doesn't. He bends and moves fast in a blur and then he has Rachel in a fireman's lift, her head and arms hanging as if she's already dead, and he's climbing down to the deck of the smaller boat.

Carmen follows. Rachel's dad's knife is down inside her boot. She's scared he'll see it if he looks up at her, even with her jeans pulled down over the tops of her boots, or the knife will come loose and fall out with a clatter as she climbs down. Or the blade will slice the inside of her foot, which is the least bad thing of all of them, except she'd get blood on her sock.

But none of those things happen. He starts the engine and unties *Orca 2*, and when Carmen lands on the deck she feels the growl as the engine changes, the grab of the propeller as the boat starts to move. There's a swell and pluming spray as they veer away from the ship, but Carmen keeps her feet. She doesn't even need to hold on.

Rachel is on her side on the deck, her face wet from the spray. She could nearly be someone in the recovery position, someone washed up on a beach, except for the cable ties. He's tied Rachel with the same cable ties as Carmen uses, with her ankles together and her hands behind her back.

The boat speeds towards open water, away from the blotting-out shapes of the other ships. He'll head to the south of Wadjemup and bypass the island and the crowds staying over from the race. He'll head for the deep canyon at the edge of the continental shelf, and Carmen knows why. The girl will be below by now, along with the other things he needs.

Carmen needs to get down there before they get to where he wants to go.

She feels the knife hard against her foot. She will only get one chance. She's not a hero. She can't save the day. Alexis has always been right about her. But she can show him what she's really like. And there's the boat to get away on, after. She doesn't have to get caught.

She bends over Rachel. Wipes a clump of heavy wet hair out of her eyes. And Rachel blinks and groans and wakes up.

*

Rachel's eyes are huge and her breathing is quick as a bird as she looks at Carmen. There's no way to talk, not with the engine noise and spray and the bumping of *Orca 2* on the swell. With him driving the boat from inside the cockpit. That might not be the right word but it's the one Carmen's brain comes up with.

She bends close to Rachel's face, bracing herself on the moving deck. Inside the boat, he's hunched forwards over the wheel and the low lights of the instruments, in a hurry to get where he wants to go. He glances up, moving his head this way and that like a snake, and Carmen's not sure if he can see her and Rachel in the dark. She grabs a clump of Rachel's wet hair in her fist and says, 'Don't move. Your head will hurt.'

She leaves Rachel, with her staring eyes and wet skin, her mouth opening like a fish, and crosses the dark deck to the steps. They're passing the island now – Carmen can see the reflected glow of the airport and settlement, the lighthouse light making its sweep. Apart from that, the southern edge of Wadjemup is dark, a low black shape against the stars, a pale line of sand and white water. The Milky Way is up there, and the clouds coming in to cover it up like they've been doing every day for the past week.

He is lit up brighter than he knows by the instruments as he drives. Carmen doesn't know why he's left her free to move around as she wants. It annoys her, that he doesn't see her as a threat, but it's useful, this annoyance; she lets it build. He's like Leo, a typical man. She could slip up behind him now and take the knife to his throat and he wouldn't see her coming. You have to be strong to cut someone's throat in one go, even with a knife like Rachel's dad's. She knows she could do it.

She doesn't, though. It's not time. And it's not the right way to do it.

She takes the steps to the deck below. The first space is a galley kitchen and the smell of dead rancid flesh and oily blood is like being punched in the throat. Carmen sways back against the step, lifting the neck of her T-shirt over her mouth and nose, because she does not like that smell. But it's bait, that's all. She knows what it's for. She keeps going. There's a narrow corridor with doors either side and one at the end. The first cabin is storage – a spare paddle for a surf-ski, wetsuits and wet-weather clothing, a shark-repelling device like the one he's already wearing up on deck. It's tidy when she steps in there, everything strapped down and in its place. Opposite is a bedroom, empty, the bed made. Next door a tiny bathroom with the door locked when she tries it. 'Hello?' she says at the door. No answer.

The door at the end. That's where the girl is.

Neil told Carmen Rachel's sister would be left unhurt in a safe place if she brought him Rachel. But after Carmen saw him carry the girl onto *Orca 2* this morning, she wasn't sure any more, about the plan. What if Neil had lied, and Rachel's sister was already dead? Or she was saved but Rachel would never see her again? That's why Carmen told Rachel to stay behind.

Rachel thinks it's her sister in there, and maybe she's right. But Carmen's been wondering, ever since she saw him move the girl. There was something about the shape of her head, and that ponytail, even in the dark.

She twists the handle and the door falls open with a lurch of the boat, and she's right.

The girl is Alexis.

'You?' Alexis squeaks. 'What are you doing here?' Carmen could say the same thing but she's too busy thinking. Alexis is wearing the same outfit from three days ago – her black yoga pants and top. She's scared, crabbing sideways on the bed. It's dark in the cabin, the only light leaking in from the door behind Carmen.

Alexis is supposed to be dead. She was the body in the garages. But that's not what happened, because here she is.

'You have to help me,' Alexis says, quick and breathless. Her eyes shine with panic, darting from Carmen to the door and back again. The boat is still going, no change in speed or direction, bumping on the swell. 'He'll come. He'll . . . We can't be here when he comes. You have to!'

Carmen doesn't like being told what to do, especially not by Alexis. She's cable-tied the same way Rachel is, but there's a dark mark on her cheek, and her top lip and one eye are swollen and bruised and big. Carmen got bitten by a mosquito once on her eyelid and her eye went like that, but Alexis's eye is not down to a mosquito. There's a moment Carmen lets herself think they're in worse trouble than she thought, that there might not be a way out of it, and the fear down inside her pulses like a flare. But it's only for a second and she shuts it down. She has the knife in her boot, after all.

Still, she's not sure she wants to help Alexis. And Alexis, she can see, has guessed this. 'Is he up there?' she says. 'You've got to help me. We're sisters, for fuck's sake.'

Carmen's never heard Alexis swear before. Mrs G has a zero-tolerance policy for swearing.

'We're not,' Carmen says, and watches the lump go down Alexis's throat as she swallows.

'Carmen, please,' she says. 'I'm sorry, all right? I know I haven't been . . . sisterly.' Her eyes slide away across the cabin. 'I'll make it up to you. Reparations. We can talk about it. Money, anything you want. But not now!' She squeaks again on the last word. He's going to hear her from up on deck and she'll be sorry.

'Who died in the garage?' Carmen says.

For a moment the real Alexis is back, a little curl in her swollen lip as she says, 'Ha. So you thought it was me. Predictable. But wrong.' She looks again at the door, lifting her head off the bare mattress. 'Goddammit, Carmen. I'll explain. But first you have to help me!'

'Explain now.' Carmen steps back from the bed and shuts the door. She can feel the engine through the walls and the floor. 'Who got killed in the garage?'

Alexis huffs, impatient, even now in the predicament she's in. 'It was some woman who'd been evicted from one of the units. I don't know. She'd been sleeping in that empty building, protesting about the developers.' She shakes her head and makes a face. 'To be frank with you, I did not *care*. I shouldn't have taken your keys and gone there, granted, but I was suspicious. And then I found your little torture chamber. The man was bleeding badly, he needed medical care. He looked *broken*. But I'd left the door open. And then ...' Her breathing gets faster, her eyes wider. 'He was so angry. I didn't know he was a ... Did you know who he was? He killed that woman.' She shudders.

'He blackmailed Leo, you know that?' she says. 'Into saying he did those murders. Said he could have me back if he confessed to them. He's much worse than you think. He put those things in your room too, after he set the fire. I knew you'd think it was me. Please Carmen, get me out of here. We can talk about this. Whatever you want, I'll do it. I'll—'

'Tell me about *that night*.'

That shuts Alexis up. Carmen watches her battle with herself inside her brain. 'You want to do this now? At least cut me free before I tell you.'

'I don't have a knife,' Carmen lies.

Her eyes narrow to slits like little fish. 'Fat lot of good you are. Help me up then. I need to be vertical for this.'

Carmen doesn't want to touch Alexis, but she does want to know the truth. So she does what she asks and gets her upright on the bed, propped against the headboard. Her narrowed eyes are fixed on Carmen, her good one and her puffed up red-going-purple one. 'All right,' she says. 'I lied about that night. I had my reasons.'

Alexis tells Carmen she woke up that night with a man's hand in a glove over her mouth and his other hand around her neck dragging her off her bed. She must have left the patio door unlocked. The lamp fell off her bedside table and made a crash and then Carmen came to the bedroom door. 'It woke you up,' she says. 'That's why you came. And he saw you and dropped me.' Carmen feels a nudge at the base of her spine, a stirring of memory and alarm. For the first time, after wanting to know for so long, she's not certain she does.

But Alexis doesn't stop. 'I hit my head, and things after that are confused. But you picked up the lamp, because I suppose you were planning to hit him with it, or threaten him, and he ran. But when I came to, your hand was around my neck and I thought . . . I really thought, Carmen . . . All right, he was gone, and you'd saved me, in a way, but now you were going to hurt me regardless. And you had good reason. So after all that, when Mum and Dad came to the door and assumed, well, I—'

'You lied.' Carmen doesn't remember, not fully, but she can

hear his voice saying, 'Not her,' and she understands now he was talking to himself, not to her. He was telling himself he'd picked the wrong girl.

Carmen sags back against the door. He did come for her, but not to stop her killing Alexis or to tell her to kill another girl. Not because they're the same. Because he'd seen her with Christine's body and thought she'd seen him too. So he decided to take Carmen first.

She can see her hand twisting Alexis's pyjama top, and now it makes sense. 'I was trying to pull you,' she says. 'Back up onto your bed. I wasn't trying to kill you.'

Alexis stares at her and Carmen stares back. It's like a balloon that's been holding them up for the whole of the last year, or longer than that, has popped. They don't know where they're going to land. It might be a long way from where they started.

'I'm sorry I lied,' Alexis says in a small voice. 'But I thought you wanted to hurt me. And I couldn't let Leo know there'd been a man in my room, that I'd left the patio doors unlocked. He's not . . . trusting.'

Alexis was more scared of Leo than she was of a man dragging her out of bed in the night. Even Carmen can see this is not normal.

Carmen's breathing like she's run a race. Things inside her brain are ripping and tearing and reorganising. All she can think is she didn't try to kill Alexis *that night* and she didn't go anywhere after Alexis's room. She didn't hurt Rachel's girlfriend.

She hasn't killed anyone.

She did the opposite. She stopped him from killing Alexis. The man in her room.

It doesn't feel good, not at first. She doesn't know if it's okay or not. But she has the knife, and Alexis is right there. Maybe she can still do it.

And then the door opens at her back and shunts her onto the bed.

The person at the door is Rachel.

She sees Alexis on the bed and stares at her, mouth open. She's got herself down here with her hands still cable-tied behind her back and Carmen doesn't know how she did it, how she got her feet free and didn't fall on her face down the steps.

'Did he see you?' Carmen says.

Rachel shakes her head. 'He's still driving.' But she's focused on Alexis. 'What's she doing here? Have you seen my sister? Is she here?' but Alexis shrugs and says no, it's only her, and Rachel's face falls.

The dip and rise of the boat bumps the door shut and Rachel leans on it. 'We got it wrong, Carmen.' Her eyes are round and dark. 'About Lock. Do you know?'

Carmen nods. But she doesn't want to think about him, about *that night*, about other things she's got wrong. Things she doesn't understand that are waiting to rush over the horizon towards her. Like why he's left Carmen free to move around the boat. How Rachel has got down here in one piece without him coming after her.

'Why the fuck did you hit me on the head?' Rachel says.

'It was a better plan than your one.' But now Carmen's not sure it was.

Rachel touches the back of her hair and winces. 'See, the thing about a plan is, you're meant to tell the person.' She

299

glances at Alexis. 'Carmen,' she says. 'You remember what happened that first day on the ward, right?'

Carmen's muscles go still all at once. She shakes her head, fast. 'No.'

'Yeah you do. You stopped the bleeding when I'd carved myself up. Called the staff and saved my life. I didn't die that day because of you.' Rachel looks at Alexis. 'She stopped me from—'

'Thank you. I got that,' Alexis says. 'But do either of you have a fucking knife?'

It's the third time Alexis has sworn and it makes Carmen jump.

'You're not a killer, Carmen,' Rachel says. 'That's what I'm saying.'

But Carmen is numb. It's too much in one go. If she's not the person she always thought, who is she instead? Her brain is going to do what it does and she won't remember any of this. Still, she pulls the knife from her boot and drags herself to the bed like it's the hardest thing she's ever done, which it might be. Alexis cowers and flinches and makes a drama out of it as Carmen raises the knife and cuts her free, and then Rachel too. And then she tucks the knife back into her boot as Alexis swears for the fourth time and rushes past her out the door.

Which Carmen reckons is a big mistake.

'I didn't want to do that, Rachel,' she says.

'I know. But now we go back out there and we finish this.'

Carmen stares up at Rachel from where she's crouched on the floor of the cabin. She has to tell her. She has to do it now. 'Did you hear what she said, from outside the door?'

'She lied. You didn't hurt her. There was a man.'

Carmen nods. 'It was him in her room that night.' She frowns. 'Lock.'

Rachel's face goes white. 'How?' She glances at the door Alexis has gone through. 'Tell me later. We don't have—'

'No. I have to tell you now.'

Because now Carmen knows she didn't hurt Rachel's girlfriend. Didn't take her and lock her in somewhere and forget so she couldn't get out. But it's still her fault, what happened to her. Fully Carmen's fault and no one else's.

It's the reason she's felt connected to Rachel all this time, but it's a bad reason.

She tells Rachel fast, as fast as she can, because Rachel's right and there's no time. She tells her he ran from Alexis's room that night because of Carmen. She tells her again Christine Watkins the year before wasn't the first one.

'He didn't kill her. That one was a shark, Rachel. I already told you.'

Rachel doesn't get it, Carmen can tell. It's frustrating.

She says the worst part. She didn't think it would be so hard.

'He had Alexis. He would have taken her but I stopped him. Maybe I hit him with the lamp, I dunno.' Carmen huffs, annoyed. 'That part doesn't matter. Do you get it?' she says, stepping close to Rachel. The closest she's ever been so she can see the freckles on her nose. 'He went back out that night. Later. It was the same night, Rachel. The night he took your girlfriend. Piper.' Names don't matter to Carmen, but this one does.

'She was the first one he took,' Carmen says. 'And it was because of me. Because I stopped him taking Alexis.'

And then there's a thumping down the steps from the deck, and the two of them turn at the same time. There's nowhere to go. No time to make a plan at the door. Their eyes meet and Carmen knows they're both thinking it – *Who is driving the boat?* – because the sound of the engine hasn't changed, *Orca 2* cresting waves like before.

Carmen pulls Rachel away from the door but he still comes through it.

He fills the frame. Carmen can't see a lot of his face but she knew, as soon as he stepped into the cabin up on the ship. He doesn't seem that much older, but he's an inch taller, his bearing different. He's got his arm out of the sling but the sling is fake and there's no getting away from it – he's left-handed. Rachel and Carmen are both staring at the speargun he's holding. At his black neoprene gloves and, curled around the grip of the speargun, his flexing left thumb.

'Final requests?' he says, 'Or not yet?' with his head tipped to one side again like that butcherbird. And now, at last, the storm comes raging over the horizon inside Carmen's brain, because she remembers where she's seen that speargun before. She knows where she first met him, why he came for her *that night* and why they're all here.

Things have got out of control very fast. It's like flipping over a rock and getting a big shock at what's underneath. Carmen tries to pin down when things went wrong. Was it when she took too long explaining things to Rachel? Or when Alexis was too slow saying why she lied? Or when Carmen hit Rachel too hard on the head?

No, it was before all those things. It was being wrong about Neil. Thinking he was *The Shark* when all along it was this man, his father, even as far back as *that night*. When Carmen is never wrong about things like sounds and smells, but the two of them have the same voice and the same smell, or near enough she couldn't tell the difference. That's why Neil didn't recognise her in the garage.

Neil was never the killer. He's a disappointment, like she thought. He was trying to keep them safe, the way he told them on the news. Driving the streets at night to stop his father from taking girls and killing them. But it wasn't enough and it didn't help.

Neil is driving the boat now and watching them all; Carmen can feel his eyes on her back. He doesn't want to be there, but he's not doing anything about it.

Worst of all, Carmen knows how it started, and how it kept going. That day when Neil's father came to the school and spoke to her class. How he showed them the speargun and played them videos of the deep canyon and what lived down inside it. Neil's father the marine biologist in his dark blue AQWA uniform. Talking to Carmen, once she started in with her questions – how sharks detect prey, how they make themselves invisible, how they attack – like he was there for her and no one else.

She only saw him that one time. It was dark inside the classroom and they were watching the videos, but still, she was listening to every word and she should have remembered him.

Carmen knows there's no point in this, that she needs to be looking forwards instead of back, but when she tries her mind goes blank, like an empty whiteboard at school. She can't have it happen here, what happens when her senses peel away from her so nothing is real. Not now. She needs to be one hundred per cent alert and ready.

But for what? She still doesn't know which way things will fall.

They are at the edge of the deep canyon, a long way past the island now. If Carmen cranes her neck towards the bow she can still see the distant blip of the lighthouse beam. This must be the place because Neil's father has dropped anchor and the boat isn't moving, not apart from a rhythmic rocking on the swell. He's making everything ready and it's the perfect night for him – flat calm with no breeze, the moon full. She'd have explained about the moon to Rachel but it wasn't the right time. The night is cool compared to the day and reminds Carmen of the boathouse – the slapping water, the sense of it underneath her, stretching into the dark. But it's not calming, not reassuring, not with him making all the preparations when Carmen knows what he has planned for her.

There was a bright fervour in his voice and face when he brought her up from the cabin. 'Are you ready? These last three are yours, Carmen.'

Three. That makes Rachel, Alexis, and Neil. Even Neil. None of them heard him say it, which at least buys her some time. All Carmen can think is, *Not yet.*

That's what he said when he was in Alexis's room that night. Instead of *Not her* it was *Not yet.* He'd come for Alexis but decided Carmen wasn't ready. Carmen was special, after all. The other girls, all of them – he has killed them for her. Everyone who was unkind to her in one way or another.

Except for Piper, who was different, in the wrong place on the wrong night.

Rachel and Alexis are secured to bolted-down cleats on the deck with enough space between them there's no chance they can help each other or talk, each with the cable ties back on their wrists and ankles. Carmen watched from the back corner of the deck as he tied them down. They're quiet now, both of them, and wide awake. She's surprised Alexis hasn't screamed the place down, or tried to make a deal to save her life.

Rachel hasn't looked at Carmen once, not since she told her about her girlfriend and *that night*.

He has Rachel and Alexis facing the open ocean so they can see what he's doing. That will be what he always does, what he enjoys, but there are other reasons. When you have to watch, when you sit watching the black water and it slowly dawns what he's waiting for and what will happen to you, that's when your body responds in all the ways it does. Adrenaline, blood flow to the brain and muscles, pulse rate, respiratory rate, all your senses heightened. Carmen knows because it's happening to her now. Fight or flight, but none of them can fly, and fighting will only make them die quicker.

If Carmen doesn't do what he says, he will kill her too.

She watches Neil in the cockpit, slumped in the driver's seat. He's watching his father and won't look back at her. Does he know what's going to happen? What his father has planned for them?

She thinks he won't do what he's done before with the bodies once they're dead. He won't take them in close to shore and let them wash up onto the beach. That's what the surf-ski is for. For paddling the bodies close in to shore so no one can see you. Not the water police patrols along the coast, not the officers watching the shallows, the locals on the beach or the surf club volunteers. Not if you're silent, dressed head to foot in black neoprene the way he is now.

No, he won't do that. Not with three of them. It's too big a risk. He'll let them drift. He'll let them go, right here on the edge of the deep canyon, whatever is left of them.

Neil's father reckons he's safe because of the black box strapped to his ankle and its trailing rope of antenna that repels the sharks. It's long, that antenna. A tail he's careful not to step on as he moves.

He has been throwing bloody, chopped-up bait out of a bucket into the water for a good fifteen minutes now. He is not being subtle about it, but he's not trying to attract small fish. The moon makes a bright wide trail on the ocean which every now and then disappears when the moon does, behind layers and stripes of cloud, and Neil's father has placed a pair of camping lanterns at the stern of the boat.

Carmen watches the oily trail the blood leaves on the water. She can smell the blood. She's always been good at smelling blood.

A part of Carmen knows this is the right way for her to die. To go into the ocean, a part of the food chain and all the big predators she loves – the sharks that outlived five mass extinction events, survivors exactly like she is. A part of her is curious about what it will be like – she can't help that. They can't have much longer to wait. Her brain is working fast. Which one will have to go first? Alexis, she thinks. He'll save Rachel for later, make her watch.

The canyon is deep here, and the moon makes things show up clear and sharp from underwater. Carmen's not the only one who's good at smelling blood. A great white will detect it five kilometres away, but there'll be sharks closer than that. People say they smell your fear, but that's not true. They sense things. The electrical activity of five beating hearts will be enough.

Carmen sees the moment Rachel figures out what he does. Her pupils are huge and black, her body arching against the cable ties. Her mouth twists in disgust and fury and pain, and Carmen knows she's thinking about the other girls, all of them. She's like she was in the garage the first night, with Neil. Carmen watches her form the word before she says it.

'No, Rachel. Don't.'

'Fuck off, Carmen. *Coward*,' she says to his back.

He stops mid-throw. He puts down the bucket.

Rachel mustn't talk to him like that. But she does. 'You're not even a killer. You're a *joke*. You both are.' She twists to glare at Neil where he looks down at them from the cockpit. 'Like father, like useless fucking son.'

The father turns around. He can move fast when he wants to.

'Now, Carmen. You want to see how this works?' he says.

Behind him, she sees the first shark.

18

Raych

The one that got away

He doesn't like me calling him a coward. I'm not scared of him. I'm not. Not Carmen either. Only what's in the water behind them. Even now I know who he is and how wrong we've been – because yeah, we cut the thumb off the wrong dude. I swear at him and lunge and snap my teeth until my cable-tied wrists pull me up short. I reckon he's coming in to hit me and I think, Good on you, dickhead. Hit the woman you've tied up so she can't fight back. The woman whose head feels split open as it is, who's dizzy and trying not to puke up, thanks to Carmen.

But he doesn't hit me. He gives me a good long look – he holds eye contact, unlike his son – and he stalks to where Alexis is tied on the deck and cuts her free. He yanks her onto her still-cable-tied feet, drags her to the stern and stops. 'Now, Carmen,' he says again. 'You've been patient. I know how hard that's been for you.'

My stomach makes a fist like it knows before I do. This is not happening. No way. 'Carmen, what the fuck?' But she's turned away and I can't see her face. Alexis hangs from his grip on her upper arm. Her eyes are like planets, her mouth trying to talk but there's no sound and what it does is make her look like a fish. I'm so freaked out I'm going to laugh. Or faint. I can't. I can't laugh at this.

It happens so fast. Carmen steps forward and muscles between them like she can't wait to get her hands on Alexis. And she does. One pale long-fingered hand in the centre of Alexis's chest, against her black top. For a second that hand is writhing, spidery and huge and I'm thinking of the oil stains in the garage, the blood under the chair. Alexis's two hands come up and grip Carmen's and they struggle – the two of them grappling, pushing and pulling with their heads so close they could be sisters whispering secrets.

But they're not sisters. And Carmen straightens her arm in the push, and it's done.

Carmen throws Alexis off the back of the boat.

Alexis doesn't make a sound. Doesn't get the chance. But I do, an animal whimper. There's a roiling swirl of black bodies and black water and then nothing. A string of bubbles on the surface.

Carmen steps back from the stern, her chest heaving. I stare at the place Alexis went in and it's like I've been hit in the solar plexus with that speargun he's holding. There's the sound of breathing, hoarse and shallow, that I realise is mine.

He turns to me. 'Your sister made a mess. Thrashing. Some of them go that way.'

'That's a damn lie!' She wouldn't have, she's braver than me. She'd have held it together.

He stares at me some more, expressionless. A triumphant glare at Carmen, still breathing hard. 'Well done.' And then at Lock, up at the helm behind us. 'Anyone else for a demonstration? I thought not.' Then he goes back to the task in hand.

Alexis doesn't come back up.

Okay. I'm shaking hard. It takes me some time to be able to string thoughts together. But I have to, so I do. Don't rile him up. Don't look at Carmen. Piper's flying fish is in my pocket. Max is not on board. Keep it together. I checked all those cabins. For now at least, I have to believe Max is alive.

There's a metal swim platform at the stern of the boat below the level of the deck, which is where he's been standing most of this time, throwing stinking fish guts or whatever the hell it is into the water. He's got his back to me now and he's gloating, his spine arched, watching the same patch of water.

Lock is sitting there at the helm. I can't get him to make eye contact. Is this all for him? Because of that boy who was killed twenty years ago? I don't know if he's here for punishment or to be shown how it's done, but I get the sense he's up against Carmen too. His face is bleached of colour – blood loss or shock, I can't tell.

His father wears a wetsuit with a full hood, grips the speargun left-handed. He's the same build as Lock but but taller, and there's that wiriness under the black neoprene I remember from the news footage – muscles weathered and hardened by sun. His voice, the voice I heard inside his house, is deeper than Lock's but the tone is the same. The same black eyes too, in a window of wet skin. But there's no softness there, not like I saw in Lock in the garage.

Carmen's watching the same patch of dark ocean. Two of us left, one against the other. Is that always how it was going to go? The double or triple cross? There's blood matting the hair at the back of my head – I know because I got a feel of it before he tied me up the second time.

It's light years from what I imagined, all those times I imagined it, when I was hunting him.

It's cold out here on the Indian Ocean. Never thought I'd say that in the middle of February. The lights of Rottnest disappeared a way back; we are truly at the edge of Perth's known universe. Sheets of high cloud across a full moon, and I remember again about him only killing on nights like this one. It'll be to do with the sharks. How they hunt. Carmen will know.

The wooden boat creaks and rocks but I don't have the lurch of seasickness I had in the dinghy, which is still tied to the stern of *Orca 2*. Ahead, pitch black ocean all the way to Africa, apart from the dorsal fins I watch surface and slide away, surface and slide away. Above us, the stars I won't look at because it hurts to move my head even though it might be my last ever chance.

I can't get the image of the original *Orca* out of my head. Quint's doomed boat in *Jaws*. That final scene where the shark is in the boat with him, and most of Quint is in the shark. My gut clenches and my hands spasm into fists. It could be worse, right? We could have seen it all, graphic and bloody, instead of Alexis going straight down.

Max is safe, that's my mantra, even though I don't know if it's true. I have to believe she's somewhere out there with the race crowd or on the river in Dad's boat. That Dad will be left with one daughter. The better one, the one that's been no hassle, except I get a feeling that might change.

I don't hold out a lot of hope apart from that. The phone Carmen gave me is in my pocket but I can't reach it. The text message to Zee from the ship didn't send and there won't be a signal out here.

Carmen's in a crouch now, low on the deck in the back corner. She's eyeballing him with her body twisted away. They're not speaking. He's gone back to throwing bait off the stern.

It hasn't sunk in yet, what she told me below deck. That Lock senior picked up Piper the same night he ran from Carmen's place. Another fact for the *too hard, not now* basket. But even that could be a lie.

I watch him, scouring the surface for parts of Alexis, for evidence of what he's done. I mean seriously, what is he? An accomplice to a natural predator at best. If I wasn't shitting bricks at what just happened, I might even be disappointed. I think of all the lost girls. Piper and Genevieve, Maya and Mo and Christine. All of them, the world over, going back centuries. I tighten my fists and you know what? The fire in me is still here.

If there's a chance for Max, if I can find out where she is, I'll take it.

I check out Lock behind me at the helm and this time he twitches his head like a tic and looks past me at Carmen. I do too and that's when I see what she's doing. At first glance she's crouched there, awaiting instructions, for Lock senior to make his next move. But there's a focus to her, a tightness, with her upper body twisted and her right arm stretched back along her right leg.

She's trying to get at something near the top of her boot, up inside the leg of her jeans.

Dad's knife.

I don't know what Carmen thinks she's going to do with that knife. Save herself? Kill us all? From what I can see, Lock senior doesn't know she has it.

There's no way I can pivot again and trust her. Not after watching her do that to Alexis. And what would be the point? As soon as she does anything he'll see it.

And then he comes for me and the decision is made and everything speeds up. He gets close enough I can feel the heat off his body and smell his sweat, still pumped from Alexis going in. He gestures for me to twist my shoulders so he can cut the cable ties. 'Better,' he says. 'Good girl. Do as you're told.'

If there's one thing that'll make my head explode like someone's shot it out of a cannon it's instructions like these from a man, but I bite my lip. There's a burst of relief as my hands come free but I don't let it show. I clench and stretch my fingers, feel the blood flow back as he crouches and cuts free my feet. A curl of black neoprene and the knobs of his spine, awkward limbs that make me think again of a spider, one of those joke ones kids piss about with at Halloween.

I'm surprised he's cutting my feet free, until I remember. All of them have been swimmers, Raych – he wants you to swim for it. He didn't get enough of a rush out of Alexis, her going straight down like that. A thrust of nausea rises and I swallow it. Fuck him. Both of them. They want me to swim, I'll swim.

The boat swings – the wind has changed. Water slaps the hull. Beyond him, a dorsal fin cuts the pool of lantern light and disappears the other side. What kinds of sharks have come? Which kind of bait attracts which shark? Carmen will know that too. The oil slick of bait won't last, I know that much.

Everything has slowed down and I'm wondering if it's my brain, if that knock on the back of my head did damage. But then he straightens up in front of me and Carmen makes that noise through her nose and I realise my brain is working fine.

The huffing noise she makes when she's impatient. Or I'm wrong, or in her opinion screwing something up.

She does it twice, like a sneeze. I've never heard her do it twice. I hold still and keep my eyes on the deck – streaks of rust, beads of water.

Lock senior steps back to examine me. I tilt my head up. 'What are you looking at, coward?' His eyes narrow. Carmen makes the noise again. I don't know what it means. 'I don't do men,' I say to him. 'You picked the wrong girl.'

He recoils, and as he does, Carmen pulls Dad's knife from her boot. I see the flash of the blade at the edge of my field of view, the silent swoop of her arm.

My heart falters and kicks. Lock senior tells me to get up but I can't. He tells me again. I do it slow. Unfold my shaky legs, stagger with the tilt of the boat. My muscles burn as the blood rushes into them. I'm waiting for Carmen.

Can I trust her?

Can I? I sneak a look at Lock across my shoulder as I straighten, his eyes wide and terrified at the helm of *Orca 2*. I know what he's watching – I sense it more than see it – the long shape of Carmen unfolding from the deck.

Then she's there. As tall as Lock senior. In her other hand is the speargun and I didn't see her take it. I imagine her arm arcing up and around, the knife or the gun at his throat. But she pushes between us the way she did with Alexis.

It's me she comes for first.

Carmen's face is pale and closed. The blade of Dad's knife at my neck, the cold tip pressed to the jump of my pulse.

There's spray on our skin. The boat tipping and bumping. I'm picturing Alexis, the push from Carmen's hand. My blood is surging, drilling like rain on wet rock, and all I can think is, *Fuck you, Carmen, that's Dad's best knife.* She blinks and says, 'Rachel', adjusts the angle of the blade. Is she sorry? Lock senior is behind her and calls her name, spurring her on. She grabs my hand and flattens it open. I stare down at my palm as I wait for the burn, the slash across my open hand or my throat. But instead she switches the knife, closes my fingers around the handle.

'Yours,' she says, and steps back.

And in an instant, everything flips. I'm bewildered, because of Alexis, but there's no time for that. It's me and him. Like I always imagined it, like no one else exists. Carmen slips away with the speargun and I keep the knife flat against my thigh, the blade pointing at the deck. Has he seen it? I could do it now, flick my arm up and stick the blade in. I know I can do it.

But I want more from this killer, Lock's father, before I do it. I deserve that much, right? I have to know where Max is. I have to know about Piper. Hope for the best and prepare for the worst. Where did I get that? Zee, most likely.

I mean, what else do I have to bargain with? I bring my shaking arm up and I show him Dad's knife.

That's where it starts to go wrong.

*

He's near the top of the steps down to the swim platform when I move towards him. Carmen disappeared to the helm with that speargun and it's instinct, to put more distance between us before I do what I have to do. He narrows his eyes for a second, his focus on the knife, then steps back.

We keep going like that, one step forwards from me, one step back from him, like a dance, until we're down the steps and on the platform. The knife gives me the illusion of control but I know that's all it is. The stinking bucket of bait is there, a plastic shovel sticking out of it. The dinghy in the pool of lantern light, bobbing like an escape pod. The platform tilting, the salty air and the sound of water. My skin is alive with fear but I don't let it show.

He's right on the edge now. Is he nervous, knowing what's in the water behind him? He's shaking, but is it fear or excitement? I'm armed and he's not, but he has me right where he wants me. All it will take is a sidestep and a push. 'Don't worry, coward,' I say. 'You'll get what you want. But I want something too.'

His eyes are hard and unflinching and arrogant and I can feel the charge of his blood. One thing's for sure, he's not the mouse his son was in that garage. I stand straighter. 'Tell me where my sister is.'

There's a yell from the helm: Carmen and Lock, raised voices and the crack of breaking glass. I can't risk a glance behind. I have to finish this.

I squeeze the knife and a burst of excitement, like a rope of fire, courses up my arm. My fingers are slippery with sweat or spray or blood but I won't drop it. 'Tell me where she is, and about Piper Lee, and I'll do what you want,' I say to him. 'But not Carmen. She's not a part of this. You can let her go.'

He throws back his head and laughs, an animal roar, and I flinch. It's so out-of-control different from his flat expressionless mouth. He looks through and past me, back towards the coast. I think the narcissist in him will lay it all out for us – every killing, going back months – and I'm not sure I can take it. But he says, 'Both dead. Nothing special.' He tilts his head. 'Tell her, Neil. Tell her how you did her sister.'

Everything stops. Even the tipping of the boat on the water. 'You're lying.'

But I turn towards Carmen and Lock at the helm and I see from Lock's face it's true. Carmen has the speargun on him and he stares down at us, rigid and helpless like he was in the garage. His mouth is opening and everything inside me, everything keeping me upright, falls away.

His father talks over him. 'Went down with the boat at Deep Water Point. That right, boy? Too crowded for her to join us out here. Pity.'

He looks at me and smiles, and that's what pushes me over. Max dead in the river. Dad's boat sunk. All because of me, and his response is that arrogant smile. It makes me madder than anything in the past year.

I stop thinking. And things happen fast.

I feint left, step right. Lunge and thrust upwards – a move from Zee. The blade goes into him up to the hilt and I stare at it. There's no resistance, nothing like I'm expecting, only a brief catch like the crust of icing on a cake. The neoprene of his wetsuit, or his skin, I don't know. I've never stabbed anyone before.

His eyes react first – the pupils dilate then flicker past me to Lock. Slack, expressionless shock. There's a pounding like surf in my head, the rope of fire across my shoulders. I can feel the heat of his blood through the knife in his gut and it grosses me out. Carmen says, 'Let go, Rachel.' But all I have is my grip on that knife and I don't want to. I want to twist the blade. I want to rip it out and stab it back in. It's not enough yet.

I say, 'Didn't like me calling you a coward, did you? Well, you are one. And your pathetic son is one too.'

My face is wet but it's not tears. I'm too angry for tears. I'm shaking and I'm gripping the knife and he's looking down at my hand. He's still breathing. I can't see any blood around the hilt of the knife.

His arms float up and grip my shoulders. Why isn't he dying?

'Rachel,' Carmen says, louder and closer.

'Shut up, Carmen! This is mine. *He's* mine.'

'Your sister's not dead, Rachel,' she says.

Lock's voice comes through from behind me, the same catch in it. 'She's ... not. I couldn't ... alive when I left her.' Apologetic, to his father or me I don't know and don't care. But it gets through.

The fight goes out of me then. I sag against the knife handle and I want to let go, want to go back to shore and call the cops and find her. But it's too late for that. Lock's father's grip on my shoulders doesn't let up. He smiles again and pulls me closer, tighter. As if this was his plan all along, and my rope of fire turns to panic. The knife is pinning us together and I'm trying to let go of it, trying to do what Carmen says and detach my hand, but I can't. 'Carmen?' I say, but she's not there. She can't get to us.

And we fall together off the swim platform into the water.

My first thought when I kick back up to the surface is, This is going to be okay. The worst is over. Soon he'll be dead. Because okay, there's the shock of the cold – and believe me it's cold, worse than the coldest school holiday swimming lessons off the Thomson Bay jetty, and my teeth are full-on chattering – but when I pull away from him and get my breath, everything has gone quiet. I tread water and Lock senior floats next to me on his back, and I've still got a hold of the knife but it's not in him any more and it's going to be fine. There's no movement in the water except for the swell, the occasional wave breaking over his body and slapping me in the face, and I'm insanely grateful for the freak weather and flat ocean. I keep my head up, blink the salt out of my eyes and scan the surface, but there's no sign of the sharks that were here minutes ago. Because it all took too long. The bait has been eaten, the fish have gone and so have the sharks.

Sure, I've got this dude bleeding out next to me and maybe I should be considering that, all the blood leaking into the water. But he's drifting away now and all I need to do is get back to the boat.

Except Carmen is yelling. How long has she been doing that? I'm swimming for the boat and she's yelling at me. 'Stay there, Rachel. His ankle. The thing on his ankle. It keeps away the sharks.' I hear the alarm in her voice, the urgency, but I don't get it.

'No, it's okay,' I say. 'He's dead, Carmen. He can't hurt us. We can go back for Max.' I don't want to stay with him. I don't. I slick my hair out of my eyes and paddle one-handed. I'm shivering, and there's a lot of blood in the water, I do know that, but it's fine.

But Carmen's pointing and shaking her head and leaning out from the back of the boat. She needs to be careful. She might fall in. Her eyes are big and I've never heard her this loud. 'No, Rachel. Don't let go of him. Go back. It's on his ankle. It's repelling the shark.'

It's the look on her face that makes me understand what it takes to chase the smaller sharks away.

One big shark.

And just like that, I'm the gutless girl again. I'm the one he didn't take because she wasn't brave, wasn't an athlete, wasn't anything special. I look down where my legs are but I can't see past the shine on the surface. It feels like they're not doing anything. I'm picturing the *Jaws* movie poster, the original Chrissie Watkins with her legs kicking out behind her. 'Fuck, Carmen. I can't see anything.' My breath gets quick and shallow and I spin in circles but Lock senior is drifting. I'm nowhere near him.

Who would choose the shark? No one. It's a totally different deal to choosing the bear. Plus it's an exercise; you're not meant to actually do it. Why do I only realise this now? I feel the surge of water before I see it, the bow wave before it breaks the surface. I spin back towards Carmen too late. It explodes out of the water – the head rearing and massive, its jaws blotting out Carmen and the boat and the sky – and I'm hurled backwards.

I go under, can't tell which way is up. I come up coughing, spinning in panic, my sinuses rammed with salt. Another wave slams me. Where the fuck is it?

When my vision clears the shark is gone.

So are the swim platform and the bucket.

I gasp air and spit water. 'Carmen? Carmen are you there?' I can't see her.

And then I can, scrambling to her feet, still on the boat.

Pointing now, jabbing with a finger behind me. 'It's ... Rachel. It'll come back.'

I spin again and can't see anything. Something bumps my back and I scream.

But when I jerk away it's him, still floating. Carmen's pointing at him and saying something but my pulse is thundering and my ears are blocked and I can't hear her.

His blood is all around me now, a warm whirlpool current. The water is black with it. He's trying to talk, his mouth opening and shutting, a dark streak of drool spitting from his lips. I move closer and see his eyes darting and silvery, first to one side and then the other. His head twitching. 'Help me,' he gasps. He kicks out a foot. 'Check it's ... working.'

At last I see the thing Carmen was talking about, a neoprene pouch on a Velcro strap. I feel my way along his shin and get a hand to it, touch the dial under my shaking fingers. I know what it's for. I've seen surfers wear them. It's electrical, rechargeable. And they do, they do repel sharks. It's doing it now.

The water's gone still again, or maybe it's me that's weirdly calm. I'm safe, as long as I have hold of this device and it's switched on. I watch the surface, feel into it with my steady treading limbs – they're still there, after all; it's not my blood pumping into the water – and I keep one hand on the switch. I ignore Carmen – what she has to say can wait.

It's only then, as I'm about to get what I've wanted for the past year, that what Haze said comes back to me. *This is about you, Raych. It's to do with your mum, not Piper.* And I reckon she's right. I've always been that scared motherless girl looking for answers. I still am. But when I found Piper, she made me different. She shored me up and made me better, braver than

I'd been before. So it *is* about her; it's about her too, and it's true
what she used to tell me, that fear is only a feeling. That you can
feel it, and still do the thing.

He says, 'Help me,' quieter now.

I pull myself closer. Turn the switch from ON to OFF until
I feel the click.

'Hear that? Your magic device is off. It's just us now, us and
the shark,' I say. 'Now you tell me. You tell me about Hana
Piper Lee.'

He tells me. He struggles, because his breathing is fast and
whistling now, his skin the colour of wet paper in the light from
the stern of the boat.

I keep hold of the switch on his ankle. I won't think about
the shark. I won't think about my legs kicking, my heart racing
and frantic, the blood in the water. I will think only of Piper –
her crooked smile, her laugh, her shit singing. And I hang onto
every word because I can't have him die before he's told me.

'Kicked ... she ...' he says first, and my teeth clench.

'Yes. You made her swim.' I don't want to know but I have
to. He's nothing. A small dying man. He's never been anything,
never been powerful. That's why he chose the girls he chose.
'What else?'

'No ...' He tries to shake his head but it barely moves. 'Please.'

'Yes. You will tell me.'

'She ... kicked. Scratched. Bit me.' He tilts his chin and the
hood gapes where it's too big. I see the scars, wet and silvery
on his neck. Like she tried to take his head off with her nails
and teeth. Piper's hands, Piper's marks on him, but it doesn't
feel good.

322

I clamp my chattering teeth together. 'What next?'

'She fell.'

'Overboard? From the ship?'

'No … before. The boat.' He grimaces. 'Please.'

'You didn't do this to her?' I say. 'She got away?'

He pants a yes, and it's enough. It's enough for now. He says something I don't catch as I feel the bow wave build again from below. It's too late for the device now. I sense his panic but I'm flooded with calm at the coming shark. I backpedal steadily through the black water away from him.

But I'm too slow.

It's that same scene from the movie. The breaching shark like a high-speed train. The smell from its mouth like a well of dead things.

It takes him. And I'm lifted like a surfboard and smashed against the boat.

I can't hear a thing except thumping. Chopping. Someone pounding meat. Is it a dream? My head? A white thing flaps in my face and I shrink back. But Carmen says, 'Rachel. Give me your hand. The knife first.'

I'm still holding it? My grip is welded to the hilt and she can't prise it away.

'My hand,' I say.

'You hurt it?'

'The other one.' Broken, maybe. I cradle my wrist, the pain pulsing but far away. Everything far away.

She helps me up onto the boat, slipping and sliding. Shivering.

Dark. The lanterns are gone. Smashed and washed away.

'The shark, Carmen.'

'Gone,' she says. 'Taken him and gone.'

'Am I okay?' I can't feel anything. Too cold. 'It hit me.'

Carmen shakes her head. 'The wave hit you. Not the shark.'

There's still that thudding in my head and then I get what it is. I lift my gaze and see the light, a way off but tracking closer. 'The cops,' I say. 'Helicopter.'

Zee got my message.

But a girl's voice says, 'He called them. The man. There's a radio.' Carmen jumps and for a second there's two of her, each looking hard at the other.

Alexis. Her hair dark and wet and plastered. Back from the dead. Behind her inside the boat is Lock, staring at all three of us. She's clutching a shark device, the same as the one on his father. How did she get that? 'They'll be here soon,' she says. 'You want to do something about that knife.'

I look at it still in my grip, black blood streaked along the blade.

'Let go of it,' Carmen says. She keeps throwing looks at her sister. She leans in to take it, digs her fingers under mine and pulls it free. 'I'll do it,' she says. 'No one can know, Rachel. You don't need to tell them.'

'Okay.' I nod and shake my head and my legs go out from under me. A shock up my spine. The deck hard and wet. Scabs of flaking paint.

I get it now, what Lock senior said before the shark hit. *The one that got away.*

Piper's not alive, I know that. But he didn't get her. She fought like a demon and fell and drowned. And there's nothing good about it, it still rips me up, but he didn't get to do what he wanted. She didn't swim for him, only for herself. She's out there, moving through all that water and light, like the flying fish she wore around her neck. She was never even in that cabin. He put the pendant there for us to find – a part of the trap.

The throb of the helicopter is closer. I think of Max and then Dad. Jared and Zee. I turn to check Carmen's done it, thrown the knife overboard, but she's not there.

'Carmen?' I swing around but there's only Alexis, tall and pale and wet, standing very still where Carmen was a second ago. I'm reminded of what Carmen did back there, can't compute why she'd save me after trying to kill her sister. 'Carmen, what the fuck? Where are you? Can we go home now?'

I strain my eyes and search the dark until I see it, her pale face above the water, drifting. 'What's she doing out there?' I say, and Alexis sighs next to me. 'Carmen, what are you doing?'

'Got rid of it,' she says.

'Come back.'

'Don't tell them,' she says. There's something in her voice, and I remember. Somewhere in the history of us, I remember her saying she couldn't swim.

Alexis swears and she's climbing into the dinghy, and the helicopter is raining down sound and wind and light, and I screw up my eyes and press my hands to my ears and duck my head.

When I look back to where Carmen was a second ago, she's gone.

SIX WEEKS LATER

19

Raych

Hope Street

They pulled Carmen out.

Weirdly, Alexis helped. The police chopper and patrol boat were there the moment I saw Carmen go under, their searchlights cracking the world open like an egg. I was blinded, panicked, shivering to bust a gut by then and making no sense at all. I was on the brink of jumping overboard to swim after her but I didn't have to.

Alexis went after her in the dinghy and at the time I didn't know enough to understand why. Lock had pulled Alexis out of the water unharmed and radioed the cops. The police boat drew up alongside and the chopper searchlight found Carmen within minutes, floating long and pale under the surface like one of the sharks she loved.

Carmen was dead – drowned, but the paramedics brought her back. Good as new, according to her. But first up, Piper and Max.

Max was found safe in Dad's boat where Lock said she'd be – tied at the jetty at Deep Water Point. She'd been drugged. All Lock had needed to do was sink the boat with her inside, but he hadn't been able to do it.

The next day, after Dad had flown home and each of us had been checked over, bandaged, splinted, drugged and whatever else we needed at the hospital, Max confessed. She said it was her on the CCTV footage talking to Piper that night on the steps of the Ocean View Club. They'd arranged to meet the bar manager to plan a party for my eighteenth. I don't know what they were thinking – my birthday was months away – but when they showed up they were told the bar manager was sick and hadn't been at work that day. After Piper disappeared, Max freaked out. She blamed herself and didn't tell anyone. But she hadn't done anything wrong. They'd talked on the steps and Piper had left, and the next day Piper was gone.

Zee tells me the task force found conclusive evidence the empty container ship was where Lock senior kept the girls before he took them out to open water. He used *Orca 2* as well as a second station wagon registered under a stolen identity that he kept at the empty property across the side street from the Frangipani House. They found Alexis Glasser's car stashed in the garage there too.

The route Piper would've have taken to the club from Ronnie's party on John Street is not well lit. He'd have clocked her on the street, followed her to the club and waited while she was inside. After that, he was ready. Piper would likely have been excited and distracted. It wouldn't have been so hard.

But enough about him. I don't like to think about that part. This is about her.

The thing is, no matter what Max had told me about why Piper left the party, I couldn't get the look on her face out of my head. Spooked, startled, whatever you want to call it, at us getting together in the pool house. I didn't imagine it. I know it scared her.

But love is scary, right? And so is change. We'd been mates for years. I was scared of things changing too.

A year and a day after that fateful party, the pool house and Piper's vanishing, a day after the anniversary that will for ever blow all other anniversaries out of the water, I finally charged up her old iPod and had a listen.

I did it with Haze right next to me. I did it on the day I caved and we were planning the not-vigil-but-celebration for Piper.

There was a playlist on the iPod. For me.

Who knew?

It only had one track on it. 'Closer' by Tegan and Sara.

Our anthem, you could say. It was playing that night at the party and we could hear it from the pool house.

So yeah, this was a love story after all.

The apartment's empty when I get there Saturday afternoon but I've got my key and I know where she'll be. I take the stairs, and I'm puffing by the time I get up to the roof.

I'm avoiding everyone except Carmen, for obvious reasons. Zee and Jared, Dad and Haze, even Max. They've had the bare bones of the story out of us and that's all they're getting. Even Lock hasn't told them all of it. The truth of how he lost his thumb, for example. Carmen's different, because she knows.

The Shark

She knows how the guilt and the grief get their teeth into you and won't let go. She knows how they're always there and you can't expect them to disappear. Not in a hurry. Maybe not ever.

I come out onto the roof and she's in the usual spot, sitting cross-legged with her face practically pressed up against the railings and the little cat sunning itself next to her. There's a skink on the top rail in a standoff with the cat, and a crow in the pine tree opposite. Carmen's the crow whisperer these days. She's wearing the set of headphones I lent her and I know she'll be listening to that Halsey track on a loop. She really pissed off the neighbours doing that when she first got in here and Dad had a few complaints. It's heaps better since the headphones.

Carmen's living in an apartment in Mossie Park, for now at least. From the roof she can see Cott to the north, the ocean and Rotto to the west, and the river, Freshwater Bay and the boatsheds to the east. It's all laid out there and she likes to face north and keep it in view. Between river and sea, as the wanky real estate advertisements like to say about Mosman Park. I call it the dodgy end, because it's one of the big blocks of units on Wellington Street. To be fair, it's not at all dodgy. Dad bought the place, after all, and he's pretty anal about stuff like that. Carmen gets to live here rent free at least until she's finished school, and if I know anything about Dad, for some time after that too.

I sit down next to Carmen. Close, but not touching. Her eyes flicker momentarily from the view so I know she knows I'm here. The concrete is warm under my butt, the sun dipping and outlining the pines in gold and taking on the colour of red bougainvillea. It's going to be a speccy sunset.

Carmen's guilt is different to mine. More complicated. Mine

is over Piper, not having gone with her that night even though she didn't want me to. Carmen's is for all of them. Piper, yes – because she drove him back out onto the street the night she was taken – but all the lost girls. She's told me the story. She's convinced Lock's father killed them all for her. But I've told her a heap of times: you don't make someone into a killer.

Piper wasn't the second girl taken; she was the first. That's what Carmen was trying to tell me in the cabin on the ship. Christine Taylor-Watkins was a straight-up shark fatality. And when Carmen found her body on the beach, Lock senior, already fixated on Carmen, got off on it. He watched her take that tooth from Christine's body and he got the idea to recreate her death with another girl, and then another.

If anyone is responsible for his father's crimes it's Lock. He worked out what was happening and never went to the authorities. Deflected suspicion from the real perpetrator. He claims he doesn't remember the bull shark attack on Roman Smith at North Fremantle but whatever happened that day had a lasting impact on his father.

So did we cut the thumb off an innocent man? Zee assures me he'll be charged with conspiracy to murder at the very least.

Carmen's never been the monster she thought she was. She's someone who dissociates easily and frequently after years of neglect and trauma. She's not ever going back to that family. Not if I have anything to do with it. Dad'd have a fair bit to say about it too. Alexis might have come good out there on the ocean but she still bullied Carmen for almost two decades.

Carmen reaches for her phone, pauses the track and pulls off the headphones.

'How many out there tonight?' I ask. She counts the ships

every day. The one Lock's father used isn't a crime scene any more but it's still not been moved.

'Six. Two left yesterday. One new one.'

'Dad's invited us for dinner,' I say. 'Shall we go?'

'Will anyone else be there?'

'No. Only us and Max.'

'Okay.'

'He'll probably thank you for saving me again.'

She rolls her eyes. 'I didn't save you, Rachel.' I reckon she sees it the other way around. She gave me the knife. I killed the bad dude so she didn't have to.

But I catch the smile at the corner of her mouth. Dad and Carmen have hit it off, in a nature docos and hunting-shooting-fishing kind of way. He's treating Carmen as a hero and that's fine by me. And Dad and Max and me aren't moving to Hedland. Not yet anyway.

Our arms accidentally touch and I look down at mine. All the words on it can never hide the scars, but that's okay. 'You did save me,' I say. 'You've done it twice now.'

I haven't asked her what she was doing drifting away from the boat like that but I guess I know. There are so many things I could say that I haven't. Sorry for thinking you were a monster. Sorry for not trusting you. But she could probably say those things about herself.

I get to my feet and she does too, still frowning at the ships and the view.

'So, d'you reckon you owe me one?' she says.

'At least one, I'd say.'

She keeps one hand on the top of the railing. 'Agreed,' she says. 'Because you didn't fully die that day in the hospital. You were bleeding but not dead yet. I did die and you didn't do anything.'

'That is so below the belt, Carmen. You went in the water without telling me. And the paramedics were right there.'

She makes that huffing sound. 'I fully died, Rachel.'

'For like, all of two minutes!'

I turn for the steps but she grips the top rail with both hands and doesn't follow. She's looking down, due north, and I know what she's staring at. It's always delicate, this part of the day. Prising her away.

'Carmen, no. She'll still be there tomorrow.'

The ghost of a smile. 'She might not be.'

The view one block north is of the house and front yard where Carmen lived with the Glassers. Alexis in her little silver car, coming and going from the driveway and the street, has a schedule you can set your watch by.

Look, I'm not worried. It's harmless. Carmen was the one who gave Alexis the shark device. It's what she pressed into her hands as she pushed her, fully charged-up and switched on. She made sure Alexis got a hold of it. It had to look real, but she was never trying to kill her.

It's not like she regrets that. Not a chance. No way. There's history there, that's all.

She likes to keep it in view.

Hope Street.

Acknowledgements

This was the book I thought I couldn't write, and I have a load of people to thank who kept me going when it got tough. First up, thanks to Boorloo/Perth for being my hometown and endlessly fascinating to write about. And thanks Theo and Charlie for that chat on the foreshore that gave me so much material. I reckon there are at least a couple more books to come out of that.

To my earliest readers, Tracy Darnton, Fiona Kelly McGregor and my agent Euan Thorneycroft, thank you for telling me I was onto something when I thought I'd lost the plot. Euan, thanks for your kindness in doing what you do, answering all my questions, and asking the right ones of the right people. And to everyone at A. M. Heath for your great work on behalf of me and my books and being lovely whenever I see you at the office or out and about at book events.

Thank you, Cal Kenny, for your passion for this novel and for once again getting what I've tried to do and drawing out of me the very best (and worst!) of Carmen and Raych. I'm so happy to have you in my corner. To you, Joanna Kramer, Ben Prior for the amazing cover design, and everyone who worked on *The Shark* at Little, Brown, thank you for making this book what it is and sending it out into the world. And thanks to Vanessa Neuling for being so thoughtful in the copy-edit.

Thanks to the following people for research chats: Nick Peake from WA Police, Alison Fan on the Claremont murders, Jane Stephens for medical, Tim Styles and Phoebe Edgeworth on dissociation and young persons' psych services, Strike Training on safe self-defence, and Alex for fire and emergency services. All mistakes and liberties are mine, or because Carmen and Raych wanted things their way.

Thanks, Theo Evans, for insightful feedback on the final draft, and pretty well everyone in my WA family and friends for once again answering endless questions only locals know the answers to. Thanks to Chris Harper for keeping a roof over my head and moving me to the coast so I could swim in open water again. To all of you for being there with encouragement through the ups and downs of writing this one, to Mark for 'rocket surgery', and to Mum, Dad, Mark, Pip and Rans, who continue to believe in me when I don't always do it myself.

For the writers reading this, I began researching and writing *The Shark* in November 2021. Not at all the wild ride of the first draft of my debut, I started it from scratch five times in the first year. But I refused to give up on these characters and a premise I knew was a strong one. If this rings any bells, trust your instincts.

During the writing of *The Shark*, many huge things happened for my debut novel *No Country for Girls* to remind me I had something to say and should keep trying to say it. Thank you, Val McDermid, for the unforgettable Harrogate New Blood selection; a load of judges in the UK and Australia for

Acknowledgements

longlisting and shortlisting *No Country for Girls* for your book awards; and the Wilbur & Niso Smith Foundation, prize readers and judges of the 2023 Wilbur Smith Adventure Writing Prize, for making this debut author's dreams come true on a rainy night in South Kensington.

To all the readers who've been in touch to tell me how much you enjoyed *No Country for Girls*, thank you. Many of you have hoped for a sequel, and although this isn't it, I hope you love meeting Carmen and Raych. As for the future for Nao and Charlie: you never know.

Thank you again, everyone who bought, read, recommended, reviewed, borrowed from libraries, blogged about, sold copies of and invited me to speak about *No Country for Girls*. Thanks too to the crime-writing community and author mates on both sides of the planet. This life would be nothing without you all.

I discovered my inner true crime nerd while researching *The Shark*, and read and recommend the following brilliant books: *Stalking Claremont* by Bret Christian; *I'll Be Gone in the Dark* by Michelle McNamara; *The Red Parts* by Maggie Nelson; *Don't Make a Fuss: It's Only the Claremont Serial Killer* by Wendy Davis; *Under the Bridge* by Rebecca Godfrey; or *This House of Grief* by Helen Garner. The seed of this novel grew partly out of my admiration for my good friend Tasha Kavanagh's debut, *Things We Have in Common*, and its devastating last line. If you haven't read it, do yourself a favour.

Thank you for reading *The Shark*. We got there in the end. I love hearing from readers, and for future book news, giveaways and more on how and why I write what I write, you can find me on Instagram and Twitter/X, sign up to my newsletter at emmastylesauthor.com.

Emma Styles writes Australian crime fiction about young women taking on the patriarchy. She grew up near the beach in Perth, Western Australia and now lives on the Sussex coast. Emma has an MA in crime fiction from the University of East Anglia. Her debut novel, *No Country for Girls*, won the Little, Brown UEA Crime Fiction Award and the Wilbur Smith Adventure Writing Prize. It was a New Blood selection at Theakston's Crime in Harrogate and was shortlisted for the CWA New Blood Dagger, the Davitt Award for Best Adult Crime Novel and the ACWA Ned Kelly Award for Best Debut Crime Fiction.

THE SHARK

EMMA STYLES

SPHERE

SPHERE

First published in Great Britain in 2026 by Sphere

1 3 5 7 9 10 8 6 4 2

Copyright © 2026 by Emma Styles

A CIP catalogue record for this book
is available from the British Library.

HB ISBN 978-1-40872-241-1
C format 978-1-40872-242-8

Typeset in Caslon by M Rules
Printed and bound in Great Britain by
Clays Ltd, Elcograf, S.p.A.

Papers used by Orbit are from well-managed forests
and other responsible sources.

MIX
Paper | Supporting
responsible forestry
FSC® C104740

<Imprint>
An imprint of
Little, Brown Book Group
Carmelite House
50 Victoria Embankment
London EC4Y 0DZ

The authorised representative
in the EEA is
Hachette Ireland
8 Castlecourt Centre
Dublin 15, D15 XTP3, Ireland
(email: info@hbgi.ie)

An Hachette UK Company
www.hachette.co.uk

www.littlebrown.co.uk

Exit, Pursued by a Baron
Aydra Richards

Other Books by Aydra Richards

Series One
His Favorite Mistake
His Reluctant Lady
His Forgotten Bride
His Improper Proposal

Series Two
The Scandal of the Season
My Darling Mr. Darling
A Duke in Disguise

Series Three
The Lady Unmasked
My Deceitful Duchess
The Marquess Wins a Wife

Dedication

To the fine ladies and gentlemen of the Historical Romance Society Discord server, because you let me be weird and don't judge me (too harshly).

I know I *said* I was going to dedicate this one to my cousin Throckmorton, the skateboarder, but since I don't have a cousin Throckmorton (the skateboarder or otherwise), this one is for all of you.

PS: Sorry not sorry for all the cursed memes. You knew what this was.